HIS WILD BLUE ROSE

A.J. DOWNEY

BOOK FOUR

COPYRIGHT

Text Copyright © 2018 by A.J. Downey

All rights reserved.

No part of this book may be reproduced in any form or by any electronic or mechanical means, including information storage and retrieval systems, without written permission from the author, except for the use of brief quotations in a book review.

This is a work of fiction. The names, characters, businesses, places, events, and incidents are either the products of the author's imagination or used in a fictitious manner and are not to be construed as real except where noted and authorized. Any resemblance to persons, living or dead, or actual events are entirely coincidental. Any trademarks, service marks, product names, or names featured are assumed to be the property of their respective owner, and are used only for reference. There is no implied endorsement if any of these terms are used.

The author acknowledges the trademarked status and trademark owners of various products referenced in this work, which have been used without permission. The publication/use of these trademarks is not authorized, associated with, or sponsored by the trademark owners.

∽

ISBN: 978-1721186402

Edited by Barbara J. Bailey

Book design by Maggie Kern

Cover art by Dar Albert at Wicked Smart Designs

Model - Salvador Herrera

Photographer - JW Photography & Covers

DEDICATION

To Elka, Mary, and Barbara. For all your hard work on making this one the best it could be. Love you, girls.

PROLOGUE

Alyssa...

"Don't you walk away from me, Alyssa! You don't get to walk away from fourteen years of us just like that."

I stood, my chest rising and falling as my high school sweetheart smashed my heart to pieces behind me. I turned slowly, tears staining my face and shook my head.

"There is no more 'us', Raymond." I held up my left hand and pulled off my wedding set and held it up in front of me. "This means that 'us' was just supposed to be me and you! Not you, me, and some random whore I've never heard of, makes three!"

He strode across the newly redone floor of our condo and grabbed me by my upper arms, shaking me.

"Don't talk about her that way. She has nothing to do with us!"

I scoffed, "Are you serious? Are you kidding me? She has everything to do with us. She has everything to do with why I've had it, Ray! I can't believe you! All of those nights waiting for you to come home until two and three in the morning? You, you, liar!"

"Lys," he grated out from between his teeth, but I didn't care. I pressed on.

"You were fucking some other woman while I waited for you, Ray!

What did you think was going to happen? That I'd cover your ass? That I'd sit here, all prim and proper while you ran out on me, and pretend everything was just hunky-fucking-dory? 'Nothing to worry about here, folks! Everything's just fine and dandy, except my husband can't keep his dick in his pants and –'" He let go of one of my arms, his hand flying out and catching me in the mouth.

I stared at him in open-mouthed, horrified silence as the crack of his hand against my face echoed back from the ceiling of our condo.

We'd been together for fourteen years. We'd met just before I graduated high school, were together for four years, all through college, married as he entered law school. We'd tried for children when he'd graduated from that, but as it turned out, we had fertility issues. Well, I had them, something he was keen to remind me of whenever it came up. We'd fought about it before, argued over everything from money to babies, to where to go on vacation but never, and I mean never, had he ever hit me before right now.

We are so fucked up. We are so broken. How did I not see it?

I tried to take a step back but he was towing me forward, saying, "Lys, Lyssa, I'm sorry, I don't know where that came from. Just, Lys, stop, stop it! Don't fight me, I'm sorry, I'm sorry!"

I struggled in his grip, and when he wouldn't let go, I started screaming. I wanted away. All I wanted was away. I didn't want him touching me with her perfume still clinging to him, with the photos of them at the dinner table still displayed on my phone, attached to text messages sent from one of my employees at my flower shop.

Stupid. Just a chance encounter.

"Let, me, GO!" I screamed and he snapped again. I'd never seen him like this. Never. It was like he was caught and the mask was off. He threw me to the floor, impatience and rage on his face.

I swallowed hard. I was scared. I was watching my life, the life we'd spent so much time building together, crumble and sift into ash around us.

"I don't even know who you are anymore…" I whispered.

There was no fixing this. There was no going back.

1

Golden...

"So, you figure it out yet?" Angel dropped onto the couch beside me and I glared at my twin.

"Fuck, no. I'll probably just put an ad out on Craigslist or something."

He twisted off the top of his beer and took a swig, giving me some side-eye as he swallowed. I rolled my eyes and waited for our abuela to come out of his mouth, and he didn't disappoint.

"You sure that's a good idea? A lot of crazy people on the internet."

"Pretty sure if I put in the ad I'm a cop, it'll cut down on a chunk of the riffraff applying," I said. "I'm just grateful I have the room to rent out. I like this place, but with the way housing costs are going through the fuckin' roof around here, I might have to move."

"As long as it ain't back in with me."

I snorted, "Fuck no. Sharing a womb, then a room, all the way up through eighteen with you was enough of that shit. Besides, I hate dealing with bitches trying to get us to double-team 'em as much as you do. I've shared enough shit with you, I don't want or need to share everything."

Angel laughed and beer almost came out of his nose. I grinned and finished off the dregs of my own bottle, and reached for the second he'd brought me from the kitchen.

"Besides, you live in a fuckin' shoebox on that boat."

"So, what're you waiting for?" he asked, changing the subject with a roll of his eyes and dismissing my dis on his boat. I think he was getting too used to them out of me. I needed to up my game.

Anyway, it was my turn to give him some side-eye around the bottle in my hand, pressed to my lips. I swallowed and raised an eyebrow at him, took another swallow and with a hearty 'ah', demanded, "What're you talking about?"

"I say, grab your laptop. Let's post this thing. There ain't no time like the present."

I shrugged and set my beer on a coaster on the glass top of the coffee table. I dragged my laptop up into my lap from underneath the end table that matched the coffee table and opened it up.

"Oh, damn," I muttered at the play going down on my television's screen, and Angel and I got side-tracked by the game for a couple of minutes while the damn laptop loaded. I dragged up the web browser and went to Craigslist.

"What?" Angel demanded, when I sat there, staring blankly at the blinking cursor on the screen.

"Trying to remember my fuckin' password."

He laughed at me. "This is going so well already."

"Shut the fuck up, dude," I said laughing, too.

"Don't you use the same password for everything, like a normal person?" he asked.

"Fuck, no, that's how your shit gets hacked. I use like three or four."

"So which one is it?"

"I told your ass, I don't have to share everything and I'm not gonna." I tried one. "Son of a bitch," I muttered softly.

Angel laughed at me some more and I let him have it. It wasn't typical that I wasn't good at something, even something as low-key as remembering my passwords. Two more tries and I got it.

"Now what?" he asked.

"Shit, motherfucker! I thought you had all the fuckin' answers!"

He laughed and I smiled, shook my head, and put fingers to keys. I didn't want to make fun of him too hard. I was going to need his help. I didn't much like the idea of living with someone. Especially the kind of someone that would need a fully-furnished room like I was offering, because I wasn't about to get rid of any of our abuela's shit, which is what the second bedroom's furniture was comprised of. It was all stuff that my grandfather had built her, by hand.

"You should get a chick for a roommate," he said suddenly, and I scowled.

"Why the fuck would I want to do that?" I demanded.

He shrugged and said, "Chicks are cleaner."

I crossed my eyes and then rolled them at him. Clearly, he hadn't had the same experience I had with women, but then again, out of the two of us, I was the more-experienced in that department. I was the evil twin, as I liked to say. Even though I was one of the good guys, or at least, I liked to think I was, I was definitely the more adventurous of the two of us. If I wanted to get off, I had no trouble picking up a broad at the 10-13 for a one-and-done.

Angel, I swear to god, was saving himself for marriage or some shit. He was as his name implied, a perfect fucking angel. Me, definitely not so much.

"What the fuck should I write, dude? I don't want to come off like an asshole. I really do need someone to pick up half of the rent."

He looked at me and smiled. Chuckling, he said, "Well, try starting out with what you're looking for in a roomie. Your expectations. Write it, and I'll tone it down for you."

He went back to watching the game and I scowled. I was really hoping he'd just write the damn thing for me, but if I had to be honest, his was the better plan. If I let him write it, I'd end up running a fuckin' halfway-house up in here.

"Cool, thanks... Remind me again why this couldn't wait until after the game?"

"Because you're the one bitching about the rent getting to be too much, you cheap bastard."

"Yeah, yeah," I grumbled. I couldn't fault him there.

I stared at the blinking cursor and contemplated calling up Backdraft, to get Lil to do it for me. I hated this type of shit.

2

Alyssa...

"I told you, it's not a problem."

"I just don't feel right, Kenzie. He's just going to keep coming around, keep bothering you, and I don't think that's fair. He's my problem. Not yours."

Makenzie Higgins, one of my best friends since college, sighed, her shoulders drooping. She'd given me a place to stay after leaving the battered-women's shelter – something I still felt weird about. Not about the fact that I'd stayed there; I'd needed to. It was more the fact that I, of all people, even had a need to stay in one.

Of course, I'd needed some place to go after my hospital stay, someplace safe to heal, to find a divorce attorney, and to figure out what was next. My face had healed, so had the rest of my body. There wasn't a visible mark left on me, but there were marks. *Oh boy were there marks.* I swallowed hard and Kenzie dropped onto her couch, which had sheets and a blanket, serving as my bed. She cozied up beside me and I pressed my lips together. I'd never been uncomfortable with close physical proximity before, but now, I found that if anybody got too near my physical space, anyone got inside my bubble, my skin would just crawl with nervousness.

I swallowed hard and she scanned the listings on my laptop screen. I refreshed the page and new ones popped up at the top.

"Ooo, what about that one?" She pointed.

"'One of ICPD's finest looking for a renter,'" I read aloud.

I clicked on it to bring up the ad.

"'I'm an Indigo City beat cop looking to rent out a fully-furnished room in my apartment for half the rent. Ideal roommate pays their rent on time by the first every month (obviously), is clean, picks up after themselves, and has a healthy respect for privacy. Kitchen is a communal space, as is the living room. You'll have your own bathroom for the most part, though it's shared with any guests that come by. Bedroom is furnished with a queen-sized bed, an antique sturdy dresser, and has plenty of closet space. Serious inquiries only. Must be able to pass a background check. No illegal substances, no pets, no bullshit. Serious inquiries only. Contact Rodrigo Martinez at, blah, blah, blah, email.' You should do this one." I blinked at Kenzie and she looked over at me and smiled.

"Come on! It's perfect. You don't have to tell him your business, says right here he wants privacy, which means he'll give it right back and you'd be living with a cop. I doubt very much that Ray would bother you there."

I scraped my bottom lip between my teeth and sighed, frustrated, asking, "What do I even say?"

"Just say you're a recent divorcee florist looking for some transitional housing for a year or two while you recover financially from your douchebag ex. It's not a lie."

"No, I don't suppose it is, but it's definitely a lot more complicated than that."

She looked as unhappy as I felt.

"He shouldn't be getting away with it," she said bluntly.

I bit my lips together and shook my head.

"I don't want to talk about it," I said, equally bluntly.

"Sorry," she murmured and she cast me that worried look. I hated that I worried her, I hated that I worried me, too. I couldn't help it, though. I never in a million years dreamed– I slammed the door on that line of thinking and took a deep breath, in through my nose, out slowly through my mouth. and gently put my fingers to the keys.

Maybe Kenzie was right. I mean, what could be safer than living with a cop? I typed out a careful reply, giving my name and contact information. Letting out another careful breath, my heart pounding in my chest, I clicked the send icon and sent up a little prayer.

"I really hate that you feel like you have to do this," she said, and I nodded.

"I know."

"I wish he would just live with what he's done, respect your space, and leave you the fuck alone."

"Me, too, but I don't think he can. He feels guilty, I get that, but there's no coming back from that." I sniffed and my eyes watered. I was sick of crying over my marriage, what happened that night, and the utter indignity of what Ray was putting me through in court, all in a bid to force me to talk to him. But I didn't want to talk to him. I wanted him to go away.

My lawyer was handling it all, and was even going after him for all the court costs. I was grateful for her. She was precisely what I needed. The domestic violence shelter I'd stayed in after I'd gotten out of the hospital had put me in touch with her at my request.

She was doing better than what I could have ever asked for. It was going to cost Ray, too, in the end. She was confident that the judge would award me everything I wanted, which wasn't much. I just wanted my business and to be free of him. I'd only taken clothes and my important papers when the police had escorted me to the condo to collect my things.

I didn't want anything else but what was mine to begin with: my clothes, my business, some old photographs from before we were married, and a few other sentimental things. It'd all fit into seven plastic totes and a single large suitcase. They were all piled in Kenzie's living room, off to one side of the couch.

"It's going to be okay, Lys. I promise," she said and covered my hand with hers. I jumped at the contact; I just wasn't used to being touched anymore.

I closed my eyes, refused to let the tears spill over, and kept scrolling through the adverts for rooms for rent.

3

Golden...

I opened the front door to two women standing on my doorstep. I frowned and asked, "Which one of you is Alyssa?"

The cool drink of water who was a corkscrew strawberry blonde with legs for fucking days pointed at the shorter, pretty, if sort of plain, brunette and said, "She is," at the same time the brunette gave a little wave and meekly proclaimed, "I am."

"Nice to meet you," I said, sticking out my hand. She gripped it lightly in one of those wussy half-assed handshakes and I fought not to roll my eyes.

I looked at the strawberry blonde.

"You are?"

She smiled broadly and said, "I'm Kenzie. I'm the best friend."

"Nice to meet you, too. Come on in." I stepped aside and let the women through, all while thinking that this was a really bad idea. Alyssa's email had come through three or four days ago, pretty much right after I'd posted the ad. I'd had a couple of dudes respond the next day, but one had reeked of pot and the other had said he was between jobs but could get me the money by the end of the week. Yeah, no.

I'd sat on Alyssa's email, not too keen on rooming with a chick, but it wasn't like the offers were pouring in, and when I'd asked her availability to come see the room, she'd been cool, said whenever it was convenient for me. She'd also said she had the money up-front when I'd asked. I'd agreed to let her come see it, so I could get a better measure of her.

"I'm Rodrigo, but most of my friends call me Golden."

"Alyssa." She laughed nervously. "Most people call me Lys."

"Well, here's the living room, kitchen; dining room," I said sweeping out a hand. It was a funky layout, but I liked it. As you came in the front door, the living room was to your right, the dining table straight ahead, and the kitchen on the left. It was a bit of a jaunt around the table and straight back down the hall. The guest room was past the bathroom on the right, and my room was past the laundry closet on the left. I had my half-bath with a toilet, shower, and sink in the master suite, while she'd have the main bath out here.

I liked the exposed brick wall on the one side of the living room and in her room. It was an old building and kind of gave it some manly vibes. I walked the girls past the black couch and black dining table set. The dining table was a bit big for the space, seating six, but worth it when I had the guys or Angel and other family over. It wasn't often on that last one. I stopped just before the mouth of the hallway and turned.

"So, uh, if you don't mind me asking, what do you do for a living?"

"Actually, I own a florist shop about six blocks from here," she said. "When I answered the ad, I didn't realize that this place was so conveniently located. I could walk to work from here, which will be nice."

She drifted around the back of the couch past the shelving units built into the back wall of the living room. The guest bathroom was on the other side of that wall, a buffer between the spare bedroom and the sound system I had installed in here. I followed her with my eyes and nodding, said, "It's a decent-enough neighborhood. You have a car?" She shook her head and stopped at the bank of windows in the wall facing out over the alley and the street.

"Well, if you ever decide to get a car, the building has a deal with the garage around the corner. It's something like three hundred bucks a month to park a car in there; prices around here have gone batshit."

"You pay that much just to park your car?" Kenzie asked, and I tuned back to her. I swear, her blue eyes crossed. I laughed a little and shook my head.

"Motorcycle, and it's like less than half that for a bike, you can fit four of them into a full sized space. And before you ask – no, I'm not including the parking for my bike in the rent."

"I'm surprised they let you sublet," Lys said, and her voice was so quiet, I almost missed it. She was looking out one of the window panes. Those windows had a decent view of the mouth of the alley and into the street, if you stood at the right angle for it, which she was. She had a bit of a faraway look in her big brown eyes.

"They like having a cop in their building," I said with a shrug. "Come on, I'll show you the room; see if you like it."

She came back around to us, drifting along the hardwood like a ghost, and I chalked it up to just nerves and maybe a little heartbreak. She did say in her email the reason she was moving was because of a divorce. I thought it was a little weird at the time. Didn't the woman usually get the house and everything? I didn't get it, but it wasn't any of my business. I didn't really care, unless she couldn't come up with the rent; then I would care a lot.

"Just so you know, I don't anticipate we'll be seeing a lot of each other, which suits me just fine."

She stopped in front of me and made eye contact for, I think, the first time, her deep brown eyes sharpening, her brow wrinkled slightly. and she asked, "Why is that?"

"I work second tour, two in the afternoon to around ten at night," I said.

She looked considering, then it seemed like she was relieved and she gave a nod. I gestured up the hall, an 'after you', and let the women go first. I didn't like having unknown quantities at my back. It was never a good idea. I'd seen some shit. Some of the most innocent-looking kids could be strapped and loaded for bear, looking to kill my ass for the uniform I wore, both over there and over here. I wasn't about to let my guard down. I stopped at what would be her door and turned the knob, pushing it open and all the way back, flush to the wall. Habit.

"It's not much," I said, as she and Kenzie stepped through.

"There was no mention of a desk," she said.

"I can have it moved out if you want."

"No, actually, I was wondering if I could use it. It'd be good for me to do my paperwork at the end of the day. I don't like staying in the shop past closing anymore."

"Yeah, sure. I don't think I have anything in it. It was my abuela's. All this furniture was."

Kenzie gave Lys a sharp look. "Your what?" she asked me.

"His grandmother's," Lys supplied. "'Abuela' is Spanish for 'grandmother'."

"You speak Spanish?" I asked.

She shook her head, "Just what I remember from high school."

"Ah, fair enough."

I know it was bad, but it meant I could bitch about her to Angel, to a degree, in front of her if she got on my nerves and happened to be home.

"So, what do you think?" I asked, getting used to the idea of having a chick in my space, like, full-time.

She exchanged a long look with her bestie and sighed. "I'll take it," she said softly, and there was a note of trepidation in her voice. Somehow that made it a little easier on me, knowing she was just as dubious about this shit as I was.

"Cool, when do you feel you can move in?"

"I have her things packed in my living room, we can be back in an hour if tonight is good," Kenzie said, and she didn't sound happy about it at all.

"What's the hurry?" I asked, laughing a little.

"She's been sleeping on my couch for the last few weeks."

"It'd be really nice to sleep in a bed," Lys answered, and she looked longingly in its direction.

"You got the money, then, yeah. Tonight works for me. You'll pretty much be on your own, though. I got a tour."

"A what?" Kenzie's brow wrinkled.

"A shift," Lys supplied and I smiled. She was smarter than she looked. She reached into her purse, it hung cross-ways over her chest and between her tits, and pulled out a plain white banking envelope. She handed it over and I counted the cash inside. All crisp, fresh, one-hundred-dollar bills. It was all there.

"I'll get you a key," I said, and she smiled a little sadly.

"Okay, thank you."

"You bet."

4

*A*lyssa...

"You're sure about this?"

"For the last time, Kenzie, I'm sure." She pulled smoothly into the loading zone in front of Golden's building. It was a strange nickname, and I wondered if I would ever find out how he got it.

"Oh, wow, there he is," she said, and I rolled my eyes slightly. I loved my friend dearly, but there were times she could be a bit of an airhead.

"I know," I said with a little laugh. "I texted him like he asked me to, so he could bring down the key." He hadn't been able to find it right away and had told us to get my things. I didn't think a cop was apt to steal my money because, you know, he was a cop. I still had to admit it'd played havoc on my nerves, though.

"Hey," he said, a bit breathlessly. "Sorry about that, here you go." He handed me two silver keys on a weak wire ring.

"One apartment and one mailbox," he said, though I didn't need the explanation.

"Thank you," I murmured.

He squinted into the back of Kenzie's SUV.

"Is that it?" he asked.

"Yeah," Kenzie said. "Think you might be able to grab one?"

"Yeah, I'm good for a load up, but then I gotta get ready for work. Gimme two." He left my door and went around to the back hatch. Kenzie was out of the car and met him there. She gave him two of the totes, one of the heavy ones and another, lighter one on top. He marched into the building without as much as a backward glance and I took a deep breath and let it out slowly.

He was as tall as, and probably bigger than, Raymond, which was fairly physically imposing. He was a police officer, which meant training, and that made him scarier in my book. Unlike my soon-to-be-ex-husband, Golden moved with a surety and grace that said he was well in control of his body, beyond just an average person. He also had some impressive muscle; the sleeves of his t-shirt hugged his biceps and the clearly-defined musculature of his back rippled through the thin cotton material. I shut the car door behind me and watched him walk away. I blinked in my sudden awareness that I found my new roommate attractive.

I hadn't counted on that. It left me feeling more than a little discombobulated, even as Kenzie called out to me, "Hey, Lys, you okay?"

"Fine!" I said hurriedly. "I'm fine."

Kenzie and I double-teamed the rest of the totes and suitcase. I held the elevator while she loaded them all in, running back and forth from her car. The load zone was only good for thirty minutes, so she would have to go find a place to park. Honestly, though, I wished she would just go. I didn't think I could get settled with her here, plus, she'd already done so much for me that my guilt was working overtime.

"Okay, let's get this stuff into the apartment and then I'll go park for real." She stepped onto the elevator beside me and I let the doors close.

I chewed my lip for a second and finally said, "Actually, it's okay. If you can just help me get this stuff into the apartment, I can take it from there. There's no need for you to stay. You have things to do."

"Are you sure?" She looked torn. The elevator shuddered and came to a halt. The doors seemingly took forever to open back up.

"I'm sure," I said, stepping off and dragging a stack of totes off the elevator, over the thin carpet. Kenzie did the same with the other stack and snatched the handle to the suitcase as the doors tried to shut on us again. I glanced up the hall and realized Golden's door stood open.

"You're really sure, Lys?" she asked one more time.

I gave her a mock-frown and reminded her, "This was your idea."

"No, moving this soon was your idea. It was just my idea you move into this apartment." She gave me a conspiratorial little smile and lowered her voice. "Bonus points that he turned out to be hot."

I blushed hard and shook my head, banishing the thought and said, "I shouldn't be thinking like that. At all."

Kenzie stopped me with a hand on my arm and said, "Lys, what Raymond did to you was undeniably shitty, but you'll get through this. I promise. You will."

I smoothed my lips together and nodded. I just wasn't ready for anything, I guess. I don't know, I still needed to unpack a lot of things, and not just these totes full of clothes and belongings. I swallowed hard, and jerked my head away from the elevator toward the door of the apartment, still standing open.

"Let's just get this stuff inside, okay?"

"Okay," she agreed, but I could tell that she wanted to say more. There was a lot to say, but none of it was anything I was willing to hear right now. I picked up two of the totes and struggled up the hall with them, setting them just inside the door and sliding them across the floor to rest at the end of the dining table. Golden had set the two he'd brought up on it.

I dashed back down the hall and took the handle to the suitcase that Kenzie offered me and she said, "Go on, I'll get the last three."

I gave a short nod and wheeled the suitcase all the way back to the bedroom. –My– bedroom. At least, for now.

I paused briefly by the closed door to Golden's room. I could hear the shower running and I quickly dashed the image of what he might look like, shirtless and with water cascading down his chest, from my mind. Kenzie was right. He was hot, and I? Well, I was emotionally-wounded, not dead.

I dragged the big suitcase in the open doorway of the room I'd rented and heaved it up onto the bed in front of me. I put my hands on my hips, letting out a gusty sigh at both the accomplishment and the effort of getting it up there on my own, and surveyed the space once more, this time with an eye toward where to put it all.

"Watch yourself," Kenzie said gently, but I still jumped. I stepped aside so she could get through the door with a tote full of documents. She went over to the roll-top desk and set the tote on the deep navy carpet beside it.

"Thanks."

"No problem, you start doing your thing, I'll bring back a couple more."

I went over to the closet and slid it open. No hangers inside, damn, but it did have a row of shelves on one end, which would be useful, and a shelf all along the top.

It'd been ages and ages since I'd done a roommate situation, and back then, it'd been a dorm roommate and a single room. This would probably be easier to work with, but not as easy as having my own home would have been.

Still, keeping my business running without having to let go of any employees wasn't easy. Neither were the mounting lawyer's fees, or the fact that other bills, bills that were in my name, were piling up because Ray refused to pay them until I talked to him, even though they were for the condo he was the one living in. –That– wasn't going to go on for long. My lawyer wanted it liquidated, and I wanted my half of that money.

Kenzie returned with two totes of clothes and went around the bed to the dresser set against the brick wall below the window in here. She set them on top of it and turned around with a dissatisfied sigh, asking, "Are you sure you don't want me to stay?"

I wasn't, but I needed to do this on my own. I also didn't want to push her away or make her feel like I didn't value all she had been, and still was doing for me, though.

"I need a few things," I said, at last.

She perked up. "Like what?"

"Hangers, for one."

She started looking around and said, "Sheets, and a better bedspread would be nice in here."

"Yeah," I agreed.

"What's my budget?" she asked, with a devilish grin, and I instantly took back any thoughts I'd had about her being flighty. She'd instantly known what I wanted.

I grinned and reached into my purse at my hip. I pulled out my wallet and huffed out a harsh sigh at how little was in it.

"Looks like I have about a hundred and twenty dollars to pull it off," I said, cringing.

"No problem, if it's one thing I learned from Pinterest and forever watching those money-saving-hack videos, it's how to shop and decorate on a budget."

"I never did get why you watch those things; you make quite a bit of money."

"I also like to take vacations and go places, and the best way to do that, is to save a lot of money. A penny saved is a penny earned."

"Right, well, do your frugal best with this." I handed her the money.

She smiled and winked.

"I may or may not throw in some of my own. No arguing!" She put up her finger and wagged it back and forth when I opened my mouth to protest.

"Fine," I grumbled.

"Do what you can, I'll be back in a couple of hours."

I nodded and she came back around the bed and skirted out the door. I heard the front door to the apartment open and close and I let out a semi-defeated sigh. It would be nice, getting back to taking care of myself. I wanted so badly to find the woman I'd been before all of this. I was scared I would never get her back.

I sighed again, this time at the monumental task of getting all of this put away. With a deep breath, I started with the dresser, glad that she'd brought in the totes of dresser clothes first.

I was midway through refolding all the things as I put them into dresser drawers when a light rap of knuckles fell on my open bedroom door. I jumped and let out a startled little yip, immediately pressing my fingertips to my lips self-consciously.

"My bad, didn't mean to scare you. I'm headed out." I turned around and my mouth went a little dry. Golden stood in his uniform in the doorway, and it made him rather imposing, especially with the added bulk of the protective vest he had on over his uniform shirt but under his jacket. The blockiness of it and the bold white letters across the front proclaiming 'POLICE' was seriously intimidating.

"Oh, okay. Anything I should know?"

He shook his head, the light from the hallway catching on the damp strands of his hair and giving him an almost haloed effect.

"Nah, don't think so. Your friend coming back?"

"Oh, yeah, she went to grab me a few things like hangers and bedding. I'll, um, give yours back. Where should I put it?"

"Hall closet where the washer and dryer live; there's an open space on the shelf above them. If there's not, just leave it folded on top of the dryer."

"Okay, will do, thanks."

"No problem. I'm off at ten, usually home by midnight or so."

"Okay."

"Have a good night, then."

"I will, you too, um, have a good shift, I guess. Be careful."

He gave me a reckless grin and a nod, and disappeared from the doorway while I silently derided myself. *Be careful? Like you're his mom? Get over yourself, Lys, he probably thinks you're a total dork.*

I'd meant to say it to be nice but – oh, god, how embarrassing. I just needed to keep my mouth shut. I sighed, and went back to folding and putting things away. I really just wanted a hot shower and to go to bed.

5

*G*olden...

At the end of a long shift, I returned to an apartment that didn't look a damn bit different from the way it'd always been. Not a single thing of hers was anywhere to be seen. The door to the spare room – her room, now – was closed, and I kind of liked that it was working out this way initially. Of course, it was only the first night, but still...

Maybe we wouldn't even really see each other that much. Maybe having a chick for a roommate wasn't going to be such a pain in the ass after all. Though I had to admit, the temptation to flirt with her somewhat-airheaded friend had been a strong one. That bitch had legs for days.

I went into my room and shut the door, beat one off in the shower, and threw on some comfortable sweats before I went out into the living room to catch up on a couple of my shows. I eased back into my couch and switched on the TV, lowering the volume by half or so. I listened for a minute, but when I didn't hear anything, I felt the tension ease out of my shoulders.

I put on some sports review and just kind of vegged for a while. I didn't get many evenings alone and it was nice to just chill.

She came out, rubbing her eyes, about twenty minutes later, and headed for the kitchen. I watched her drift around the island on the other side of the dining table and open a few cupboards. She pulled down a glass and I said, "You could have just asked."

She damn near jumped out of her over-sized nightshirt, that looked like it could have been one of her ex-husband's old business shirts, and let out a little yip of surprise. I raised an eyebrow. It wasn't like I was hiding, out here in plain sight with the TV on. What the fuck?

"Sorry, I thought you were asleep," she said. I shook my head and she drew a glass of water from the tap.

"Y'okay?"

"Yeah, I'm good, I'm good." She laughed nervously and swallowed some more water, leaning back against the counter.

"Awfully jumpy, aren't you?"

"Mm, bad dream. Can't seem to shake it."

"Huh, what do you usually do for that?"

She looked self-conscious and said, "Better living through chemistry, to be honest."

"What, like weed?" I scowled.

"No." She shifted uncomfortably. "The doctor gave me a prescription..."

"Say no more." I held up my hands. "Ain't none of my business."

She cleared her throat and said, "Thanks. Anyway, goodnight."

"Night."

She padded barefoot back up the hallway and her door closed softly behind her. She'd looked way more shook than anybody should be, that I was awake and not asleep, like I'd caught her in the act or something. It was nagging at me when I went to bed myself sometime later and I decided that I would need to run her name through the system at work. After all, the background check which I'd run for a criminal record and her financials had come up clean and her credit was good, but they didn't tend to turn out a name when a person was a victim of something.

It wasn't any of my business if she was just trying to put her life back together. I had to admit, though, my curiosity was piqued as to what her deal was, now.

I turned in, and she was gone by the time I got up and wasn't back by the time I left for work. That suited me just fine.

I promised myself I would run her name, but shit got busy, like it was the full moon, or something, more psych calls than you could shake a stick at. I'd forgotten about it completely, and when I got home, she was once again nowhere to be seen, locked up tight behind her bedroom door.

I was too wired to sleep, so I showered, grabbed a change of clothes, and leathered-up for a ride.

I left back out of the apartment and hauled ass over to the garage where my bike was parked, and rode to the 10-13 to blow off some steam. It was my Friday night, so why the fuck not?

6

Alyssa...

I wasn't sure what woke me up at first, but then I heard it again. Drunken laughter out in the living room was followed by some really loud shushing. I rolled my eyes and clicked on the little Himalayan salt lamp I had on the small bedside table closest to the bedroom door.

A thud, more giggling, and stupid laughter. I swung my legs over and stood, went to my door and opened it.

"Oh, my god! Who is *she*? Your sister?"

"Nah, roommate, sorry not sorry, Lys." Golden half-slurred, and pushed open his bedroom door.

"It's fine," I murmured lamely, not sure what else to say.

"Sorry!" his date chirped, and she, at least, seemed more apologetic. He gave her a shove through his bedroom door and shut it soundly behind him. I let out a little frustrated sigh and hoped that this wouldn't be a regular thing, before I closed my door. More thumping and drunk laughing emanated from behind his closed door just as I shut mine.

I went back to bed and turned out the light, staring up at the darkened ceiling and the lines of light cast by the blinds over the window.

The rhythmic thumping and porn-star moaning started up a few minutes later. I rolled my eyes, rolled onto my side, and clapped a pillow over my head.

I had to work in the morning!

I gritted my teeth. The louder they got, the more my resentment set in. I eventually fell back to sleep despite the noise, but it was a fitful one full of nightmares and flashbacks. I hated it and I was just on the edge of hating him.

I woke up to blessed silence, but still got up a full hour before my alarm was set to go off. I tried a hot shower to fully wake up, but only caffeine was going to cure this hot mess. *If there really was any cure.* I went to the kitchen and used his coffee. Petty? Sure, but I felt like he owed me at least that much.

While it brewed, I went in and got ready for the day, getting dressed, then turning on my laptop on the desk and scrolling through open invoices. I sent a few reminders for the ones creeping up on their due date and snippier ones for the two that were past due. I sat back with a gusty sigh; it was a mix of feeling accomplished for the small tasks that were done, and frustrated for the veritable mountain of the rest that still lay ahead of me.

I knew there were growing pains to every living situation, but this was only day three. I worried that I'd made a terrible mistake, but it was too late now; I was here and I would be stuck here for at least several more months while the divorce proceedings dragged on, thanks to Raymond.

At least we weren't in a state where it was pretty much legal for a husband to force his wife to stay married to him.

I went back out to the kitchen and doctored a travel mug of coffee for myself and, my purse slung over my shoulder, my keys in hand, left to deal with work.

∼

"Um, Lyssa?"

"What is it, Avery?" I asked my shop-girl. She had been the one to text me the photos of my husband with the other woman. I still didn't know who that other woman was, but I wished her the best of luck with him. At this point, I wouldn't wish Raymond on my worst enemy.

"I think your husband just placed an order," she said, and looked like she was about to cry. She felt so guilty about what happened between me and Ray and it seemed like nothing I could say or do would convince her that it wasn't her fault.

It was his. Squarely his... and maybe a little bit of my fault too, but not for what he did to me. No one deserved that.

Then why are you covering for him? I probably asked myself the same question a thousand times a day at this point. I wasn't covering for him over the beating. The rape? I don't know what possessed me to keep that part a secret. Shame? Guilt? *The fact he cried and kept apologizing while he did it?* I just don't know, but I'd lied when they'd asked me at the hospital if it went beyond just the hitting. I swallowed hard and held out my hand.

"Let me see," I murmured. She brought over the invoice and I frowned, asking, "What makes you think this is him?"

She had the grace to look embarrassed and said, "It was a man who placed the order, and he insisted that the owner deliver it, personally."

"Okay, that's unusual," I agreed. I sighed indecisively and finally said, "Have Jeremy run the order per usual. I'll deal with any fallout if and when it happens."

"Okay," she said, and looked as skeptical as I felt about the whole thing.

"Thanks, Avery."

She nodded and disappeared from the chiller, out through the plastic curtain into the rest of the store. I continued making the arrangement of roses I'd been working on and just wished for the day to be over already.

Time dragged on, the minute hand seemingly carrying an extra burden as it made its way around the clock. Finally, Avery reappeared and said goodnight. I went out and locked up behind her and sagged against the counter once the lights were all out. I was a bone-weary I hadn't felt in a long time.

Part of it was a deep mental exhaustion, worrying and wondering over the mystery order. Jeremy had run it, said that he'd delivered the flowers to reception at a dentist's office without incident and that was that.

I didn't know what to make of it, to be honest, and I really tried to shove it aside and not think about it anymore.

Instead, I went into the cooler and finished up the boutonnieres for a wedding service the next day and tidied up before leaving myself. I hadn't realized how late it had gotten and it was dark by the time I slipped out the front door.

"Lys, can we talk?"

I froze.

"No, Raymond, I don't want to. There's an order of protection in place. Please leave before I scream."

I turned around and he stood not far from me. I cringed back into the door, and he looked defeated.

"Don't do that, I would never hurt you like that again, you have to know that."

I did know that, I think... but I wasn't about to put it to the test.

"Just go away, please?"

"Fine, but I really think we should talk; there's something I want to tell you."

"What?"

"Come have dinner with me," he said, and I shook my head.

"No, Raymond. I'm calling the police, you shouldn't be here, and honestly, I could care less about what you have to say." I pulled out my phone.

"No, it's fine! I'm leaving. Just, Lys... I'm really sorry."

My soon-to-be ex-husband put out his hands and stepped back towards his car at the curb. I huddled in on myself, scared, and waited for him to drive away. I suddenly couldn't wait to be home. I didn't know what he was playing at, why it was so important that I deliver the flowers myself, but I also didn't care.

The whole way back to the apartment I kept shivering despite the warm evening and couldn't help but look over my shoulder, wondering if he was watching, scared that he was somehow pacing me in the slow-moving traffic.

I should have called the police, asked for help, but then again... I lived with the police, now. I stepped into the lobby of the building the apartment was in and hurried to the elevator. I felt like maybe, if I moved fast enough, I could leave all of it out in the street behind me. I mean, I'd only been living with the police for three days. The last thing I wanted to do was tell my roommate, who I barely knew, all my dirty laundry.

If I told Golden now, or asked for help, he probably wouldn't hesitate to hand me back my money and tell me to go. I can't say I would blame him; it's probably what I would do if it were me in his stead. I got off of the elevator and quickly hurried up the hall to the door. I keyed myself in, my chest still heaving with panic, and shut the door firmly behind me, leaning on it heavily and turning the locks, trying to tamp down the rising flood of emotions that felt just awful, piled up on top of each other like they were.

"Where's the fire at?" he drawled from the couch and I jumped and let out a yip. I clapped my hands over my mouth to stifle the noise and turned. He sat stoically and raised an eyebrow at me.

"Okay, what's going on?" he asked when I didn't volunteer any information.

"Nothing!" I lied, knowing full well I was bad at it, so I quickly tried to make something up. "Just a creepy homeless guy out on the sidewalk. Scared me half to death."

He eyed me carefully and nodded, saying, "That I can believe. You're jumpy as hell."

A hysterical little bubble of laughter escaped me and I put my hand back over my mouth to stifle it. I nodded rapidly, my eyes beginning to swim, and forced a smile.

"I think I'm just tired," I said.

"Yeah, about that, I tend to bring home a lot of dates. I'll, uh, try to keep it down next time."

I nodded rapidly and said, "Thank you," then beat a hasty retreat to my bedroom and closed the door. I immediately kicked off my shoes and sat down at my computer to type a lengthy email delineating the exchange with Raymond, sending it to my lawyer. I felt better for it. If anything, she would know what to do about it. Maybe she would know who to call or what to say to make him stop.

Yeah right, I thought savagely. *Like a piece of paper is going to make him do anything.*

I closed my eyes and tried to get my rapid breathing to return to normal, but finally had to give up. I took one of the Xanax prescribed to me and waited for it to kick in, for the numb feeling to spread out from the middle and the chemically-induced apathy to take hold. Sometimes, like now, it was just better not to feel anything.

7

*G*olden...

I shook my head at the broad and her bizarre behavior and told myself I needed to look her shit up when I got back to work. Angel must have had his twin voodoo working overtime because my phone lit up, with his ugly mug on the screen, just about two seconds after she shut her door.

"Yo, what's up?" I greeted him.

"Had some downtime, figured I'd call and see how the roomie situation was going."

I shifted on the leather of my couch and said, "So far so good." I dropped my voice. "Chick's a little weird, jumpy as all get out."

"Huh, 'jumpy' how?"

I told him how every time I even remotely caught her by surprise she'd jump and yip. It would actually be kind of adorable – if it weren't so fucked-up.

Sometimes, it was like she just got lost so far inside her own head she just didn't fathom anyone was around or in her space. Which was hilarious, because she wasn't in her space, she was in my space, but, whatever.

When it was like that, it had an edge of cute. What wasn't cute, was when she would cower or cringe, or how her arms went up and covered her chest in an almost-defensive posture, like she was trying to hold herself in and ward something off, all at the same time. Then, it was anything but cute. It was worrisome, bothersome, *And it isn't any of your fucking business,* I reminded myself.

"Sounds like maybe she's had a rough time of things."

"Dunno, it's none of my business, really."

"Well, no, it's not, but –"

"No 'buts' about it, bro. It's straight-up none of my business. I'm off from saving the goddamn world when I'm home."

Angel sighed on the other end of the line. I loved my twin, but sometimes he just didn't have a fucking 'off' switch. It was one of our biggest bones of contention. He felt the need to be some sort of crusader for every lost cause that came around, whereas I was a live-and-let-live type. People needed help, they knew how to fuckin' ask, which I told him.

"Some people don't know how to ask," he said unhappily, and I nodded, realized he couldn't see it, and gave a heavy, exasperated sigh myself.

"Can't save everybody, and the fact they don't know how to ask is their problem, not mine."

Angel grunted noncommittally on the other end of the line. It was the classic signal for *I hear what you're saying, I just don't agree, so I'm not answering* I wasn't up for beating that dead horse of a debate, so I asked him, "What're you doing tomorrow night?"

"Same thing you're doing. Club meeting."

"Cool, I'll see you there."

"Yeah." He didn't sound too happy about the fact I was trying to rush him off the line, but tough. I didn't feel like arguing.

"See you there, Angel."

"See you there, bro. Love you."

"Yeah, you too."

I hung up and restarted the program I'd been watching, settling back and propping my feet on the coffee table.

Tonight was Friday night, but she didn't go anywhere. With the way she'd come in here, locking the front door up tight behind her, I wasn't too surprised about that. I didn't know if the whole not going out was going to legit be her regular routine yet. It was too soon to tell, but I had my suspicions.

I shoved them off to the side and didn't think about it. A few minutes later, she came out of hiding. I listened to her bedroom door open and then the bathroom door shut. A second or two after that, the shower started. I turned up the TV and minded my own business; that was harder than it sounded when the door opened back up and the damp air from the bathroom, permeated by this heady citrus-and-floral scent, crept out into the living room.

Whatever she used, she had good taste. I liked the smell.

I expected her to make herself some dinner or something, but nope. She just went back into her bedroom without a word or a sound, and I might as well have been living on my own again. Shit, that honestly worked for me.

I wrapped it up, still nursing a mild hangover from the night before, and called it an early night. I paused outside my bedroom door and waited, and sure enough, caught the faint, soft sounds of her weeping through her bedroom door. I frowned. Something was definitely up with her, but it wasn't my job to pry, unless it affected me directly. Which it didn't. I went to bed, crashed hard, and stayed down for the count.

When I got up the next morning, her door was still shut and there wasn't a sound from inside. I figured she'd gone out. I was making some breakfast when she scared the shit out of me by asking softly from the other side of the kitchen island, "Is there coffee?"

"Fuck! Make some damn noise, would you? You nearly gave me a fucking heart attack!"

"Sorry," she murmured.

"Okay, yeah, some ground rules are in order. You cannot sneak up on me."

"I said I was sorry," she mumbled and wouldn't look at me.

"It's not about 'sorry', it's about safety. I'm not just a cop, I'm also a combat veteran. Sometimes training takes over first and questions come later. I wouldn't want you to get hurt."

She gave me a long, slow blink as she processed the information I'd just given her and repeated herself once again; I was thinking it was out of some sort of habit at this point. "I'm sorry…"

"Don't be sorry, just change the behavior," I told her. She nodded and I changed the subject.

"Yeah, there's coffee. I'm making it, now."

"Thank god," she said, putting her hands flat on the kitchen island and stretching forward, yawning.

"Sounded like you went out pretty quick," I remarked.

"Yeah, combination of the crappy night's sleep the night before, a long day at work, and the Xanax hangover."

I lifted my chin and slid the first mug over to her. She looked like she needed it more than me.

"Didn't think florist work was that stressful," I said.

She smirked and I handed over the cream from the fridge and the little pot of sugar I kept on hand. She doctored her coffee while I waited, then said, "You've never had to deal with a bridezilla, have you?"

"Only when I arrested one for beating the shit out of her maid-of-honor for fucking the groom the night before the wedding."

She winced and said, "I think she earned that one, don't you think?"

I shook my head and took the first sip of my java. "I don't get paid to think. I get paid to follow the rules, uphold the law, and do shit by the book."

She pondered that for a moment and finally gave a single nod, "Fair enough."

I figured she had a stake in the whole solidarity with a fallen sister thing on the cheating front. Isn't that how most marriages ended? Cheating was usually the top of the list, but with her being the one all moved-out and renting my spare bedroom, it was likely she was the cheater, wasn't it? I wasn't about to ask, and it wasn't my place to assume shit about her, but I did wonder.

Guess it was written all over my face because she gave a bitter little half-laugh and shook her head.

"I wasn't the one who cheated," she said simply. "I just didn't want to live in a house of lies anymore. Besides, I couldn't afford the mortgage by myself, even if I did want to. Let him have it."

"I wasn't asking," I said, holding up my hands.

"No, you weren't," she said simply, then she cracked a faint smile and said, "But you were wondering."

I nodded slowly. "Fair enough," I threw back at her, and her smile grew.

She wasn't half-bad to look at when she smiled. In fact, sitting there with no makeup on, her hair sleep tousled like it was, in her nightshirt and bathrobe, I decided that she wasn't bad to look at first thing in the morning at all. In fact, she was kind of beautiful.

"So," I said in an attempt to make some small talk. "What're your big plans for today?"

"Mm." She finished her sip of coffee. "Work."

"It's Saturday, you don't get a weekend?"

She shook her head. "Not if I want to keep us all employed."

I nodded, "Well, have fun with that. I'm headed out."

"Okay, have fun."

I nodded, "Have a good day at work, I guess."

"Thanks."

I left her sitting at the kitchen island, on one of the tall stools tucked up under it, the dining room table at her back. She was reading on an electronic-reader thing, her long brown hair was up in one of those plastic clips, stray tendrils artfully draped around her face. Yeah, I had to take my earlier assessment of 'plain' back. She was a knockout when she wasn't so self-conscious.

I went for a long ride, solo. Took some wind therapy before heading into the 10-13 for the meetup. When I walked in, the sun was starting to dip below the horizon and a decent-sized chunk of the guys were already in the fishbowl around the big table. I went in and claimed an unoccupied seat. The ribbing began almost immediately.

"So, Golden, I hear you're living with a chick now." Oz had this shit-eating grin on his face and I rolled my eyes.

"Fuckin' Angel," I muttered.

"Is she now? Do tell…" Poe was grinning, too. I gave him a look like '*Really, dude?*' and Oz laughed out loud.

"Look at him, he don't know what to say."

"You're right, so I'll keep it to sign language," I shot back and gave him the finger. He fell out laughing and I let out a chuckle of my own.

"Where do you get this shit?" Blaze demanded when he caught his breath.

I shrugged.

"Oz, mostly."

Oz went into another round of laughter, rocking in his seat, and Skids banged his knuckles against the tabletop.

"all right, all right, all right! Much as I find Golden's new living situation truly fascinating, we got shit to talk about. Although. to be honest, I got no idea what that shit –is–, this time around, so. Golden: what's she like?"

More laughter and I let it roll off me like water off a duck's back. I gave a half-assed, nonchalant shrug and told them the truth.

"No idea yet, it's only been a few days, and it's not like I'm fuckin' her. She's just living there."

Youngblood rolled his eyes and snorted, "Yet."

I scowled at him. "I think I know better'n to shit where I eat, yo."

Oz, between bouts of laughter, choked out, "Didn't know you were into it that way! Oh, man." There was more laughter at my expense and I was starting to get irritated.

I just shook my head and kept my mouth shut after that. Nobody liked to be under fire, friendly or not, and that was what it had started to feel like. I tried not to care, but deep down, it bothered me some. The thing I liked about these guys is they got it when they started to go too far, and they reined it in. They could be dicks sometimes, but they were never dicks about that. Still, my mood was a bit darker and it looked like I needed to have another talk with my twin about carelessly dropping my business.

Meeting turned to this and that, talk about doing a group ride sooner rather than later, that sort of shit. Before we knew it, it was over, and I was already scanning the bar floor, looking for a mindless hookup to work out some of my underlying frustration.

"Redhead, eleven o'clock," Oz called out from behind me and I got a bead on her. I felt my mouth turn down at the corners as I considered her.

"You hit that?" I asked.

"Crazier than a Mexican lizard. Hell yeah, I hit that. Was a wild ride, but I'd hit it and quit it, boy I tell yah."

"With a descriptor of 'crazier than a Mexican lizard', I'm gonna pass, and also, fuck you."

Oz laughed his ass off and I grinned; he went up for his turn at the dartboard and I settled on the brunette friend of the redhead. So what if she sort of resembled my current roomie?

"He's goin' in for the kill!" Oz declared as I moved through the crowd and I flipped him off over my shoulder to a bunch of raucous laughter.

8

Alyssa...

Weeks went by and Golden's initial apology about bringing random hookups home and making too much noise turned out to be bullshit. He did it at least once a week, but more often than not, it was more, a lot more. He even brought them home on his work nights, which I couldn't fathom. It wouldn't have bothered me, but for the fact that I'd had two randomly open up my bedroom door, giggling loudly, and at least one throw up all over my bathroom.

To his credit, Golden had cleaned that up, but still, gross. I'd found a new appreciation for the cleanser he'd used, though. I'd never heard of Fabuloso, but it smelled really nice. I guess there was a silver lining to just about everything.

One of my biggest frustrations was that he brought these random women over when I had work the next morning. I'd been too afraid to say anything, but we were well into the second month of my living here, on the cusp of the third, and damn it to hell, I paid rent, too! So, when I was woken, yet again, I finally snapped.

It was just too much. The laughing, the thumping, the porn-star-level moaning, the slapping sounds, I heard everything. It was a struggle for me, too, knowing that I was probably way past my prime in the desirability department, not only due to my barrenness, but also thanks to my whore-mongering ex-husband. He still hadn't quit with the fucking flower orders to that damn dentist's office with the special request that I be the one to deliver them personally.

There was no proving he had violated the no-contact order explicitly; he always placed the order with Avery, not me, and there was no proof that he was placing the order, he always used an untraceable gift card to do it. I wasn't about to turn down an upwards-of-a-hundred-and-twenty-dollar order every week, not when I knew he could afford it and I was barely making it.

I lay there, listening to the laughter and the noisy kissing, and wished they would just go to his room already, when my door burst open.

"No, not that one!" he whisper-shouted, but it was too late.

I sat up and yelled out, "Enough is enough!" I threw my pillow at them and pointed at Golden, "We are so talking about this tomorrow, because this is bullshit!"

He cocked his head and shoved the girl, another brunette, back off of him and said sharply, "Playtime's over, badge-bunny. I'll see you out."

Oh, he wanted to do this now? Okay, I was game. He marched her by the hips back down the hall and I sprang out of bed. I pulled my bathrobe off the post of the headboard that it lived on, and swung it on while he dealt with her whiny protests out in the living room. I heard the front door open and shut and the heavy tread of his boots against the faux-hardwood tile that comprised the floors of the main traffic areas in the apartment.

He appeared like a dark shadow in the doorway of my room and I clicked on my Himalayan salt lamp by the bed. Funny, it didn't do a damn thing to sooth or calm me. When I turned, Golden's eyes were ablaze with dark light.

"Just what the fuck is your problem?" he demanded, and he wasn't nearly as drunk as I'd thought he'd been. That was both comforting and even more infuriating at the same time. That mollified me to a certain degree. I didn't know that such polar opposites of emotion could be felt at once.

"My problem is that I live here, too! I pay rent, I'm not a guest, and this is getting god damn ridiculous! I need sleep, Golden. I have to work!"

He snorted like it was the dumbest thing he'd ever heard and that just pissed me off even more. What came out of his mouth had me damn near frothing at the mouth.

"Because arranging flowers is so goddamn important."

"It's important to me! It's important to my clients, and it's important to the people who depend on me and my business to stay employed! God, you are such an arrogant ass!"

He stood up straighter, his chin lifting, his nostrils flaring, and he took a menacing step into the room. I didn't want the bed at my back, not when he looked so like Ray from that night, and so I turned and took a step back, the desk and wall behind me. He kept advancing and I shrank back, wedging myself between the closet and the sliver of wall between its sliding door and the desk.

I made this unbidden, animalistic, anguished noise and shrank down as small as I could.

And he froze mid-step.

"What the fuck, girl?" He sounded mystified but I couldn't bring myself to look up as the memories swamped me, rolled me, and sucked me down, down, down, into that dark, dark, place.

"Whatever," I heard him mutter, and a second later, my bedroom door slammed shut.

I dissolved into tears immediately.

9

Golden...

I was shook. Right to the core. I had never, –ever– hit a woman, and as pissed-off as she'd just made me, I hadn't planned on hitting her, but she acted like I was some big damn brute.

I'd probably meant to run her shit like a thousand times at work, but I'd just kept conveniently forgetting about it. *Not tonight,* I avowed.

Something seriously fucked-up had gone down with her, and yeah, I may not be a fuckin' superhero by any means, but that reaction had been way... *Madre di Dios*. I stood in the hallway, my chest heaving with a shot of adrenaline as I listened to her bawl on the other side of the door.

I felt this fractured ache in the center of my chest listening to that weeping, but there was fuck-all I could do about it. If I went back in there now, I'd just make it worse. She hadn't met Angel yet, and I couldn't remember if the fact I had a twin had come up in any of our casual and short conversations. So, that ruled out calling him for help. All she'd probably see in her panicked state was me coming back through the fucking door.

I didn't want to out her fuckin' business to anybody, certainly not to one of my bros in the club. So the only conclusion I could reach was to, let this shit go, deal with listening to the crying jag, and try to talk to her after I got off tour tomorrow night when we were both much calmer.

I went into my room but left the door open a crack, so I could hear. She cried like that for what felt like forever and I thought back on the last couple of months of her being here. She hadn't been a half-bad roommate, but I wasn't one-hundred that I could say the same about me.

I changed into a comfortable pair of lounge pants and listened. She quieted after a time and I felt hella guilty, replaying all the times I'd brought chicks home and knowingly woken her up. All the afternoons I'd gotten up and coffee was still sitting in the pot from that morning. The time I'd had to scrub drunk-puke out of the bathroom that was supposed to be hers, because the dumb bitch I'd been banging hadn't realized that I had a fuckin' toilet right fucking here off my room.

She hadn't said a word about it. She'd woken up and come to to pee, and blinked owlishly at me. I'd told her to use my bathroom, but she'd simply said quietly that she'd wait and asked if I needed help. Who does that? Volunteers to clean up some other drunk bitch's vomit? I'd said no, and she'd gone back to her room, but she'd fallen back asleep before I'd finished and I didn't have the heart to wake her up.

I'd felt like kind of an asshole then, but it hadn't stopped me. I'd still brought random chicks and badge-bunnies home. I don't even think she'd noticed that I'd somehow switched from blondes to brunettes. Hell, –I– hadn't noticed, until one of the guys had pointed it out last week. Fuck me if they ever found out that the woman living in my apartment was a brunette; I'd never hear the end of it.

I was still awake when her alarm went off, and I got up silently and went to my door, grabbing the handle and easing it shut silently, wincing as I did it, afraid I would give myself away. I heard her door open, the smart little kitten-heeled pumps she wore with her prim-and-proper skirt and blouse sets and business-appropriate dresses clicked down the hall past my door, and she didn't even stop in the kitchen. I heard the apartment door open and whump lightly shut, and that was it.

I went out and checked, and sure enough, she'd keyed the lock and deadbolt shut behind her. I doubled-down on my guilty feelings for some reason at that and went back to bed. I fell into an uneasy sleep that didn't really do me much good, right until my own alarm went off.

I dragged ass into work. My partner took one look at me and stated the obvious.

"You look like shit."

"Thanks, Captain Obvious."

"Seriously, should I worry?"

"Naw, man. Just had a fight with the roommate, stewed on it way longer than I should have. I'm not hung-over. I tend to pick 'em up drunk, and play drunk without actually being all that drunk myself, you know?"

"Just looking to hit it and quit it?"

"Yup."

"Dangerous game, you ask me," one of the old-timers on the force chimed in.

"Good thing I didn't fuckin' ask you, then, huh, Romansky?"

He didn't take it personal, just chuckled and walked out the locker room. I turned back to my partner, Pruitt.

"I'm actually with Romansky on this one. That's how you end up on a rape charge due to buyer's remorse."

"Never had any buyer's remorse. You must be doing it wrong," I said.

"Ha ha, fuck you. Seriously, though. You're playing with fire on that, bro. All it takes is one."

"Okay, Mom. Jesus."

"all right, all right, lecture over. See you at muster." He slammed his locker door closed and it was a domino effect. I shook my head and stowed my shit in my own locker. My apartment was conveniently located three blocks from my precinct, so I tended to walk over here in uniform for the most part, just with a plain bomber jacket in place of my patrol coat. I had to keep my weapon secured at all times, which meant on me or in my gun-safe at home. I didn't leave that shit in my locker. I did leave the rest of my duty belt in it, though.

I switched out holsters, made sure my backup was secure down around my ankle and switched coats. I followed the rest of the guys out of the locker room and took formation to stand through another boring briefing before we were released to hit the streets.

I followed Pruitt down to our patrol car, and he said, "I'll drive."

I didn't argue. I was tired. Instead, all I said was "Coffee or bust, man."

"Sounds like a plan."

When we got down to the car, I took the passenger seat and swung the laptop around to face me.

"What're you doing?"

"Looking something up."

"Oh yeah, what?"

"Tell you in a minute, maybe. Just drive."

"We keeping secrets now?" he demanded, and I looked into my partner's very serious blue eyes.

"Not my secrets to tell, man."

"Dude, –what happened–?"

I debated for a minute while the system worked its magic.

Finally I sighed.

"You swear to keep your fucking mouth shut?"

"Hell, yeah! You know you can always count on me for that shit, dude."

I told him about Lys and the drama from the night before. He gave a low whistle and agreed, "Yeah, that reaction is –what you would expect, Golden. You aren't a small guy." He sounded judgmental, but I let him have it. I felt like shit about what'd happened but at the same time, he hadn't seen her face, the panicked, haunted look like... like, *Not again!*

"Something had to have happened, bro. You weren't there, and–. Bingo! I think I just got something."

"Her name popped?"

"Yup. Just as I suspected, as a victim."

"Of?"

"Pretty gnarly domestic violence call. Shit, no wonder she left him."

"There pictures?"

"Yeah," I said grimly.

She'd been beat to fucking shit. One side of her face was misshapen and unrecognizable. The pictures had been taken before the bruising had even had a chance to set in. Everything was red and swollen, her eye was puffy, her lip fat all down the left side of her face. She had a cut up in her hairline and blood at the corner of her mouth. She stared forward into the camera, grim defeat, her whole world seemingly stripped away. If I had thought her brown eyes had been pain-filled and listless the day she'd moved in? In the pictures, her one good eye was positively dead. Nothing was in there, nobody was home; the pictures were haunting.

I turned the laptop back to my partner, who pulled up to the curb outside our favorite quick-mart. He scanned the photos, his mouth set into a grim line and read off the list of her injuries, out loud.

"Multiple contusions and abrasions, four millimeter scalp laceration secured with steri-strips, no stitches required. Concussion, sprained wrist, fractured left ocular orbit, and a busted left zygomatic. Shit, this guy worked her over, but good. Wait a minute..." he scrolled down and really frowned.

"What?" I asked, looking out the window, rage seeping out from the cracks around the vault I kept it in.

"Suspected sexual assault but victim did not submit to a rape kit. She fully cooperated where the beating was concerned but wouldn't let anybody examine her further."

"Jesus Christ," I muttered and closed my eyes.

"Looks like he violated the order of protection a couple months back. Her lawyer reported it. Showed up at her place of work as she was closing."

"That's enough," I said. "I already feel like I've pried too much."

"Dude, you think she moved in to your place on purpose?"

"Uh, yeah. Seriously. If you were her, wouldn't you?" I just wondered why she didn't say anything.

"Yeah, but I wouldn't tell anybody," Pruitt said.

"Why not? Don't you think someone you were moving into their house should know something like that?" I demanded. I was a little pissed and that anger was growing the more I thought about it.

"Do you think anyone in their right mind would let her move in, knowing something like that?" Fuck. Touché. I know a couple months ago, I would have said 'Nope, not today, Satan. Not today.' Knowing her, though? Granted, not even knowing her that well, I don't think I would have changed my mind.

After last night, though? Watching her cower from me like that? Yeah, no. I couldn't turn her out, but we would need some kind of a come-to-Jesus meeting, because shit couldn't go on like this. If it did, it would only get worse.

I made it through the rest of my shift, but only by the skin of my fucking teeth and by the grace of a partner who fuckin' got it, and let me sleep on our lunch break while he drove around to cover my ass so I could do it.

I took myself up to my apartment, soaked by the rain that'd started pissing down on me as I'd left work. I paused inside my front door. Hers was standing open, the soft glow from that ridiculous bedside rock lamp of hers glimmering faintly along the floor. I went to my room and changed into something dry before I did anything else. I wasn't keen on wet clothes. Never had been.

I stopped in her doorway and took her in. She was in that light blue nightshirt thing that looked like it could have been her ex-husband's. She was sitting on top of my abuela's dresser, her legs out in front of her, leaning forlornly against the brick wall, her head laying against the edge of the window as she watched the rain on the other side of the glass.

My bottle of good whiskey was perched next to her thigh, a glass at her hip. I had to smile at that. I heaved a heavy, silent sigh and tried to figure out how to get her attention without scaring the shit out of her.

Easier said than done.

10

*A*lyssa...

He cleared his throat behind me and I jumped. I don't know why I jumped. I knew he was home. I'd seen him walk past the mouth of the alley, had heard him come in the front door. Still, I jumped, and then I closed my eyes and felt my shoulders droop in defeat.

"Hey," he said, haltingly, and I opened my eyes again to watch the rain lash the window and trickle down the pane.

"Hey," I intoned back.

"I see you found my good whiskey."

I snorted a derisive laugh and said back, "Yeah, well, I figured you owed me a stiff drink." I picked up the glass at my hip and took a sip. The bite of the alcohol was strong, the flavor very oaky, but pleasant as the warmth trickled across my tongue and down my throat.

"That's fair enough," he said and I sighed, lifting my head from the wood window frame and turning it slowly.

He stood in my doorway, hands stuffed into the pockets of a pair of jeans, the button undone but the fly mercifully up. He was shirtless and comfortable, and looked entirely too delicious. And I really couldn't believe my brain was even going there right now. Then again, if I drank enough, I might become attractive to him, too. That's the way he seemed to like them. Drunk and horny, not a lot of class.

I swallowed my bitterness and turned to face back out the window. He sighed and I heard him pad barefoot across the carpet in here. He came into view, leaning a hip against the dresser near my feet.

"You know," he said softly, "You're doing this all wrong."

"Oh, yeah?" I challenged him. "How's that?"

"The kind of pain you're trying to drink away? It's the straight-from-the-bottle kind. No need for a glass."

He picked up the bottle by the neck and took a swig, wiping his mouth with the back of his hand. He held the bottle out to me. I took it, and the peace offering that it stood for, and took a swig myself. He picked up my glass and gave me a nod.

"There you go."

"I suppose I owe you an explanation," I said, a bit ruefully.

"You don't owe me shit," he said flatly. "But if you want to tell me, I'm here to listen."

No, I did. I most definitely did. I'd been so embarrassed, the more I thought about it throughout the day, and it wasn't fair, me living here like this and him not knowing. This entire time I felt like I was using him, and that wasn't totally far off the truth.

"I was with Ray for fourteen years," I said softly. "Married for ten."

"Yeah?"

"Yeah. Never, not once, did he ever hit me until that night."

"What happened?" he asked and I could tell that he didn't believe that last part, that it'd never happened before.

"I guess it started years ago, when I couldn't conceive," I said and took another pull from the bottle. I figured I might as well let it all hang out, but damned if I was going to do it without some liquid courage first.

"Ray always wanted a big family. I mean, it's not like I couldn't imagine his disappointment when I couldn't get pregnant. It's all I'd ever wanted, too." I closed my eyes and swallowed hard.

"Tough pill to swallow," Golden said and I could tell he was uncomfortable, but he wasn't especially awesome at being comforting. It just didn't seem to really be his thing. I got my shit together and pressed on. No need to make him suffer any longer than he had to with me and my pity-party. I'd really like for it to go back to being for one.

"The sex dropped off pretty quickly after that," I said with a bitter, self-deprecating laugh. "I should have known, when it became nonexistent and his work hours got longer, that he was getting it somewhere else, but, stupid me." I sighed in an attempt to let go some of the bitter feeling breeding virulently in the center of my chest, but it didn't work. I took another swig of his booze to try and drown it instead, but I should have known that wouldn't work, either.

"That night he was 'working late' but my employee, Avery, she was supposed to go out to a really nice dinner, you know? It was all she could talk about all day, that day. It was her and her boyfriend's fifth anniversary, and he had made reservations at Cipriani's – that expensive five-star place. I was at home waiting for Ray, and I get these text messages from Avery, saying she was sorry but that Ray was there. She sent me pictures and he was, with another woman."

I felt just as crazy over it now as I did that night and that was so stupid, wasn't it? I hated it.

Golden's hand fell lightly on top of my foot and I jumped. He didn't take it away, though. He just smoothed it comfortingly a third of the way up my shin, and back down, back and forth a few times before he just left it on the top of my foot, like he was an anchor to the ground.

I stared at the ceiling and took several deep breaths while the feelings overwhelmed me and swept through me. They washed over me like a tidal wave and swept me under. I was caught in a maelstrom, a riptide, and I felt like I was drowning, except for that one, tiny, little lifeline that was his hand on the top of my foot.

"I confronted him when he got home, things got heated and he hit me." I pressed my lips together and he waited me out, patiently, staring at me with solemn, dark eyes. Not judging, just listening. "He threw me to the ground and we argued some more and then…"

I still couldn't say it out loud, still hadn't said it to anyone. Golden pursed his lips and nodded, and I took a leap of faith.

I said it.

"He raped me."

Golden bowed his head and nodded again. I couldn't even begin to identify the look on his face. I'd never seen something so determined, yet so angry before.

"Let me guess," he said, putting his hands flat on the dresser top and hauling himself up and back onto it in a sitting position, feet dangling over the edge. "You thought moving in with a cop would make you feel safer."

I nodded, and returned my gaze out the window. I was suddenly too ashamed to look at him. His hand returned to the top of my foot and he rubbed it lightly back and forth, a reassuring gesture that I appreciated, but one that stirred up something else. Something I didn't know if I was ready for or ever would be ready for again.

"I'm not mad," he said finally, and I looked at him. He raised the glass that I'd been drinking from and downed the last sip or two of whiskey out of it. He held it out and I poured for him.

"I was going to say, I'll move out if you want."

"No," he shook his head. "I don't want that, but I do want to help you."

I barked out a bitter laugh, my stomach queasy all of a sudden, and I laid off the whiskey for a minute.

"I don't think there's anything out there that could help me."

"I disagree. I can think of a few things off the top of my head," he said with a reckless sort of grin that was watered way down from his usual one.

"Like what?" I asked.

He shook his head. "Not tonight," he said, pressing his hands flat to the dresser's top and sliding back further. He brought up his legs and crossed them Indian-style, pressing his back against the exposed brick on the other side of the window. He leaned his head back and put his hand back on my leg, this time curling it around the back of my calf. He let out a gusty sigh and said, "Tonight, I think I'd rather just stop being a self-absorbed dick, and I want to try my hand at just being here for you."

I leaned my head back against the wall above where my shoulder was fetched against it and sighed with what I think was relief.

"I'm afraid it's going to be awfully boring for you," I murmured and he gave me a half-smile and hitched a bit of a laugh.

"I'm all right with that."

Hmm, we would see. I didn't want to get my hopes up, you know?

11

*G*olden...

Well, it wasn't boring. I ended up holding her hair back as she puked into her toilet. Girl was not a drinker. I tried to make an off-color joke about being here before, but she spit and said, "I don't want to hear it, because I made it to the toilet."

I laughed. She had me there. What I did do was make sure her hair was in no danger of getting hit by any stray spit or vomit while I ran cold water in the sink and soaked a washcloth. I wrung it out, much like her story had wrung out my heart, and folded the wet cloth into thirds. I laid it over the back of her neck for her.

"Oh..." She sounded equal parts grateful and miserable and I couldn't help but chuckle. I'd been there, I don't know how many times. I wet another wash cloth and went to her, pressing it against her forehead and holding it for her.

"You are going to be seriously hung the fuck over," I said, with another little laugh.

"Maybe I should just take the day off of work."

"I think that'd be a good idea," I agreed. "I'll call my asshole brother, have him bring you some sub-q fluids. It'll help speed your recovery along.

"I don't know about all that," she said, dubiously.

"Trust me. Some IV fluids and you'll feel right as rain."

"I'm sure I would, but I'm also pretty sure I've earned this hell." Her voice echoed back from the toilet bowl, and I laughed and shook my head.

"Maybe for wasting some of the best whiskey that money can buy, but not for anything else that I can think of."

"You're being too kind," she moaned into the basin and finally, after a moment or two more and a few more spits, she groped for the lever and flushed. I helped to ease her up into a full sitting position and she took over the washcloth on her forehead.

"Hold it right there," I said gently and stood up. I went to the sink again and plucked her toothbrush from the holder, hit the water and ran it under real quick before loading it with paste. She looked up at me in gratitude, her watering eyes making her look like that pathetic orange, computer-generated, cartoon cat from the kid's movie. It was actually pretty adorable. Never thought I'd think that about a woman who'd just had her head in a toilet bowl, but here we were.

"Thank you," she mumbled around her toothbrush as she stuck it in her mouth.

I ran the washcloth from her forehead under some more cold water in the sink while she brushed.

"Just spit in the toilet, don't try to get up yet," I told her. She nodded wearily and I handed her down a glass of water. She sipped and spit and while she worked on her oral hygiene, I replaced the cloth on the back of her neck with a fresh cool one.

"Thank you," she said dully, her eyes slipping shut. She looked wrung-out, not just from puking, but likely by all of the emotional talk leading up to it.

I gave her a free pass. She'd been through some shit. Heavy shit. Still, she wore the burden of it on her shoulders like wings. She had some quiet strength, some solid resolve, as far as I could tell, anyway. Not many women I knew could keep their shit together this good, carrying the things she did. Despite the cracks in her veneer, she did it with some grace. I had to give her that.

"I think I'm ready to get up now," she said after I rinsed her toothbrush and put it back. I took the glass from her, poured the last dregs of water down the drain and set it aside. I dragged my hands over the seat of my pants to make sure they were mostly dry before I tried to help her up.

She took my hands and I hauled her to her feet. Too fast; she braced her hands on my shoulders and closed her eyes, swaying on her feet, her eyes closing as she tried to regain her equilibrium. The hair stood up on the back of my neck and goosebumps marched down my arms and across my chest at her touch, and I cleared my throat awkwardly.

"You all right?"

"Yeah," she said softly. "Just dizzy. Trying not to get sick again."

"Take your time," I told her, and she began to give a faint nod, but stopped mid-motion, going a touch pale.

"You good?" I asked and she licked her lips, the smell of peppermint wafting over to me as she let out a slow breath between them.

I was suddenly fixated on those lips as she said, her eyes still closed, "I think I'm good."

"You sure?" I asked, and I was worried it came out hoarse, but her eyes flicked open and she gave no indication she thought anything about me was out of sorts.

"Yeah, I'm okay."

"Okay, let's get you into bed." I helped her inebriated self back to her bedroom and pulled back the blankets on her bed. She got in, but moaned and stuck her foot out, touching it to the floor. I fought down a laugh, but it still edged my voice when I asked, "Room spinning?"

"Yeah."

I tucked her in and shook my head.

"Sleep it off, Lys. We'll talk more in the morning."

"Can we just not and say we did?" she asked, and I smiled down at her, her arm was thrown over her eyes.

"No can do, Chica. You opened this Pandora's box."

"Not a good analogy," she said.

"Why not?"

"Pandora opened the box and released untold troubles into the world," she said.

"Yeah, okay, I see your point. Bad analogy," I agreed, even though I didn't. It just wasn't worth arguing over right now. She'd released a whole lot of ugly truth into the night, and what she'd told me? I couldn't be sure it wasn't going to be trouble. Trouble for her, and trouble for me, but at least it was the kind of trouble I was good at handling. It was my job. I could see why she'd chosen to move in here. I guess I was a little put-out by her not being upfront about it, but I could see that shit from her perspective, too. If I'd known, I probably would have said 'Hell no' but now? It felt a little late for that and somehow, I just couldn't be mad.

For now, I told her, "Just sleep. We'll get shit handled when you're sober and feel like you can deal a little bit better."

"You can be nice when you want to."

"Yeah, I guess I can."

I left her door open and went across to my room. I left mine open, too, and found some pajama bottoms and switched out of my jeans. I got into bed and listened for her, smiling when she began to lightly snore.

God, she was a hot mess. I had a few ideas on how to straighten her out some, but 'sober' came first. The talk would be much harder without the liquid courage, but I had a pretty solid idea now that she was a tougher nut than I'd initially given her credit for.

12

*A*lyssa…

"Mm, god, why!?" I half-cried, half-moaned, and stuffed a pillow over my head. A truck was backing up in the alleyway below my bedroom window and the backup beeps were positively shrill. The tones went shrieking through my skull, and every time I even remotely tried to make a move, it felt like my brain was sliding along an icepick in my head. I couldn't remember the last time I'd had any kind of hard alcohol to drink, and now I was remembering why. This was miserable.

A low masculine chuckle and a couple of sharp cracking noises went off next to the bed and I flinched.

"Easy," Golden said. "It's just me. I got a pair of creaky knees. Help for that hangover is on the way."

"What are you talking about?" I groaned through the pillow and he pulled it off of my face.

"That was probably my brother and his partner backing their rig up."

A knock fell at the front door and I watched his well-muscled back as he padded out of my room and down the hall. I blinked when two of him reappeared.

"Whoa, she really tied one on."

"I think I'm seeing things, or are you identical twins?"

The second Golden chuckled lightly and hefted a padded square tote, like a soft-sided cooler, off his shoulder and onto the floor by the bed.

"Guilty as charged," he said. "I'm Angel."

"Oh. my God," I closed my eyes and let my head fall back. "This is so embarrassing."

"Not the first hangover I've remedied. Give me your arm."

"You're seriously going to do this?" I asked, holding out my arm, palm up. I would pretty much give anything to feel better at this point. I squinted past Angel, who had taken up Golden's crouched position by the bed. Golden leaned nonchalantly against the door frame, arms crossed over his stomach which was just as impressively muscular as his back. An amused look crossed his face and I realized I'd been caught looking. I covered my eyes with the arm that his brother wasn't inspecting and felt my face flame hot, which just made my head throb even more.

"Got a vein. It's always harder when you're dehydrated," Angel mused as he sat back on his haunches. I swallowed hard; I hated needles, especially after all of the painful failed fertility injections. I listened to him sanitize his hands and pull on a pair of surgical gloves. He tied off my upper arm and said, "Make a fist."

He felt around with his fingertips at the crook of my elbow and warned me, "Sharp pinch." I sucked in a breath and let it out slowly, hissing between my teeth.

"There you go," he said and taped it to my inner arm. "I'll get this drip going and you'll feel better in no time."

"Thank you," I murmured, but I still wouldn't come out from under my other arm. This was so embarrassing, yet he was being so nice. Still, what a way to meet a person for the first time.

"I don't do this often, you know," I said softly and he chuckled.

"Not here to judge, just here to make you feel better. It's what I do."

"Thank you," I said and swallowed hard.

"Get some more rest. Golden knows how to undo all of this when it's done."

I took my arm away from my face, realizing how childish I was being. Just because I couldn't see him, didn't mean he couldn't see me. He gave me a reassuring little smile and stood up, hefting his bag back onto his shoulder.

"Don't worry about the stuff," he told me. "I'll just damage it out. Happens all the time. Plus, it's pennies on the dollar for what they actually charge patients. It's fucking ridiculous."

I tried a timid nod, not trusting my voice. I was getting pretty emotional. They were both being so sweet and caring, and somehow that was making me feel even worse about so many things. Like, *why couldn't my husband have been this way? Why on earth were things with him ending like this?*

Also, selfishly: *I wonder if I will ever find anything similar again or if I'm going to live the rest of my life and die alone.*

Melodramatic? Maybe, but I'd never really done 'alone' very well, and the prospect of it was more than a little overwhelming, when it forced its way up through the middle of the mountain of hurt already in place.

"Come on, Bro. I'll show you out."

"Yeah. Sleep tight, Lys. It was nice to meet you," Angel said as he slipped past his twin and out the bedroom door.

"Nice to meet you, too, and thank you," I called faintly after him.

Golden shut my door with a nod and I heard them retreat down the hall. If either of them said anything, I missed it. Either that, or they were speaking so low I couldn't hear. I was okay with that. I was tired, and I just wanted sleep.

Alas, it didn't seem like it was to be, because it felt like no sooner had I closed my eyes, than my bedroom door opened with a loud cacophony of voices arguing. I winced and Kenzie stood there open-mouthed, astonished.

"See, I told you. Food poisoning. Last time I checked, wasn't she the boss?" Golden demanded, unimpressed.

Kenzie drew herself up to her impressive six-foot height, dressed to impress as she ever was, in a light-gray pencil skirt, expensive blouse, hose and smart pumps. Her designer outer-wear jacket was belted at her trim waist. She looked like that actress, the one who'd been married to Tom Cruise for years way back in the day- Nicole-something.

"Lys, why didn't you call somebody?" she demanded and I pushed myself up into a sitting position. I realized I must have been asleep for longer than I had thought because the IV was gone; I could feel the familiar pressure and pull of a cotton ball and tape at the crook of my elbow. It was conveniently hidden, of course, by the sleeve of my night-shirt. I kicked my brain into gear and squinted up at my best friend, catching onto and holding the excuse that Golden had provided.

"Bad Chinese," I said. "I spent most of the night heaving into my toilet."

I would likely tell her the truth; that I'd been drunk as hell the night before, at some point, but right now Golden was trying to spare me any more embarrassment and I didn't want to embarrass him in return by outing him for giving me a cover story.

Kenzie sat down on the edge of my bed and pushed some of my hair back behind my ear. She went from worried friend to sympathetic in a heartbeat.

"You look like hell," she said and her face crumbled into lines of compassion. She raised an eyebrow at Golden and made a shooing motion. He raised his eyebrows in turn and said, "I'ma let that slide and get ready for work."

He let go of my doorknob and it rattled as it twisted on its mechanism. I jumped at the sudden sharp sound, and Golden gave me an undefinable look, unhappy with a dash of calculating.

"Thanks for helping me out," I said, and he gave a nod and closed the door behind him.

"Wait, what'd he do?"

"Babysat me while I puked," I said honestly.

Kenzie shook her head in amazement.

"Can't picture it," she said and I chuckled softly.

"I know he's rough around the edges," I said, "but once you get to know him, he's not half-bad. He's a good guy, really."

"I guess you have to be to be a cop. Still, you should have called Avery. She's held down the fort, but was worried sick when you didn't answer your phone. I left a meeting when I couldn't get you to answer your phone."

I looked around and spotted it on my desk; I thrust my chin at it and she brought it over.

"Deader than a doornail. I must have forgot to plug it in. I am so sorry, Kenz." I groaned and flopped back down onto my back.

"It's okay," she said, plugging it in for me. "Guess this proves you have people that still care about you, though."

I looked up at her and frowned. "I knew that," I said softly, borderline offended.

She sighed and sat back down.

"We've been worried about you, Lys. You've been so down, so depressed since this happened, and it's scaring some of us a little."

"My marriage fell apart, my husband beat me half to death, and... and I think I have a reason to be depressed."

"You do, but you're also getting a divorce and he's definitely not worth stewing over. We just want to see you get back to your old self again."

I knew she meant well, I knew she spoke with nothing but the best of intentions, and I wished I was brave enough to tell her the whole story – but I wasn't. I don't know why I had told Golden last night.

Maybe it was the alcohol. Maybe it was because he was a cop and he knew things like this happened all the time, he didn't have the shiny hopefulness about humanity that Kenzie still bore. I don't know, but I still hadn't been able to tell her about the sexual aspect to the assault, even though I knew she suspected it. I swallowed hard, wracked with guilt, not just for hiding that from her, but also for making everyone worry.

"Oh, hey, here now, don't worry about any of it. You busted me out of a boring budgetary meeting that I didn't want to sit for anyway." She sighed. "Want me to help you clean up?"

I gave her a flat look. "It's a gnarly case of food-poisoning; I'm not a total invalid."

She laughed a little, "Fair enough."

"Besides, I'm pretty sure Golden is in the shower and if I got into one right now, I'd steal all the hot water. We found that one out the hard way and trust me, it wasn't pretty."

"First world war roommate?" she asked.

"Yeah, funny now, but it hadn't been then. He was so mad!"

She laughed a little, the fine lines of worry back again, tightening around her eyes.

"He just yelled and cussed a lot," I told her frankly. I didn't tell her that I shut off the water and crouched in the bottom of my tub with shampoo still in my hair until I'd heard the front door slam, my heart in my throat the whole time.

"Okay, fine, then we wait. You hungry yet?"

"Yeah, maybe just some broth and saltines, though. Until I know my stomach isn't going to rebel again."

"Okay, I'll run out, you get cleaned up."

"Okay."

Sounded good.

13

Golden...

I let myself into the apartment and Lys was wrapped up in a blanket on the couch, used tissues scattered around her and a half-eaten carton of ice cream in one hand. One of the small, personal-sized ones. She looked like a deer caught in the headlights, and had she not clearly been crying, I probably would have found it adorable.

I stopped short and asked, "What's wrong?"

She faintly raised her hand and pointed at the TV, and were her nose and cheeks not already red from crying, I probably would have picked up she was blushing. I stepped further into the apartment after shutting the door, and looked. Some sappy romance was playing out on the screen.

"Jesus, nearly gave me a fucking heart attack." I took off my patrol cap and went over to the couch, dropping onto it beside her. She set her ice cream on the coffee table and was hastily snatching up her tissues. I went in for the kill.

She laughed a little and said, "Oh, gee, just help yourself."

I'd already stuck a gob of chocolate-chip-cookie-dough-and-vanilla ice cream into my face, and I said around it, "Don't mind if I do," as the credits rolled on the screen.

"I swear you're home early," she said and I nodded.

"A little. Got done with the paperwork early. Had a little bit of an incident out there, tonight."

"Oh, no. What happened?" she asked, standing and letting her blanket fall away.

"Mm." I held up the spoon in a bid to get a minute while I worked on my overzealous bite of the sweet, cold, dairy product in my mouth. "Dude bit my partner. Somehow, he crashed into the top of the patrol car and busted his nose when I put him back there. You know, business as usual. Just, any time someone gets hurt while on duty or in custody, it's a ton of C-Y-A paperwork."

"I see, is your partner going to be okay?"

"Pruitt? Aw, yeah. Comes with the job. Didn't even break the skin this time."

"What about you? You ever been hurt on the job?"

I rubbed my leg through the rip-stop fabric of my tactical pants. She'd opened up to me the night before, I guess turnabout was fair play. I nodded.

"Yeah, that's how I got my road name."

"Your nickname? 'Golden'?"

I nodded again and tried to divert from the rough stuff for a moment, as she came slowly back around the kitchen island from tossing her used tissues in the trash under the sink. I shoved another bite of her ice cream in my face, suddenly thinking real hard about how fucking good it was. She drifted over, light on her bare feet against the faux-wood tile and came around the back of the couch. I tried not to think about how good her legs looked under that nightshirt of hers and how much better she would look in one of my shirts, as she retook her seat and arranged her blanket in her lap for modesty's sake.

"What did you call it?" she asked and I was glad for the extended reprieve from talking about my elephant in the room.

"A road name. It was given to me by the club," I explained.

"The Indigo Knights?" I couldn't remember if we'd ever talked about them, but then again, she'd seen me come in and out of here in my cut more than a few times and she was a smart cookie.

"That would be the one," I said, laughing.

"We've never really talked about them before," she said defensively at my laughter. and my suspicions were confirmed.

I nodded again and said, "You're right. We honestly don't talk about a lot of things."

She winced and went further with, "We don't really talk about anything."

She wasn't wrong. I just wasn't that guy. A talker, I mean. If I wanted this to work out for me and her, what I had cooked up, I guess I would have to be.

I told her, "Fair enough. I can work on changing that." Her shoulders eased down from their constantly guarded position and she dared to even smile.

I was developing a plan based off some observations I had about her. It was like, she had an eye for details, like my club name on my cut, but she didn't have a clue when it came to her surroundings as it related to her personal safety. The girl was smart, but there was a vast difference between being book-smart and street-smart. I had the feeling she was the former, and I had an eye towards making her the latter... if she was interested and would let me. I didn't bring it up quite yet. I was waiting for a good place to do it where I figured she might be more receptive to the idea.

"I think I would like that," she said, of talking together more.

I put my feet up on my coffee table and she crossed her legs under her blanket and leaned back against the arm of the couch. Guess there was no time like the present when it came to communicating and telling stories. Might as well get it over with.

"The guys gave me the road name Golden because around the time I earned my cut – the leather vest with all the patches– I was the Indigo City Police Department's golden boy."

"You don't sound proud or happy about that, how come?"

I pressed my lips together and blew out my cheeks. *No time like the present*, I reminded myself.

"Because it didn't matter, the guy I tried to save, in the middle of the giant shit sandwich we got caught in, died anyway."

She flinched and her soulful brown eyes dropped to her hands in her lap.

"I'm so sorry to hear that," she said, and unlike a lot of motherfuckers, she sounded like she really was.

"anyway, I got shot, too. In the leg, twice. Got lucky, one was a through-and-through, and the other one lodged in the bone but somehow didn't break it."

Silence stretched between us and I could tell she wanted to ask. I just wanted to know if she was going to be brave enough to.

"Do you mind if I asked what exactly happened?"

Huh, I hadn't thought she was going to do it. I guess I underestimated her. I bobbed my head and put the empty carton and spoon back on the table. I flopped back against the couch and slid down some so my head was supported.

"Beat cops do plainclothes work too, sometimes. anyway, I was with a bunch of detectives, serving a warrant on this dude up for assault and battery charges. We do the usual shit, bust down the door, go charging in, and we're trained – but believe me, ain't nobody trained for the level of firepower and the amount of gangbangers in that place."

I choked up, but didn't want to seem like anything less of a badass than I was, so I didn't let it show. I just cleared my throat and said, "We got pinned down in the kitchen. It was bad. Dead 'banger here, two of ours dead over there, and one of the detectives, a dude less than two years out from retirement, is layin' there gasping on the floor. I get him up, go to move around the island, and take one in the leg. I went for the stairs and took a second one in the back of the leg. I was out of ammo by then, and there's this shotgun and I fell, fallin' on top of this guy I'm trying to save. I snatched it up and pointed it at the 'banger coming to finish the job and... man. I'll never forget the look on his face or how his chest opened up."

I looked over at her. The silence in the apartment as deafening as the silence after the roar of that sawed-off I'd grabbed up. Her eyes were wide, her hands gripping her ankle through the blanket in a white-knuckled grip as she listened.

"I got Rubin out front, but he'd taken one in the neck. He was dead before I even got him out of the house. I tried, though."

"I'm so sorry," she murmured, and I looked up from where I was playing with a loose thread near one of my cargo pockets, into some very serious brown eyes filled with hurt.

"Don't do that, Chica."

"Do what?"

"Hurt for me. I can handle that all on my own, I'm a big boy." She sort of shrank in on herself a little, and to take the sting out of my words, I gave her a sort of half-smile and added, "Besides, you got more than enough hurt all on your own to handle, eh?"

She sighed and it was a heavy, tired thing. I slapped the shit out of myself on the inside for reminding her. She gave me a slightly watered-down, charmed little smile and said, "Don't we make a pair?"

I laughed slightly and nodded. "Yeah, tonight we do. Tomorrow's a new day, though, and you know what they say…"

She shook her head and asked, "No, what?"

"'Tomorrow is the first day of the rest of your life.' One day at a time, with shit like this." She thought about it and nodded, and I sprang my idea.

"I'm going to be off for a few days, you working tomorrow?"

"Yeah, I need to."

"Cool, I'll be by to get you when you're done. You got gym clothes?"

"Yeah, why?"

"Tomorrow, I start teaching you how to make sure something like what happened to you, never happens again, that's why."

She laughed incredulously, "Me, stop a guy the size of Ray? As big as you?" She shook her head. "Impossible."

I gave her a look and smiled myself. "Bigger they are the harder they fall. Violence comes up, when it comes to someone like you and your size, you don't fight fair, Chica. You fight to survive. I'm going to teach you every dirty street-fighting trick in the book, and throw in some legit moves the Army taught me, too. Also, there's a chick that travels the states teaching the departments how to deescalate situations and how to temper their use of force. She's some kind of Krav Maga queen. We have some of her training DVD's at the department. I'm going to see about scoring some copies and I want you to study them. Knowledge is power."

"You're serious," she said in disbelief.

"As a heart attack, chick. Never again."

I met her eyes with mine, and she repeated softly, "Never again."

I nodded, "That's my girl."

She rolled her eyes and snorted, swinging the couch pillow at me; I caught it and hugged it so she couldn't take it back. She got up, gracefully despite the unwieldy blanket, and managed to keep those long legs hidden as she went around the back of the couch.

"You getting a shower?" she asked.

"Nope."

"Good, because I wanted one."

I smiled as she called back from the hallway, "Good night, Golden."

"Night, chick. Get some good sleep."

That, of course, ended up being wishful thinking on my part. A couple hours later, I found myself staring at my own bedroom ceiling, wondering just what the hell I was thinking taking on something like this... but I'd already committed. I couldn't pull back now. Besides, I was suspended for a week. Could possibly be without pay, I wouldn't know for a bit. I'd more than busted the guy's nose when I'd shoved him into our patrol car. I'd snapped off some teeth. "Excessive force" was probably going to go into my jacket for this one and I couldn't say I'd left the brass much of a choice. He was handcuffed, and by that point had stopped resisting, all except for his shouting.

Lys didn't need to know any of that, though. I needed to get her used to the idea that, like it or not, violence was a part of everyday life and could rear its ugly head at any moment, but I needed to do it without scaring the shit out of her, either. I wasn't one-hundred-percent on how exactly I was going to accomplish that, but I'd figure it out.

She was already pretty well wrapped around the axle and still jumpy as shit. I didn't know if putting some agency back into her own hands was going to be enough, but it seemed like a good enough place to start.

I sighed, as much out of worry as out of frustration at my inability to sleep. We'd see if she would commit to the course of action I had planned, too. She seemed a little taken aback when I'd suggested it out in the living room, and hadn't looked too thrilled at the prospect of my picking her up from work.

I finally managed to fall asleep, probably just before her damn alarm went off for her to go to work, but by then, I was so tired, my mind wore out from running on its hamster wheel, that I didn't even come close to waking up when it did. I slept right through it.

14

*A*lyssa...
　　I thought about what he said, about training me to be prepared and I thought to myself, *Yes, I'd like that. To be prepared means to not be afraid. Or, well, not –as– afraid.* I went to bed feeling much better, now that I potentially had something concrete to cling to, and when I got up the next morning, before I even got dressed, I went and found my exercise leggings, sports bra, and a loose-fitting exercise tee.

　　I was used to cycling or running on a treadmill for my exercise, and I was afraid that in my exercise clothes, I looked like one of those women who was wearing them more as a fashion statement than for their intended purpose. I was also pretty self-conscious about wearing them where I could be seen and I would go to the exercise room at our condo only when I knew no-one else was likely to be there. I had a lot of self-image issues. I knew that about myself, but I figured, what woman didn't?

　　I tried to remember when those issues had first appeared, and I was both surprised and not surprised to realize it had started after I had given up the fertility shots. That's when Ray had stopped wanting to be seen with me, when he had started spending more time out of the house than in it, when spending time with the guys had become more paramount to him than going out or being seen with me...

When I started to feel neglected. Alone. Un-beautiful to my husband. I thought it was just a phase; that we would work through it, that he would come around eventually. I had been woefully naïve.

I dug my running shoes out of the bottom of the closet, and with a sigh, set everything on the desk chair, neatly folded.

I thought about what to do, as I got dressed. I wanted Golden to know that I was serious, but at the same time, I was nervous. I was scared of failure like you wouldn't believe, which was almost laughable, considering the monumental failure my marriage was.

That wasn't you... I thought, and it was true. I wasn't the one who cheated. I wasn't the one to give up on us, to stop even trying. Except, I had. I hadn't told Ray how I felt. How I felt alone, devalued, and so much less at his rejection. I hadn't made him talk to me, or told him how much his silence killed me.

I'd just patiently waited, and for what? My inaction was partially to blame, but I wouldn't be that way anymore. If I didn't learn from my mistakes I was doomed to repeat them. That's why I left, why there would be no apology great enough from Ray to ever make me go back. No matter how much it hurt to be alone, no matter how much it ached to give up.

Except you didn't give up. I shook my head as I picked up my things and went out to the dining table. I set them in a neat pile on it and went over to the end table by the couch and picked up the legal pad full of random scribbles and figures. I had no idea what it was for but I needed to leave a note.

I hastily scratched out what I wanted to say.

Golden –

I get off work at six, I don't have a gym bag or anything, but I wanted you to know I was serious. Go left out the building, up two blocks, then left, and down four. My shop is on the corner of Bowker and 67th. I'll see you then.

Lys

I left the pad next to my clothes and took a determined breath.

I went to work and spent a long day, dealing with customers who were either dissatisfied or couldn't make up their mind. I was as patient as I could be with the latter, because I certainly knew how they felt. I must have gone back and forth, waffling between whether or not I was ready to really do anything about my situation. The fear, the anger, the hurt, all balled up into a Gordian knot of emotion, weighting my heart like a stone.

I was mopping up a water spill when the bell above the door chimed. I straightened and turned, to see Golden strolling in. He had a gym bag slung over his shoulder and wore sweats, like he was ready to go running.

"Hey," I said, sweeping a stray lock of my hair out of my face and tucking it behind my ear.

"Hey, you almost ready?"

"Mm, should be in just a few."

"Cool." He held out the bag. "Go get changed; I think starting with cardio is the way to go."

"Oh, okay."

I took the bag from him and turned, handing the mop off to Avery and asking, "You're okay to close up?" She was staring at Golden open-mouthed, and nodded absently.

"Avery?" I asked, to make sure.

"Yeah, yeah I'm good, go, go!" She shooed me toward the back, and I smiled and shook my head.

I went into the bathroom and changed.

Golden nodded his approval when I came back out, and I asked, "What should I do with this?" indicating the gym bag of my regular clothes.

"Leave it, you got keys. We'll come back by and get it." He was staring at his phone and frowning slightly, tracing along the screen with a finger. I took a peek at the screen and he seemed to be setting up an app to give us a route. I slid my own phone into the pocket for it in the leggings, blessing whoever had thought to include the slim phone pocket in the design.

"I'll see you tomorrow."

"Thank you, Avery."

"No problem."

I followed Golden out onto the sidewalk and looped my keyring around my index finger, palming the keys. He slid his phone into an armband and said, "Come on, let's warm up."

He set off in a brisk pace down the sidewalk and I wondered what he was thinking but was honestly too nervous to ask. Guys hated to be peppered with questions and it was a bad habit of mine, one I had forever been exasperating Ray with, when we'd been married. *Wait and find out. Watch the movie. Jesus, Lys! Listen and you might get your answer.*

"How was your day?" Golden asked, and it jolted me out of my reverie.

"Long," I said, and laughed a bit nervously.

He nodded and said, "Rule number one of any situation is "Know Your Surroundings". Don't let yourself get lost in your head. People who are comfortable with doing violence to another person won't hesitate to exploit a weakness like that. Don't give them the opportunity."

"Right, sorry," I murmured and he shook his head.

"Don't be sorry, be safe. You're not a person who has dealt with much violence, or has even been aware of it until what happened, happened. Now, it's our goal to make sure, not that it won't happen again, but that you're prepared to handle it if or when it does. Baptism by fire has already occurred. It didn't end well, you got hurt. If there's a next time, we want to make it so you either don't get hurt, or barring that, you get hurt less."

"Easier said than done," I said with a nervous laugh, and he nodded.

"You're learning already."

He broke into an easy lope and I picked up my pace into a light jog to keep up. It was a gradual ramping-up into a hard run that took us in a big loop, ending a few blocks from the shop, where he slowed back into a cool-down walk.

"Now what?" I asked, when I finally caught my breath enough to speak.

"We get your shit and we go home. I'm starving."

"I'll cook, if you'd like."

"After we hit the showers, sure."

"Okay."

We stopped at my shop and picked up the bag with my work clothes. Golden took it from me and slung it over his shoulders and across his chest.

"We're gonna run three to four times a week like that. Every other day or so. Building up your endurance and stamina will only help you in a fight, but that's not what I want to focus on for you."

"Oh? What do you want to focus on?"

"First of all, I want to focus on you getting away from a violent situation. We're going to work on you recognizing and escaping violence before it can start, or getting away from it once it's started. I want you to be able to disengage and outrun an assailant. There's no reason for you to engage with a dude trying to hurt you. You call 9-1-1. That's what we're paid for."

"Truthfully, I'm relieved," I admitted. "I want to be able to defend myself, sure, but I'm not a fighter. I never have been."

"I'm less concerned with you being physically prepared as I am with you being mentally prepared. We need to work on that. Get to where you can think through a situation, to where you don't panic."

"Okay," I said nodding.

"This is about survival for you. Survive and thrive."

"I don't know about that last part," I said, miserably. "Lately, I feel like I've just been barely hanging on."

He lightly gripped my elbow and stopped me just outside the lobby door. I looked at him and he said, "What happened to you was a lot more than most people ever have to go through in their entire lives, let alone all at once like you did. You're doing pretty well, all things considered."

"I don't feel like it," I confessed.

"Not surprised, Chica, but I promise, you are."

"Thanks," I murmured, at a loss for what else to say.

We went up and he handed me the black-and-blue gym bag with my things in it. I murmured another quiet thanks.

"No problem. You go on and shower first."

"Okay."

I took my time and luxuriated in the hot water, but I did make sure to save him some, and put my hair up in a plastic clip to keep it from getting the back of my fresh nightshirt wet. I pulled on some dark heather-gray leggings on under it, for modesty's sake, and rolled the long sleeves back up to my elbows before I padded out of my bedroom and into the kitchen. I heard Golden's shower start up midway through my getting dressed and contented myself with preparing dinner.

I liked to cook, I just hadn't had much occasion to since finding myself single again. That, and I'd found myself lacking in the appetite department more often than not.

He returned to the kitchen in a pair of low-slung lounge pants that looked like they were about to abandon ship from the ridges of his hip bones any second, and I fought not to stare. Blushing furiously, I turned back to the stove and shook a little pepper over the stir-fry I was making.

"Like what you see?" he asked mildly, as if he were asking about the weather.

I turned sharply, giving him a bit of a glare, and replied, "I don't know how to answer that."

He raised an eyebrow, a cocky smile on his face. "How about honestly?"

"Does it matter?" I asked, trying to weasel out of answering.

"To me, it does."

"Why?"

"It's nice to feel appreciated?" he hazarded.

I closed my eyes for a second, my nose tingling in that familiar way that said tears threatened, but I resolutely blamed it on the pepper in my own mind. Still, it didn't stop my mouth from betraying me. I said out loud, "I wouldn't know."

"What, that it's nice to be appreciated?"

"I haven't been, for a very long time. So, I guess so? Why are we even having this conversation?"

"Because I caught you lookin', and went fishing for a compliment."

I snorted and laughed asking, "Are you always this frank?"

"No, I'm always this Golden." I turned around, taking my eyes off the stove top for a second, to see him perched on top of one of the tall stools up under the counter. He smiled at me and winked and I rolled my eyes.

"Is this how you pick up your drunk girls at the bar? By being a big damn dork?" I asked and almost immediately wanted to take it back. I mean, *how rude!*

He grinned and said, "Dork? Ouch. You may have just hurt my feeling."

"Feeling?"

"Yeah, all one of 'em I got left. Uncle Sam beat the rest of 'em out of me a long time ago."

I shook my head, smiling a touch ruefully, and said, "I'm sorry, that was really rude, when you've been nothing but helpful lately." I turned back to the stove and stirred the food to keep it from sticking or burning.

I caught him shaking his head out of the corner of my eye and he said, "Don't apologize. I've earned some of it. What I'm more interested in knowing is..." he trailed off and I cocked my head.

"What?" I waited but he didn't say anything. I made sure the food was okay and turned around and jumped, he'd come around the island and wasn't too far from me. He had a curious look on his face and held out a hand, palm up in an invitation to take it.

I looked at it for a moment before extending mine over it, but for some reason, I couldn't bring myself to lower mine any further, to actually touch him. It was like I was blocked by some invisible internal force. That force was fear; fear of rejection, fear that he would pull away at the last moment and say 'Just kidding!' My heart was suddenly flung into such a tumult.

"Hey." His voice was soft and my eyes jerked from our hands, so close but not touching, to his warm brown eyes.

"What?" I asked.

I jumped slightly when his middle fingertip grazed the underside of my wrist in a faint touch. Gooseflesh immediately swept up my arm in a tingling wave, the hair standing on end and my breath stilling in my lungs.

He stepped into me slightly, his other hand cupping the side of my neck and my mouth went dry as his thumb grazed my cheek, so soft, so gently. I let my eyes close and pretended for just a moment...

He stepped into me again, even closer, his lips grazing my hair on the opposite side from where his hand rested, my other hand still hovering above his, the heat and energy transfer between us a gentle thing.

He whispered into my ear, "Sometimes, I wondered if you might've been jealous."

I froze and pressed my lips together. I didn't answer, because he was right. I had been, but not about the fact it wasn't me in their place, specifically, more about how easy it was for them to be free with themselves and their bodies, about the fact that I didn't know if I ever would be again.

I took an abrupt step back, and he let me go with a nod. I turned back to our cooking food and turned off the water that had begun to boil, pouring in the measuring cup of rice and dropping a lid on the pot.

I swallowed hard, my movements jerking, halting, as I hovered between the place of wanting to move towards him and wanting to move further away. I closed my eyes and huffed out a frustrated breath, drew another, and let it out much more slowly.

"Beer?" he asked softly, opening the fridge.

"After last time? No, thanks," I said with a bitter laugh.

He smiled and pulled a Corona out of the fridge and put it against the counter, gave it a hearty smack and busted off the cap.

He went back around the center island and retook his stool like nothing at all had happened while I still shook on the inside. I felt ripped open, gutted, and achingly realized that I was jealous. That despite what I thought would be normal, that I shouldn't want to ever be touched again, all I wanted was to cuddle up close with someone and build new, sweeter memories around intimacy. It ravaged my soul when I felt like I would never have something like that again, and that sudden flood of strong emotion surged, making my face hot and blurring my vision. I switched off the burner beneath the stir-fry, turned my back to Golden and pressed my fingertips to my eyes, my palms to the rest of my face.

I heard his stool scrape and I stiffened but didn't jump. A moment later, I did jump when his hands landed lightly on my shoulders and he turned me around. I didn't want to come out from behind my hands, and he didn't make me, just kind of carefully stepped in, as if he were approaching a skittish cat, and put his arms around me, hugging me awkwardly.

I either put my arms around him, too, or stepped away, and goddammit, I needed the comfort. I'd been doing this, carrying it all by myself for so long and I just needed a goddamned break for a minute. I hugged to him, and cried it out and he didn't once tell me to shush.

Instead, he gave a heavy sigh that sounded genuinely sorry, and said, "I'm sorry I pushed."

15

Golden...

"I'm sorry I pushed. I'm sorry," I murmured, but I wasn't. I couldn't be. I needed to figure out how many tunnels this rabbit-warren of a mess had. It wasn't just about feeling safe for her. I'd seen her jump or twitch any time her friend Kenzie touched her, too. I think she'd probably just gone too long without touch, so long, that every touch had become startling. Something about that killed me. Something about that wrung me fucking dry.

She was soft where I held her against me, and smelled like coconut and lime, tropical and fruity with this light herbal base. Like a woman, fresh from her shower. I closed my eyes while she trembled against me and breathed her in and willed myself not to get hard. Now was hardly the time to get aroused, but she was arousing, beautifully arresting. At least my heart was starting to think so.

I'd watched her, so solemn, moving like a ghost around here for more than two months now. Listened to her soft voice on the phone as she spoke to her friend, or conducted business. I'd sometimes come in late at night and see her through her open doorway, sitting at her desk, and I'd want to stop and follow the curve of her neck, sweeping up to the messy bun she had her hair in, her pencil between her teeth as she balanced her books. The way she sat in that damn chair, one leg curled under her, the toes of the opposite foot tapping on the carpet? Shit, there was just something simply alluring about it. Normal about it.

She had class. She had grace. She was nothing like the bimbos or bitches I'd paraded past her door. She was the kind of woman you settled down with, the kind of woman you made a life with. And the fact someone had hurt her, abused her, even if she were telling the truth and it was just the once... it was fucking heart-rending and I couldn't fucking tell you why it bothered me as bad as it did, but it did.

I wanted to fix it, and I couldn't, and it drove me nuts, but there wasn't anyone in the world that could fix Lys but Lys. I just had to show her that it could be done, that there was such a thing as life and light on the other side, but I wasn't sure I was the right man for the job. Surely not me. I was too down, too dark, and too twisted for a job like this.

Madre de Dios, this was the kind of job for Angel, not me.

She pushed back from me, calmer in that way that only a good crying jag could give a chick. I never understood that shit, but I'd seen my moms and my abuela do it enough times growing up to know it was a thing. I ripped down a paper towel off the dispenser and handed it over to her. She mopped at her face and sniffed saying, "I'm sorry."

I shook my head. "Don't be. It's not your fault. Life doesn't come with a playbook, Chica. We just do the best with the shit life hands us."

"I'm afraid I'm not very good with that at the moment," she said.

"Doing better than some, a little worse than others. You're doing you, that's about the best anyone could ask of you right now."

"Well," she said, and didn't sound like she was quite convinced. "Thank you."

"You're welcome. Food smells good." I changed the subject, giving her an out, and she nodded and went for plates. I leaned back against the counter and stayed out of her way. Lys dished up the food and set it on the breakfast bar, I went around and took my stool and she hopped up on the one next to mine. I thought about it and figured if she cooked, I would clean. Seemed like a fair trade. I wasn't used to actually engaging with someone I lived with, who wasn't family. So far, Lys and I had fended for ourselves. We hadn't really done a meal together or anything like that. We'd just been two people occupying the same space. It wasn't like family or anything.

I wasn't at all used to living with anyone in a domestic capacity. When I moved out at eighteen, it was straight into the military and bunking with a bunch of dudes in the barracks. I stayed single then for a reason, that reason being most bitches couldn't stay faithful to save their lives while dudes were on deployment. It wasn't worth it to me to blow my money on a broad fucking some other dude. I saved that shit, got out, got my own apartment, signed on with the ICPD, and had lived alone up until now. It was strange even occupying the same space with a woman who wasn't my mom, my abuela, or my sister.

We were quietly enjoying our meal, only about a half-a-dozen bites in, when a knock fell at the front door. I straightened, and said "I got it," as I slid off my stool. I went to the door and peeked out, raising an eyebrow.

I opened it up and said, "I was just thinking about you a minute ago."

My sister, Maria, looked past me and her eyebrows went up. "Sorry to just drop by like this, I didn't realize you had company, but it was Julio's day to take Manolo and he cancelled on me last minute and I have to work tonight. I picked up an extra shift."

I opened the door further to reveal my eight-year-old nephew, Manolo, and sighed. "Angel?" I asked quietly.

"On-shift, I wouldn't ask if I didn't have to."

I shook my head. "You never have to ask," I said.

She switched to Spanish and asked, "*And what about your whore?*"

Lys choked behind me and my sister paled. I laughed and said, "That's what you get, and she's not a hookup, Maria. She's my roommate, she lives here." I stood aside and motioned for my sister and nephew to get in. Maria walked past me, blushing with embarrassment, and Manolo followed her, grinning like a fool. "Maria, Manolo, meet Lys. Lys, this is my sister and my nephew."

"I am so sorry," Maria rushed out. "I didn't know – " She shut her mouth and looked like she wanted to melt into the floor. I bit back a laugh.

"Manolo," I said. My nephew looked up at me. "Next time you want to speak Spanish in front of a gringo so they don't know what you're saying, I want you to remember this, ay?" Manolo grinned from ear to ear and Maria looked like she wanted to straight murder me. I smiled at my sister and she glowered back.

"It's, uh, nice to meet you," Lys said charitably, a little pink across her cheeks and nose.

"I'll be back to get you in the morning, Miho." My sister bent down to hug her son and he hugged her back.

"'Kay," he said. "Love you."

"I love you, too, son."

"Thank you," she said to me, rushed, and before turning, gave Lys a grudging nod.

I rolled my eyes and debated calling her out for not really apologizing, but decided to let it go. She looked harried as it was, and I knew it wasn't a mark on Lys, but rather on me, and probably more than a little misdirected anger at Julio. I could take it. It wouldn't be the first time.

Angel and I had been seven, and my mom pregnant and about to give birth to Maria, when our dad got killed. After that, it was just us, mom, and my dad's mom, our abuela. Maria never had the father-figure growing up. Our mom did her best, but Maria had nothing to go by except stories. Like a lot of fatherless girls, she got herself knocked up in high school. Unlike a lot of fatherless girls, Maria had tried to make it work with Julio and kept him in Manolo's life.

Julio just couldn't seem to get with the fucking program.

He kept bouncing on his weekends and was in and out of jail. I'd even arrested him myself, once. That had caused all sorts of family drama for a minute. The point is, Maria had it hard, but didn't often complain about it. She made it work. She relied on me and Angel some of the time, but not often enough to put a cramp on our respective lifestyles.

She shot a worried look over her shoulder and glanced from me to Lys and back to me. I rolled my eyes at her and she frowned and shut my front door. I would head that drama off at the pass, once I got Manolo settled.

I turned, but my nephew had disappeared. I heard him call from up the hallway, "What did you do to my room!?"

"It's not your room, Hombrecito! It was the guest room, and it's Lys' room now. You can either bunk with me or on the couch."

"I thought she lived with you!" he called back, and I shook my head while Lys stifled a laugh with her hand.

"Get out of there, and come back here!"

He came wandering back into the living room and dining room area of the apartment and looked up at me with attitude, a miniature version of his mom. If my mom, his abuela, had been alive, she would have been begging Mother Mary for mercy. I went over and lifted his backpack off his narrow shoulders and he relinquished it, shrugging out of the straps while he stared at Lys.

"Are you a stripper?" he asked.

"Manolo!" I barked.

"What? That's what my mom said about the last girl you had around here that I met."

"Dios mio, kid. You're killin' me with that mouth tonight. You and your mom both."

Lys was killing me, too, trying, and failing miserably, to suppress her laughter, but she gave my runt of a nephew a pass and answered his question.

"Not a stripper," she said. "I'm a florist."

"What's that?" Manolo wrinkled up his face and jerked his head back. To be fair, he was an inner-city kid. The closest he's probably ever really been to flowers and a flower-seller is the florist department of a grocery store.

"I arrange flowers for a living, and own my own flower shop," she explained.

"You can make a living off of that?" he cried, incredulous.

Lys laughed, "It isn't easy, but yeah. Mostly on wedding arrangements, sometimes funerals, but we do bouquets for all occasions."

"Like what?"

"Well, like corsages for dances, um... center pieces for catering companies, and flowers for hospital patients to help them feel better."

"What kind of flowers?" he asked suspiciously, and I stopped him just long enough to ask him if he had dinner.

He rolled his eyes and said, "Yeah, but I can always eat!"

I went over to dish him up some food while Lys listed off a bunch of flowers I don't think I'd even ever heard of.

"Where do you grow them?"

"Oh, I don't grow them, but a lot of them come from local farms, nurseries, and green houses. It also all depends on what is in season."

"Sounds kind of cool," Manolo said, taking off his jacket and putting it over the back of one of the chairs at the table. He came over and climbed up on one of the stools on the other side of Lys.

I set a bowl of rice and stir-fry in front of him and got him a fork. He picked around the vegetables for a moment and asked suspiciously, "What is this?"

"Food, now shut up and put it in your face," I said, smiling.

"Okay, geeze."

Lys was back on her stool and I retook mine. We ate and I listened to her patiently answer all of Manolo's questions, and that kid had a lot of questions. Reminded me of Angel, when we were kids.

"What's that?" he asked, for like the millionth time, when she named a Phalaenopsis orchid.

"It's a flower native to swamp lands and tropical regions. They're really pretty but require a lot of care and specific conditions to thrive. You have to keep them indoors here, preferably by a window that gets the most sun. They like a lot of sun."

I felt a sudden stab of sympathy, watching them together. I had to admit, Lys would have made a great mom. I was pretty sure she was feeling every minute of it right now, too, even though she didn't show a bit of discomfort talking to my sister's kid. There wasn't a trace of sadness in her eyes or on her face. It made her knock-out beautiful.

I smiled to myself, happily munching away on my dinner until there was a natural lull in the conversation.

"Hey, Manolo," I said, finishing a bite.

"Yeah, what?"

"Wanna watch a movie?"

He gave me a gap-toothed grin and asked, "Desperado?" excitedly.

"Mm, you sure you don't want to watch something else?" I asked.

"It's our movie," he said almost indignantly, the way that kids do, you know?

"Desperado?" Lys asked, an eyebrow raised.

I shrugged a shoulder, "It's our movie," I said like it explained everything.

She let out a sigh that sounded a lot like *Why am I not surprised?* and I winked at her. She tried to suppress her smile, but failed.

"Okay, Desperado it is," I said, and Manolo gave a stoked grin.

"Cool!"

"That's all you two," Lys said. "Too violent for me."

"Really?" Manolo asked, wrinkling his nose.

"Mm-hm."

"Oh, come on!"

Lys smiled and asked, "Don't you have school in the morning?"

He rolled his eyes and said, "It's Friday."

"It is?" she asked surprised, and I laughed at her and nodded.

"It is."

She shook her head. "I don't know what I was thinking."

"Eh, you've got a lot on your plate."

Manolo frowned and said, "No she doesn't," while looking at her actual dinner plate.

Lys and I shared a laugh.

"What's so funny?" he demanded.

"Tell you when you're older, kid."

He rolled his eyes at the effective conversation-ender and Lys shot me a grateful look over his head. She even did the dishes so I could keep Manolo entertained.

I kind of liked playing house with her. Maybe a little too much.

16

*A*lyssa...

Golden's week off went by in a blur, but it was definitely eye-opening. He didn't so much teach me how to fight as he did to recognize potentially violent situations and how to avoid them altogether. What he was teaching me was more valuable to me than how to hit, or punch, or kick someone, because let's face it, I wasn't exactly a physically-imposing specimen. He was of a mind that self-awareness was key, and that getting away and calling him or the police was the best thing I could do.

I was sad when he went back to his regular schedule and we went back to being ships passing in the night. Except things were still different. He would look in on me when he got home from work, check in and see how I was doing, and when I fixed my supper, I made sure to fix extra so that he would have something when he got home. I wasn't always awake when he got home, but when I was, we talked, and it was nice.

One Thursday night, when he got home, he knocked lightly on my bedroom door before pushing it open. I lowered my reader into my lap and looked over, curiously, from where I was sitting up in bed. He sort of half-stepped in the room sideways, still in uniform. I tried very hard not to think about just how damn handsome he was in that uniform and, I confess, I failed miserably.

"Hey," he said.

"Hi."

"I was wondering, can you give the whole six-day-a-week thing a rest this week?"

I frowned. "What, take Saturday off?"

"I was thinking more like tomorrow, since it's my Saturday."

"Um, let me think a minute here." I set my reader aside and picked up my phone from the bedside table. I scrolled through my day on my calendar function and didn't see much, if anything, that Avery couldn't handle.

"I think so," I said. "Let me just text Avery, and make sure that she's comfortable manning the fort all by herself."

"Cool, let me know."

"Sure."

He ducked out my bedroom door and went into his room, closing the door softly behind him. I didn't even think to ask him what he had in mind. I probably should have.

Avery texted back almost immediately, saying that it would be fine and that she wished I took more time off, that the shop wouldn't burn down without me. I smiled wryly and thanked her and told her to call me if she needed anything or if anything came through that needed my attention, that I should be able to handle it from wherever I was. She told me to go have fun with whatever I was doing.

By the time the text exchange was through, I heard Golden's shower running so I picked up my reader and tried to get back into the book I'd been reading. He came back out to check in with me, delicious in just those damn black cotton pajama pants and no shirt, rubbing a dark gray towel over his wet hair.

"We good for tomorrow?" he asked.

"Yeah," I answered softly. "What are we doing?"

He gave me a reckless grin and said, "I figured we'd go for a ride."

I gave a long slow blink, wondering if I'd heard him right. "A ride? As in on your motorcycle?"

"Well, there's another type of ride I give; I'm just not a hundred-percent certain I'm your type," he said dryly and again, I gave a disbelieving blink.

"Are you flirting with me?"

He laughed, "Maybe I am." He turned and said back over his shoulder, without looking, "Maybe I am."

I sat there staring at his closed bedroom door for several heartbeats before I set aside my mystery novel and clicked out my lamp. I didn't think sleep would find me very quickly with how my mind raced with speculation. I mean, I hadn't said 'Yes' but I hadn't exactly said 'No' either. To either.

I lay in the dark hush of my room and wondered what exactly that meant.

THE NEXT MORNING, Golden woke me up by crouching beside the bed and waving coffee under my nose.

I groaned and winced back, asking, "What time is it?"

"Early," he said with a chuckle.

I pushed myself up slowly into a sitting position and he put the coffee into my hands. I sipped gingerly, relieved when I found it both not too hot and doctored to my liking. Meanwhile, he stood, his knees popping like rifle cracks in the small space of my room, though it didn't seem to bother him in the slightest.

"Doesn't that hurt when your knees do that?" I asked.

He raised an eyebrow. "Nope, just a holdover from military life. They make a lot of noise, but I haven't had any problems yet." He knocked on my bedside table and I smiled at the little superstition.

He looked amazing, as usual, in a pair of faded Levi's that hugged his legs and tight ass and again I was trapped between lusting and being mortified, wondering if I even should. I shook my head to myself as he opened my closet doors and, whistling, slid hangars along the rod.

"Ooo! I'll take it." He pulled down a leather jacket of mine and laid it over the back of my desk chair, before rooting around in the bottom. He tossed first one, then the other, of some stylish, above-the-ankle black boots over each shoulder and stood up.

I watched him, amused.

"Are you having fun?" I asked dryly, and he grinned, giving me a wink. I rolled my eyes and he went around to my dresser, opening and closing drawers. He opened my underwear drawer and stretched his mouth like *Yikes!* I laughed.

"Ah, here we go." He pulled out a pair of jeans and laid them across the foot of my bed.

I raised an eyebrow and said, "Why stop there? Might as well finish the job."

He laughed, but rather than leave me to finish dressing myself, he finished going through my things, pulling out socks and underwear: a lacy bra and panty set I hadn't worn in ages. I rolled my eyes and he gave me a look.

"I'll leave those to you, then," he said, and put them back. He went back to my closet, picked a tasteful white blouse to go with the jeans and turned, raising an eyebrow.

I smiled and laughed, and gave a nod.

"Good choice," I praised and he grinned.

"Excellent. Finish your coffee, braid your hair or something, and let's go." He bounced on the balls of his feet in his motorcycle boots a couple times, like an excited kid, and I couldn't help but laugh again.

"Okay, okay!"

He scuffed across my carpet and went out the door, closing it behind him. I shook my head and marveled. I don't think I'd ever seen him so pleased or excited over anything before. I shook my head and gulped my coffee. I was a Twizzler stick of anxiety. On the one hand, I didn't want to keep him waiting, while on the other, I was really nervous about what he had planned. Each one was wrapped around the other and wound tight.

I went to get dressed, picking out a camisole to go under the sheer blouse and a nude bra as opposed to the black one he'd chosen earlier. I finished putting on my clothes, swallowed the last of my coffee in three big gulps, and slung my purse and jacket over my arm, remembering at the last minute to grab my phone.

I found Golden in the kitchen, rinsing out his coffee mug, and as soon as I appeared, he held out a hand for mine. I slid it across the kitchen island at him and he looked me over.

"Hair," he reminded me and I started.

"Oh, right!"

I ditched my things on the dining room table and listened to my boot heels clack against the tile on my way to the bathroom. They sounded a lot more self-assured than I actually felt, but I swallowed hard, brushed my hair, and carefully wove it into a French braid tight to my skull.

I tied the braid off, looked at myself in the mirror, and rolled my eyes when he called from the living room, "Lys, come on! Are you ready yet?"

"Hang on, hang on, I'm almost done!" I swiped on some natural lip balm, rubbed my lips together, and marched out and back down the hall.

"Good deal," he said, dragging open the front door, already in his chaps and leather jacket.

"I don't know about this..." I trailed off, ducking into my purse strap and hanging it cross ways over my chest. He watched me settle the strap between my breasts and raised an eyebrow. I put on my coat and zipped it up, tying the leather belt securely.

"Your body language suggests otherwise, Chica. Come on. No time like the present." He picked up a helmet off the entryway table by the door and bent, opening the little cabinet underneath and retrieving a second. He held it out to me and I stared at it for a long time. I finally stepped forward and took it from him.

He winked at me and held out his free hand. Another moment of terrified reluctance passed, and I took it.

Oh, my god. Was I really about to do this?

He gave my hand a reassuring squeeze at the elevator door and bounced his eyebrows, letting go to punch the button. I tried a smile, but I was afraid it came out weak. His got bigger at it, and he gave me a nod as the doors slid open. He jerked his head in the direction of the elevator car and I took a deep breath and stepped on.

I half expected him to give me an 'Atta girl'.

"Okay, so some things to remember..." he started, and then proceeded to fill my head with everything motorcycle safety, all at once, as we briskly walked up the sidewalk before turning at the corner. Two buildings down, he stopped at a side door and asked, "You think you can handle that?"

I swallowed. "Lean with you, not against you, don't stiffen up," I repeated.

"And?" he prompted.

"Watch the pipes when getting on and off."

"Atta girl!"

I smiled, I couldn't help it. He dragged open the door with a grin of his own. I followed him down the stairwell, down and down, until he stopped and pulled open the next door. We went through and found ourselves in a chain-link cage. He rattled through his keys, found the right one, and stuck it into the lock, giving it a twist and shoving open the fencing. I followed him through and he shut it, making sure it was locked behind us.

I followed him down the dimly-lit rows of cars to the end, the dirty fluorescent lighting muted but still buzzing loudly overhead. He stopped at a row of motorcycle spaces and went to one, pulling off a cover and bundling it up, stowing it in one of the saddlebags.

I swallowed again at the sharp gleaming chrome and satiny-black tank. The leather seat shimmered faintly under the dull lighting, with a buttery soft luster. It was a beautiful machine, but still, intimidating.

"Here, let's get you fixed up." He gently took the helmet from my nerveless fingers and dropped it on my head, his swift, sure hands working at the nylon straps beneath my chin. He smiled at me gently and I tried to wrap my head around just how jazzed he was.

He put on his own and swung a leg over the bike, settling on the front seat and sticking his key in the ignition. He turned it, the lights coming on, and thumbing the switch, the bike chugged to life. I jumped. It was loud. In the enclosed space of the garage, the rumble of the engine reverberating from the cinder-block and concrete, my whole body vibrated from the bass thrum of the engine, an echo down to my very soul.

He held out a hand and I rubbed my lips together and took it. He helped me on behind him and I settled, making sure my feet were where they needed to be. I let my arms wind around his body and swallowing hard, held on tight.

"I'll go slow to start," he called, heeling up the kickstand. "Hold onto me. And – here we go!"

My heart was in my throat as we powered up the ramps winding around and around towards the surface streets. I held onto him and followed his directions to the letter, feeling that same mixture of excitement and anticipation as when you climbed in a roller coaster, poised at the top, and ready to go over, in the center of my being.

Excitement fizzed in my veins as he pulled his wallet from his jacket pocket and held it against the black pad at the garage's exit kiosk. The arm raised and we were suddenly out on the street, the sky reaching far above, the buildings stabbing towards it like fingers, held in the palm of the city's hand.

This was so different. Without the bubble of a car, it was the difference between watching the scenery and being a living breathing part of it. I felt myself grin and before I knew it, I couldn't stop smiling.

We rode through the city at a sedate pace and rolled up to a stoplight, where he turned and asked me, "What do you think, you want to go faster?"

I bit my bottom lip in an effort to contain my enthusiastic smile and nodded. I think I failed miserably, because Golden threw back his head and laughed.

"'Kay, hold on! We're gonna hit the freeway!" I got settled, held on, and he turned in the direction of the freeway's on-ramp.

The wind had already washed over me and through me, a cleansing sensation that lifted some of the cobwebs and stripped them away, but the speed of the freeway? It lifted the final strands from me and sent them spiraling into the ether, never to be seen or heard from again. I suddenly very much understood the appeal of these machines. Bonus points that, had I still been together with Ray, he would hate that I got on one.

A bubble of laughter rose from the center of my being and escaped through my lips, and that joy was so irresistible, I couldn't help but whoop and laugh and cheer out loud. I felt Golden laugh in front of me, and I felt so secure, I even let go with one arm, trailing my fingers in the wind's stream like one would through an eddy of water.

We rode out over the Bay Bridge and even though I had no idea where we were going, I didn't care. It just felt entirely too good to let loose and so I did, and simply enjoyed the ride, grateful that he'd seen fit to bring me along.

17

*G*olden...

I was doing Skids and Reflash a solid, heading down to a distillery in Virginia to pick up a few bottles of some liquor they used in one of their specialty drinks. They weren't out, just wanting to restock, and I'd been itching to go for a ride anyway. The idea had struck me out of the blue to take Lys with me, and hot damn, it'd been the right idea. She was all but bursting with joy on the bike behind me and her mood was downright infectious.

I boasted a smile of my own as I navigated the long stretch of freeway ahead of us, ticking off the directions in my head, enjoying a decent cruising speed and the stillness that came with the hypnotizing rush of wind and road. Peace settled in my being and the two-or-so-hour ride flew by as if it only lasted minutes.

I took the exit we wanted and navigated cracked roads through countryside-looking areas. The distillery was tucked back along a river, trees reaching towards the sky, nature replacing the concrete and steel of Indigo City as if we'd passed from one hand to another, from father to mother.

There was something decidedly gentler about the surrounding scenery. Idyllic. The colors were more vibrant, the water placid as we passed over the old-fashioned covered wooden bridge and up the sweeping lane further into the hills. The distillery was tucked away, and even though it was a tourist spot, it wasn't too busy, not on a Friday. We came around a bend and suddenly there it was, an old brick building that probably dated back to Civil War days.

It hadn't always been a distillery. It'd served multiple purposes over its lifetime: tobacco, munitions, a field hospital at one point, all manner of different manufacturing gigs, until finally, about thirty or forty years ago, the distillery, looking for more space, moved on in.

They had a good tour, all about the history of the building in addition to the distilling process. I couldn't be sure, but I was hoping it would be something that Lys might like.

I parked and shut off the bike. She got off of it carefully and stood, eyes closed and face turned to the sun, breathing in the clean air. I took a second or two longer than I probably should have to soak in the sight, still trying to decide exactly what this was.

I'd certainly dug chicks before, but this was somehow different. I was less concerned with banging her than I was with seeing her smile. When she did, smile, I mean, it was like my whole world flipped upside-down and inside-out and got lighter somehow. I wasn't used to that shit. I mean, she was attractive, beautiful, even, but I'd been around chicks that were pretty before, and it'd never felt like this.

"What are we doing here?" she asked, opening her eyes and fixing them on me. They may have been brown but they were anything but boring; a deep brown with amber highlights in the right light.

I smiled and said, "Needed a good ride, promised Skids and Reflash I'd pick up a few bottles for their bar. They're getting low and their distributor is out. They called down here and the distillery has them, but something about Virginia law prevents them from shipping."

"Have you been here before?" she asked, turning to look up at the building, working at the unfamiliar strap at her chin with its 'D' rings.

"Come here, let me do that," I murmured. She obediently stepped up to me and I reached up to work the straps free, saying, "And to answer your question, yes. I've been here before. They have a really good tour, and I thought you could stand to get out of the city for a bit."

She gave a gusty sigh of agreement and nodded, as she ducked out from under the helmet I held in my hands.

"I didn't realize how oppressive it was beginning to feel," she said. "Not until we hit the bridge and the whole world felt like it suddenly opened up."

I nodded and smiled, hanging her helmet off one of the handlebars and reaching up for my own.

"Sometimes you just need to get out. Get away, even for just a day and experience something new."

She was staring back up at the building, eyes distant, seeing but not seeing, as she took in the hush of the lightly-rustling trees, the distant babbling of the river lending the serenity only the sound of cascading water could provide.

"I used to go to the botanical gardens a lot when I felt like I needed to reconnect," she said.

"Oh, yeah?"

"Mm, they closed Indigo City's down for renovations, then everything happened with Ray and I forgot to check to see if they've reopened yet." Her expression darkened at the mention of her douchebag soon-to-be-ex-husband's name, the light dimming in her eyes. Then I saw something unprecedented. She swept her gaze from the building back to me, and the light that'd dimmed returned full-force, like the sun having been temporarily hidden by a scudding cloud.

I think I forgot to breathe for a second. The weight of that moment was profound and definitely something I'd never felt before. I mean, I couldn't... I didn't... shit. I didn't know what to do with the fact that I felt like I lived to see that look on her face when she looked at me, all the time. I swallowed and found myself smiling back like a fuckin' dope.

"What do you say? Wanna take a break from life and take a tour with me?"

Her smile grew and she bit that bottom lip of hers coyly and my heart quickened in my chest.

"I'd love to," she said and I stood up in one fluid movement, swinging my leg over the bike and standing firm, both feet on the ground. It helped ground me and kept my head from swimming with these sudden, strong, and newfound emotions.

I didn't think, I just –did–, and held out a hand to her without thinking about it. She took it, sweeping a stray lock of her hair away from her check where the breeze had picked it up. She tucked it behind her ear and fell into step beside me. All the while I couldn't stop thinking about how alluring that simple gesture had just been to me. Sexier than a full-on striptease.

"Other than the botanical gardens, what're some of your favorite things to do?" I asked, curious.

She laughed a little and said, "I can't believe we haven't talked about this stuff before. Um..." she trailed off and I liked that she was really thinking about what I'd asked as we slow-walked it up to the building's entryway.

"I used to love gardening. When we first got married, we bought a house just outside the city and I used to garden." She looked wistful for a moment and said, "Oh, you should have seen it. I managed to get some Himalayan blue poppies to grow along the front flowerbeds. They were beautiful against the white paint of the house."

"Why'd you move into the city?" I asked.

"Well, Ray got the job at the firm that he did, and the commute was becoming unbearable for him. We were going to start a family, and the schools in the city were, surprisingly, better." She chewed her lip. "We reasoned that if we had kids, I wouldn't really have time to garden like I used to, and Ray agreed to let me start my flower shop to sort of mitigate that loss for me..." she trailed off and sighed.

"When we found out about the fertility issues, we'd already sold the house and bought the condo, and the rest, I guess, as they say, is history."

I nodded gently, absorbing her words, her story, like a sponge. She took a deep, cleansing breath and let it out in a great sigh, her body relaxing marginally, making me realize she tensed any time she talked about him. I couldn't blame her. His name was now synonymous with the single worst moment of her life thus far. Surrounded, it sounded like, by dozens of other smaller moments, no less damaging in their own way.

"What about you?" she asked.

"Me?" I laughed a little.

"Yeah, you." She stopped and tugged a little on my arm, indicating I should stop, too. I did, and faced her. She looked into my eyes, her face openly curious and asked, "Why do you sound like it's so hard to believe I would want to know things about you, too?" she asked.

I blinked, bewildered, "Did I?"

"Yes, you did," she said unequivocally.

She's calling you on your bullshit, Martinez. Time to 'fess up.

I rolled my lips and said, "I guess it's because I can't be quite sure when the last time somebody asked me that was. I mean, asked me that, and really meant it, you know? Like, was seriously and legitimately wanting to hear an answer. Not just going through the motions."

She frowned and her expression darkened with that same sort of sadness, as if another cloud had passed over the sun that was her heart.

"How incredibly sad for you," she murmured and it sort of blew me away. I felt like a deer caught in the headlights.

"I never really thought of it that way before, but yeah, I guess you're right. Still, I don't want or need you to be sad for me, Chica. Today is supposed to be a good day."

She smiled and it held a bit of whimsy to it. She said to me, "So far, it's been one of the best days that I've had in a very long time."

I smiled, my chest nearly cracking in two with how much it swelled with fuckin' pride. I nodded and said, "I'm glad for that," as I dragged open the door to the distillery. Lys smiled at me and went through, and I followed her in.

To borrow a phrase from Oz, I'd pretty much follow her straight into hell in gasoline boots, if it would make her smile like that more often.

"Hello! Welcome in." I looked up at the cheery greeting from the girl behind the counter and listened to Lys shyly return it.

"Hi."

"Have you been here before?" the girl asked.

"I have, she hasn't."

"Okay, well –" I tuned her out, only half-listening, and watched the light and shadow play through Alyssa's eyes as she listened, nodding along.

I wasn't one-hundred-percent sure on how to do the whole relationship thing, having never done it with much practice or regularity. Hell, I was a grown-ass man in my thirties, who had never held a relationship beyond a few months here or there.

Probably because you just hadn't met the right girl.

And was Lys the right girl?

You already know the answer to that, asshole.

I wondered for a minute if I did. I mean, if I did, really, and what's more, what made Lys the right girl out of every girl that had come before.

Let's see, she's successfully living with your ass, putting up with your shit, and doesn't whine or complain about trivial things. Hell, she doesn't tend to bitch or whine about the big things until they get so overwhelming she has a total meltdown.

True.

Also, she's responsible, stable despite the hell she's been through, and Manolo seems to like her and that kid's just like you. He don't like anybody.

Also true.

I nodded, smiled, and agreed with something the counter girl said, and paid the nominal fee for the tour for the both of us. Lys looked like she was having the time of her life and that made me smile.

That, and you gotta love a chick who is smart –and– easily entertained.

I had a hard time not laughing out loud at that last thought and let myself be swept along by the two women and the history of the place we were in. I couldn't deny it was a pretty cool place. It all seemed brand fucking new watching it all through Lys' eyes.

That will probably also never get old, my inner voice said and I honestly couldn't disagree. Still, I had a lot of self-doubt, and I only knew of one place to turn to get help with something like this.

I was never going to hear the end of it, either.

∼

SURE ENOUGH, when we walked into the 10-13 later that evening, Pasquale was the first to have something to say. Then again, Pasquale always had something to say.

"Well, I'll be goddamned!" He stood up straighter from behind one of the two tall tables by the dart boards that we tended to take over. Chrissy, Aly, and Lil looked over, and everyone just sort of froze while Pasquale went on saying, "I ain't never seen you bring no broad –in– to this place before."

"Hey!" I gave him a stern look. "Be nice." He reared back, surprise painted on his face thicker than his outlandish makeup. I ignored his melodramatics and said, "Lys, this is Pasquale, that's Chrissy, Lil, and Aly."

"Hi," she murmured shyly and gave this adorable little wave of her hand.

I hefted the canvas pack full of booze bottles higher onto my shoulder and said, "Shouldn't be more than an hour. Order something to eat, the food is good." I gave Pasquale and the girls a sharp look and said, "Try not to give her the third degree."

The girls laughed and Pasquale crossed his arms and gave me a look that said he was so not impressed. I raised an eyebrow at him as I passed and reminded him sharply, "Be. Nice." He rolled his eyes at me.

I shook my head and finished heading for the fishbowl, past the pool table. A bunch of the guys were watching the whole thing through the glass, and my twin was among them, a faint smile on his face. I scowled at him, asking with my eyes what the fuck his deal was. He quirked an eyebrow, barely, almost imperceptibly, a direct answer of *You know what I'm talking about.* I rolled my eyes quickly at him and dragged open the fishbowl's door.

"Well that's a first, you bringin' a girl –in– here," Skids remarked.

I frowned at him.

"You got ears out there I don't know about?" I demanded, knowing full well the fishbowl was pretty well sound-proofed from the rest of the restaurant.

"Now, you know I ain't, why?"

"Pasquale said the same damn thing, almost verbatim." I gently swung the army green canvas pack off my shoulder and held it out to him by the top loop. "Here's your booze for the bar."

He took it.

"Thanks, how much I owe you?"

I named off the figure and he nodded, "Write you a check when we get out of here."

I sat down, and Oz demanded, "So, who is she?"

"That'd be Lys," Angel said and I scowled at him, our classic look for *'Thanks for narcing me out, bro.'* He gave me a shameless shit-eating grin.

"What, the roommate?" Poe asked.

"Yeah," I answered, and shifted a little uncomfortably. Youngblood and Backdraft exchanged a look.

Youngblood asked, "You catching feels?"

"Like the goddamned flu," I confessed.

The whole table went into stunned silence. If Angel's face split into any more of a grin the top of his fuckin' head was going to come off. I rushed forward. No going back now.

"I'm out of my depth here, boys. I actually really don't want to fuck this up, and I'd appreciate it if you'd all keep the jabs to a minimum this time."

More silence. Skids let out a sigh and leaned back in his seat, his blue eyes trained out the window at the knot of people around the tall table furthest from us. Lys had slid up onto one of the stools next to Aly and it looked like the girls were doing their thing, welcoming her as one of their own. Pasquale had even lost some of his hard diva edge. I thought maybe some of his nursing instinct had kicked in. Lys did still have some of that wounded vibe around her.

"What's her story?" Driller asked softly, and I realized she telegraphed it like a reader board. Even from here, you could see it. Her shoulders were slightly hunched, rounded forward, her mannerisms timid and uncertain. A tightness was around her eyes, that hadn't been there earlier when it'd been just me and her.

"Just a second, hang on." I got up and went to the door, dragged it open and called out, "Lys!" She looked up, and I called out to her, "Situational awareness." She nodded, smiled, and looked around. She asked Pasquale something and he kind of half-reared back, but obliged her, switching her seats so that she could see the door.

I watched it all as I went back to my seat. Some of her tension had eased. Sometimes she just needed the reminder. She was still learning, still getting used to it. She did much better about it when she was on her own, and I took it as a mark that she trusted me to look out for her, that she forgot about it sometimes when I was around, unless we were actively working on it together.

I sat back down and sighed, trying to buy myself time to figure out where to begin. "Just because y'all are my friends, doesn't mean I feel free to speak her business, you know what I mean?"

I heard grunts of affirmation around the table and I knocked a knuckle thoughtfully against the wood surface. I looked from one to the next to the next of my brothers and said, "You didn't hear any of this from me. You don't know a goddamned thing."

Nods and affirmations went around and I laid it out. There weren't a lot of surprised looks around the table. That was the cost of doing business when you were full time heroes, though. We knew how bad it got, how deep the evil of this world ran. That was why, when you found beauty in it like Lys, you hung onto it.

"So, what's the problem, then?" Driller asked, shifting uncomfortably in his seat.

"How the fuck do I even do this?" I asked laughing. "I've never really wanted to try before, so it's not like I have any fuckin' practice."

"Seems to me you're doing just fine," Angel said and there were some nods of agreement.

"Why her, of all people, bro?" Oz asked.

I raised an eyebrow and shrugged, "She's lived in the same place as me for the last couple three months and hasn't run screaming yet. That's a start." Chuckles swept around the table and some of the guys exchanged some amused looks.

"Lemme ask you something," Skids said, leaning forward and putting his elbows on the table. "What're you more afraid of, hurting her or getting hurt?"

I answered immediately, "Hurting her, she's had enough."

"If everything's different this time, prove it," Backdraft said with a wink.

I frowned.

"The fuck I do that?"

"Hearts and flowers, dude. Hearts and flowers," Oz said, grinning at me.

"Easier said than done; she's a florist, owns her own flower shop."

Laughter went around the table and Angel said, "I got you covered. We'll talk."

"Yeah, I figured you would," I grumbled.

"All seriousness, though. Glad you came to us," Skids said. Serious expressions and serious nods went around.

"You don't ask for help as a general rule," Reflash said finally. "The fact you'd ask about this, says just how serious you are."

I shifted uncomfortably and gave a grudging nod. He wasn't wrong, and the fact the guys weren't making fun of me and giving me a ration of shit about Lys meant a lot. I hadn't given a fuck when they'd done it over my man-whoring ways, because I didn't really give a fuck about who I was sticking my dick in. I hadn't so much as touched Lys that way but this time I cared. I hoped that meant I wasn't turning into some kind of a pussy.

I turned around in my chair and cast a look through the glass. Everyone at her table was looking at me. As soon as I frowned, they all busted up laughing, which made me scowl harder.

"What the fuck are they laughing at?" I growled and the guys around the table laughed.

"You, they're laughing at you. Who the fuck knows why," Oz said, laughing at me too.

"Pasquale," like four voices said in unison.

"That queen is more trouble than he's worth sometimes," I muttered, but didn't mean it. Pasquale and the club's favorite game was getting on each other's nerves.

I turned back to the table and huffed a sigh asking, "anyway, where were we?"

The guys exchanged glances and Skids said, "Well, I do believe we were in the middle of working on your problem, which, it seems to me, ain't really a problem at all."

I nodded, I got where he was coming from. Still, I told him and everyone else, "I'm open to suggestions, boys. In fact, I'm all ears…"

18

*A*lyssa...
"Okay, so, inquiring minds really want to know. What in the hell is it like actually living with that gorgeous, yet infuriating, man?" Pasquale demanded. I think it was just his way, like his outlandish choice in clothing and makeup.

He was wearing a corset and long, elegant pants that looked like they belonged with a high-end pantsuit. They didn't touch the ground, but only by virtue of the patent leather, platform, spike-heeled boots. Over the corset and pants, he had a long black cardigan-wrap-thing that, like the pants, flowed and floated if he had the occasion to walk. He was bald, his eyebrows penciled on, high and dark in a perpetual look of surprise. His silver eyeshadow was done all the way up to them.

I was jealous of his perfect cat'seye black liquid liner. I wished I was half as accomplished at it as he was. He tapped a perfectly-manicured black acrylic nail against his deep maroon-painted lips and waited, with his not-so-patient eyes trained in my direction.

"Um, it's okay now, but at first it was..." I groped for the correct word, and finally settled on one he used that was, sadly, pretty accurate. "Infuriating."

"I knew it! Oh, darling girl, you simply must tell us everything!"

"I don't know," I said, hedging. I knew Golden was fairly private, and I didn't want to share anything out of turn.

Pasquale tutted and heaved a melodramatic sigh. "Okay fine, let's start with you. Why on earth did you move in with the likes of him?"

"Um, well, I'm going through a divorce and I needed someplace to stay and, um..." I gave a nervous laugh. The door across from us opened up; we heard the sound of it scraping across its metal lintel. None of us paid it any mind, but then, Golden called out my name. We all stopped then, and looked in his direction.

When I looked up, he fixed eyes on me and said two words: "Situational awareness."

I nodded and he went back inside and Chrissy rounded on me and asked, "What does that mean?"

"Um, it means I need to move. Can I switch seats with one of you so my back isn't to the door?"

One of the things Golden and I had discussed when it came to safety and my feeling safe was special and situational awareness; there were things I could do to feel more in control of my surroundings, and be in more control over my person and my personal safety.

Pasquale stood up, and with a knowing smile, said, "Absolutely. If it puts me facing all that delicious leather-dipped man-candy up there, I have no problem switching you spots, honey."

"Thank you, it just helps my anxiety, not having my back to the door."

"I understand," Chrissy said kindly, and Aly and Lil exchanged a look.

"Um, my husband got violent with me once. Only the once, but it was bad and I had to stay in a shelter for a bit. I was living on a college friend's couch for a while and the ad for a room for rent came up, and I kind of figured it'd be safer living with a cop, you know? Well, Kenzie, my friend who I was living with; it was her idea, actually."

I chewed my bottom lip nervously as Chrissy looked on kindly and the other two women blinked owlishly at me. Pasquale looked empathetic and patted me on the hand where it rested on the table.

I jumped slightly and he said, "Well, hold on, now, Sugar. Ain't nobody here gonna harm you so, just relax." He tsked again and sighed. "All that, and you land in his place. You poor, poor, thing."

I smiled, "He's really not so bad once you get to know him."

"Rough start, I take it?" Aly asked innocently, but not at all surprised.

"A little. I didn't realize there'd be a different girl coming through every time. That was a little,..." I made an 'eee' motion with my mouth and cringed a bit, and knowing smiles and glances were exchanged.

"So drunk, right?" Lil asked.

"Oh, my god, so drunk."

They all laughed.

"I'm really surprised he hasn't ever ended up on the wrong side of some charges with that," Chrissy said casually. She sipped her drink and I frowned. "Don't get me wrong!" she cried. "I'm glad, believe me I'm glad he never did, but I think we all worried about him."

I nodded and thought back on some of the girls he'd seen out the door, how most of them weren't even like 'Call me', they were just 'Thanks for the good time' and that was it. I think Golden was a bit better at picking them than he was getting credit for. However, on the flip side of that coin, all it took was one who was packing crazy, and as Ray had proven to me, anyone was really capable of anything at any given moment.

"I don't think you have to worry much now," I said faintly, staring at the back of the chair Golden was in through the glass.

Pasquale jumped on the statement like a dog on a bone. "How's that?" he demanded.

"He hasn't brought anyone home in weeks," I said.

Everyone looked in Golden's direction and Pasquale said, "Well, fuck me. There may be hope for me to get in there for some beef jerkies, after all."

"What?" Lil demanded.

"It's what he calls a hand job or a reach-around," Chrissy said dryly, and at that moment Golden turned to look at us, looking at him, as we all burst out laughing. I shook my head and couldn't stop grinning at the timing of it.

"As tempting as you are, I don't think he'll take you up on it," Lil said, staring at the back of Golden's head.

"Oh, and who asked you, Ms. Smut Writer?" Pasquale asked.

"Me!" Aly cried excitedly. "I want to know! Why do you say that, Lil?" Pasquale gave Aly a flat look.

"I say it precisely because I'm a smut writer," Lil said smugly and she gave me a wink.

I felt my brow wrinkle in confusion. *She wasn't suggesting...* I shook my head and passed the thought right out of my mind.

"We're just friends," I said.

"That's how Backdraft and Lil started," Aly said, helpfully.

"Motherfucker," Pasquale muttered, and shook his head in denial.

Chrissy laughed at him. "To be fair, I think Golden's already declared his adoration for the fairer sex," she said.

"Bitch please." Pasquale positively glowered at her. "Ain't nobody fairer than me."

Laughter erupted at the table and I had to agree: Pasquale was absolutely, blatantly fabulous.

"So, what do you do, Lys?" Lil asked.

"Oh, I'm a florist. I own my own flower shop."

"Oh, yeah?" Aly lit up.

"Yeah," I smiled. "Indigo Blooms."

"Oh, nice!" Lil said. "Do you do event arrangements?"

"Like weddings?" Pasquale hazarded.

Lil rolled her eyes. "Oh, my god! Eventually, but not yet. I meant like dinners and galas, and maybe if I ordered some arrangements for my next book signing. That sort of thing."

I smiled and nodded, "Yes, I do all of that."

"Fabulous!"

"So you're an author?" I asked. Aly and Chrissy sort of laughed, and Lil beamed at me and nodded.

"I write romance novels."

"Only, like the best romance novels of all time," Aly said around her straw.

Lil rolled her eyes and sighed, "You're going to probably find out anyway. I'm Timber Philips."

I bit my bottom lip. "The name sounds familiar, but I don't really read romance. I'm more of a mystery kind of girl. Sometimes true-crime."

"See!" Lil crowed triumphantly. "Not everybody knows who I am."

I laughed, glad she wasn't insulted. The conversation diverted from Golden and from me, for which I was grateful, and instead turned to books, which led into television shows, and movies, which then led into music.

Eventually, when the conversation reached a natural lull, I asked, "What do they talk about in there?"

"Who knows," Pasquale said with a gusty sigh. "Probably about each other's penises."

Chrissy scoffed, "Wishful thinking on your part."

"Bitch, you know it."

This of course led the conversation to exactly how Pasquale ended up hanging around in a cop bar with a cop motorcycle club. Chrissy's story was a sad one, and yet also gave me some hope. I mean, if she could look so put together and be so successful after something so horribly violent, I could too, right?

Right. It just took time and dedication and non-stop exhausting work on myself. All of which, well, most of which I was willing to do; and the rest? Well, even if I didn't want to do it, I was doing it anyway.

The door scraped and we all looked over as the guys came filing out of the glassed-in banquet room. They flowed down the ramp and down the stairs, a leather-and-denim pyroclastic flow of hot men. I think all of us around the table stopped talking, and took the time to appreciate. I know my temperature went up a few degrees; I could feel it in a faint blush across my cheeks, though for some reason, my eyes kept gravitating to Golden, as if he had some sort of magnetic pull.

I reasoned it was because I knew him best out of everyone there. I had met a few in passing, when he'd had them over for some game on television, but it was only briefly, as when I had come home from work that night I had been tired and had stopped to eat on my way home, so I had just gone in to bed. Not even their rowdy cheering had made me stir. Once I'd been out, I'd been out.

"Hey, Lys. Nice to see you again."

I smiled and said, "Hello, Poe. Hi, Angel. Nice to see you, too."

"What about me? What am I, chopped liver?" I smiled a bit more.

"Hi, Oz."

"So, you got right intentions by our girl?" Pasquale immediately demanded of Golden, hand on his narrow hip.

"What the fuck you talking about?" Golden demanded back.

"We've decided we like her," Lil declared.

"That's right," Aly agreed enthusiastically. "We've adopted her."

A man almost as short as she was went to her and put an arm around her waist. He laughed and hugged her to him, and the display made me smile.

"Come here, you." One of the tallest brothers, broad through the shoulders, went to Lil and bent to kiss her and the way he looked at her made my heart melt for them with happy. Of course, with the sweet, comes the bitter, and it hit me in the form of a pang of jealousy, though, I had to admit, the pain of it was much less pronounced than it would have been, say, a month, or even a week, ago.

I was getting better, gradually, but better. Golden winked at me as a third man went to Chrissy and kissed her.

"Oh, you guys are all adorable together," I said putting my hands over my heart. It was true, even though my own emotions had begun to churn in a vicious tug-of-war in the center of my chest. Once upon a time, I'd had that, but not anymore. I slammed the door inside my head on that awful little voice that tried to whisper *Maybe never again...*

I didn't want to believe that, but for now, while everything was still a disaster and the divorce wasn't even final, it was easy to believe that particular serpentine hiss of negativity. My line of thinking was interrupted by Golden, who asked, "Did you eat?"

I smiled and shook my head, "I'm still full from lunch, thank you, though."

"Yeah, me too," he agreed.

We'd stopped at G&M before traversing the Bay Bridge back this way. It was a place famed for their Maryland crab cakes, although they were more like crab bombs, about the size of a softball and so, so, good! Still, they were super-filling and I just didn't have the appetite to go for another meal so soon.

"You ready to go?" he asked, and I nodded but Pasquale had something to say.

"Now, hold on there, Casanova! We were just starting to get along with our new friend, and she was about to tell us all your secrets, you can't deprive us like that!"

"Shut it, tramp!" Golden shot at Pasquale, with a grin to take any of the sting out of the insult, but still, Pasquale jerked back as if he'd been slapped, and made a horrified gasp.

"Now you listen here, whorebiscuit! That was uncalled for –"

Everyone surrounding the table burst into riotous laughter, including Golden. Oz was bent double and came up, clapping Golden on the shoulders and giving him a shake back and forth.

"Look! Look here!" Oz gasped and wheezed for breath, almost laughing too hard to be able to speak. "She called you 'whorebiscuit'!" and he bent back double, dropping his hands to his knees, gasping and wheezing between gales of laughter.

I couldn't breathe either, it had just come out of nowhere, and everyone else laughing had just fed it, and as soon as we thought we were done, someone would start giggling or laughing again, and would start it all over again.

"I'll be here all week, no, really, tip your waiter," Pasquale said dryly, snapping his fingers. He didn't look a bit fazed, but you could tell by the sparkle in his eyes and the slight upturn to the corner of his mouth, he was pleased at everyone's reaction.

People were wiping tears out of their eyes, and Golden grumbled,

"Oh, come on. It wasn't –that– funny," which set everyone off some more.

The older gentleman that ran the place approached from the bar and handed Golden a check for the alcohol we'd brought him. He asked "What's so funny?" and everyone looked at each other, and it started a whole new fit of laughing and giggling.

I laughed so hard my sides hurt, and oh, how I needed that laugh. Golden was smiling faintly as he looked me over, and I nodded. While the laugh was needed and very nice, I was about peopled-out. It had been a very long day and I was ready to go home.

"Okay, you guys have fun, we're going to head home. It's been a long day. A good one, but a long one," Golden declared. I nodded in agreement and picked up my coat from where I'd draped it over the tall bar chair I'd been sitting on.

There was a lot of moaning and groaning and 'Aw, come on's from everyone, but Golden waved them off.

"It's not his fault," I said. "Honest. I have to work tomorrow and I'm not a twenty-something anymore, believe me."

I suppressed a shudder. I hadn't tried to drink since the debacle with Golden's whiskey a couple of months before. In fact, I somehow doubted I would ever want to drink whiskey ever again, after that. The girls and Pasquale all lined up and hugged me, which was nice.

"Please bring her back here," Aly begged, and Golden smiled and jerked his head down in a nod.

"You got it, Aly cat."

And with that parting shot, we departed. It was chillier than it had been when the sun was out, but it wasn't too bad. At least, not until we started moving. I was glad we only had to go across the city and that the traffic, though it wasn't awful, slowed us down enough to keep the evening air from getting too biting.

He pulled up in front of our building to let me off and I swung a leg over, stepping up onto the curb. He paused, then shut off the bike, leaning it onto its kickstand before getting off himself. I cocked my head, questioningly.

"I'll walk you up," he said and I smiled.

"It's okay."

"No, I really want to walk you up, make sure you're good."

I nodded and he took off his helmet while I took off mine. We went upstairs, the elevator seemingly taking forever and the silence between us thick, almost palpable. I wasn't sure what was up, but there was something hanging over us, between us, and I grew uneasy with not knowing what it could be.

Had I done something? Said something? Oh, no...

He stopped me, his hand finding mine, just in front of our door. I faced him squarely and his hand came up, his fingertips light along the side of my neck, thumb grazing the underside of my jaw, just so.

His eyes were intense where they bore into mine, searching, and I silently willed him, aching, to kiss me.

"I don't want to screw this up," he murmured, and it was as if he were committing every line of my face to memory. I imagined it was how I looked when I stared at a particularly beautiful bloom in the conservatory. I felt my breath catch and though I wanted so badly for him to bring his lips to mine, my voice betrayed me.

"Then don't," I whispered.

His lips curved into a sad little smile, and he nodded softly. He dragged my forehead to his lips and pressed a kiss there, murmuring against my skin as my eyes sank shut and peace descended over me from the crown of my head all the way to my feet in a light, tingling rush.

"This is not where this story ends."

I nodded faintly against the press of his lips and he drew back. It was suddenly hard to look at him.

"It was a good day," I murmured, changing the subject to a slightly different track. "One of the best days I've had in a long time."

He smiled and nodded, saying, "More ahead if you want."

I smiled and nodded and with a wink, he turned and strode back down the hallway calling, "Be back as soon as I park the bike."

"Okay," I called at his back.

I let myself into the apartment with a heavy sigh, slightly frustrated with myself for chickening out at the last second like I had. My stupid words echoed back to me. "Then don't," I muttered under my breath with disgust. "Way to go, Lys. Way to go."

∽

Life went back to business as usual, only much nicer, over the next week. We were still ships passing in the night, but on the nights I was still awake when he got home, we would talk. I would ask about his day and it was quickly becoming the same answer, he would smile this secret little smile that could mean anything or nothing and would say, "I wanna leave that shit out on the street, out at the curb. Tell me about your day."

And I would; I would tell him about my day, while I watched him visibly relax and unwind from his. Then I would ask if anything funny happened to him during his. That would usually get him talking about something or other, but at least once he just shook his head. A serious look came over him and he said, "No. No, nothing funny happened tonight, Chica." I learned vthen it was just best to let it go. I'd pushed, gotten my head bitten off, and he'd gone into his room, slamming the door.

I'd teared up, had gotten very upset with myself, my heart racing, hoping I could somehow fix it, but had tried to give him space the rest of the night. When I'd gone to bed, his door had opened behind me as I had opened the door to my bedroom. He'd apologized, and we'd stayed up far too late talking about it, but it was worth it just to have the communication.

That had been two nights ago, and tonight, it was his Friday. I half expected to find him on the couch when I got home. Okay, I was super hopeful I'd find him on the couch when I got home. It was going to be a nice change. I stopped at the mailbox in the lobby and opened it with my key, shuffling through the letters as I got into the elevator.

"Rodrigo Martinez, Rodrigo, Rodrigo, and Rodrigo. Hm," I muttered as I went through them. Nothing for me.

I tossed the letters up on the breakfast bar and set my tote and purse on the end of the dining room table. My feet were aching and I tried to remember what had possessed me to wear that particular pair of pumps this morning. I fished out my dirty Tupperware from my bag and loaded it into the dishwasher, and went around to my laptop, which I had left on the bar that morning. I slid myself up onto the stool and sighed tiredly just as the front door opened.

Manolo burst through and made a silent and sullen beeline for Golden's room. I looked over at Golden, and he looked unhappy, shaking his head.

"Hey," I murmured. "What's going on?"

"His dad's in jail again," he said softly, and I felt my shoulders drop.

"Mail come?" he asked.

I nodded.

"Just missed me grabbing it."

I nudged the short stack of business-sized envelopes at him and he came over and swept them into his hands. He went through them, one, two, and at the third one he stopped gave a triumphant nod and slapped the stack against his other hand.

"Something you've been waiting on?" I asked.

He nodded and said, "Thanks for grabbing it," but didn't elaborate. He headed for his room and called back over his shoulder, "You hungry?"

"You cooking?" I asked wearily and he laughed.

"Yeah, I'll cook, just hold on a minute. Manolo!" he rattled off something in Spanish at his nephew, too fast for me to keep up. Something about washing up, I think.

I shook my head and smiled to myself as Manolo smarted back in English, and thought that he was just like his uncle in that regard and that this had to be some form of cosmic karma for Golden, if only in small dose.

When they came back out, Manolo was quite a bit less angry and quite a bit more reserved.

"Hi, Lys," he said, dully.

"Hey," I said back. "Tough day?"

"Yeah."

"Wanna talk about it?"

"No."

I smiled and gave him a nod and said, "That's okay, too. I have days like those. So does your uncle."

"Yeah," he said glumly.

"*Desperado*?" I asked and he scowled at me.

"I thought that was too violent for you," he said, rolling his eyes.

"I think I can take it – if you don't make fun of me for hiding behind my hands."

He smiled and nodded. "Popcorn, and you have a deal."

"What's a movie without popcorn?" I demanded.

"Tío! Lys said she'll watch *Desperado* with us but only if there's popcorn!"

"Oh yeah?" Golden called from his room. "Sounds good. Dinner first, buddy!"

I smiled and updated my spreadsheet with the day's numbers, tracking my profit and loss while Golden fixed dinner and Manolo talked my ear off about El Mariachi. It wasn't quite the Friday evening I had envisioned.

It was better.

19

*G*olden...

I swapped my Saturday with a dude from another shift for Sunday so that I could get a rare Friday, Saturday, and Sunday combo off. I wanted a three-day weekend, and to take Lys out on a date , a real date. First, I needed to work up the nerve to ask. It was Friday, and I headed down to her flower shop. One, I wanted to check it out because it was so much a part of her life, and two, I wanted to ask her. I was nervous as fuck about the second one.

Bright blossoms decorated the sidewalk outside her business. She had them all up in big old tin milk-cans and washtubs, rustic and simple, on rolling wooden frames so they could be brought into the store and locked up at night. It was a cute little place. Small and narrow, right on the corner and down in the basement of the old building. I went down the three steps to the door which was propped wide open and stepped into a world of polished cement floors and more greenery and blossoms than I thought Indigo City could hold.

"Hi, welcome in! Can I help you find something today?" Avery, the girl behind the counter, was adorable, and once upon a time would have even been my type. Waifish with a short blonde pixie cut, she was busy arranging roses in a vase and gave me a winning customer service smile from around the salmon-colored blooms.

"Uh, yeah, I was actually looking for Lys. She's my roommate."

She blinked big green eyes at me in total shock, quickly recovered, and stammered out, "Uh, yeah... Oh my, God how embarrassing, I totally forgot. Um, she's in the chiller, through there." She pointed down a back hallway and I gave a nod, and I have to admit, my best panty-dropping grin. She blushed furiously and I made my way through the flaps of thick clear plastic into the colder, refrigerated section of Lys' shop.

Lys looked up from where she was clipping the end off of a stalk of gladiola before stuffing it in a giant vase overflowing with greenery.

"Hey, you!" She smiled warmly and it did things to my insides. I didn't think the whole 'butterflies in the stomach' thing happened to dudes, but yeah, apparently it did, because I had them. The phone rang out front and I heard the shop-girl pick it up.

"Hey," I said. I jerked a thumb over my shoulder and said, "I guess I haven't been here in a minute, Avery forgot who I even was." I laughed a little and she smiled and nodded, and looked a little nervous.

"I hope you're not terribly offended." I chuckled. Somehow, I didn't think that was the real reason why she was nervous, but she didn't have anything to worry about. I was still working on proving it, though. I'd talked to Angel; I'd even had a few text conversations with a few of the other guys. I had this big master-plan but fuck, I was nervous as hell.

"No, not at all," I said.

"What brings you all the way over here?" she asked, leaning against the stainless steel work table in the center of her cooler.

"Was curious, I wanted to ask you something."

"Oh, yeah? Must be pretty important to come all the way over here."

I laughed, "You act like I trekked across the Arctic Circle; I walked six blocks, Lys."

She smiled, shook her head, and opened her mouth to say something, but her assistant, Avery, came through the flaps keeping the cold air in here.

"Sorry to interrupt, Lys. You asked me to tell you if he ordered this week, and he just did."

Lys's face fell and I frowned.

"Who ordered?" I asked.

"We think it's her ex, he's been doing it for weeks, same request that Lys delivers it personally."

I turned from Avery back to Lys and demanded, "Do you?"

Lys rolled her eyes. "No. I send my deliveryman, Jeremy. Doesn't stop him from making the requests, though, and I'll gladly take his money." She heaved a heavy sigh of frustration. "I can't turn down a sale."

I held out my hand for the slip in Avery's hand. "Give it to me. I'll make the delivery this time."

"Oh, Golden, I don't know…" Lys' voice trailed off and I could hear the distress.

"This is harassment, Lys. You have an order of protection in place for a reason."

"Can't prove it," Avery said sadly. "He isn't using his credit card and I somehow doubt that my recognizing his voice on the phone is something that will stand up in court."

"Happens all the time," I assured her. "Gimme the flowers, and the address." I waggled my hand at Avery for the slip and she looked to Lys.

Lys sighed and her shoulders sagged. She nodded and Avery handed it over. I looked over the address and asked, "What am I taking?"

∼

I TOOK a car service using an app, the dude dubious about the arrangement of roses between my knees. I showed him it wasn't too full, tried to not call him a pussy, and got my ride to some dentist's office in the ritzier part of the city.

I got out and told him to wait, and he said sure; at least I had that going for me. I went into the dentist's office and a natural blonde looked up from behind the front wrap. Her eyes lit up and she laughed, putting her hands together and pressing her fingertips to her lips.

"I keep telling him to stop this, but he won't hear of it. They're beautiful." I set the dozen red roses on the counter and she stood up. I felt my stomach drop at the sight of hers. She was definitely pregnant and definitely showing.

Son of a bitch. That was just fucked-up.

"Where's Jeremy, though?" she asked me. "He usually delivers the flowers."

"I'm Rodrigo, I'm the new guy. Say, what does your boyfriend do for a living that he can afford to send flowers every week?"

She looked taken aback at the question and looked me over. I was in faded, comfortable jeans, a worn but comfortable gray tee, and my jacket and cut. She smiled and said, "Oh, Raymond? He's a lawyer. Corporate stuff." She waved her hand dismissively.

I got out one of my business cards from the ICPD. I wrote on the back of it and handed it to her.

"I'm not trying to start anything, you seem like a nice person, but it's real fucked-up that this guy buys you flowers every week from his ex-wife's flower shop. She has an order of protection against him for a reason. You give him this, and tell him to pick a different florist from now on."

I handed her the card, her expression stunned and hurt, but probably not half as bad as the one that would be on Lys' face when I told her what her douchebag ex's master plan had been. I didn't know what the fuck he was thinking or what he was up to, trying to shove his pregnant mistress in her face. I stopped and raised my cellphone right before walking away, and snapped the bitch's picture.

I was pissed, and yeah, it probably wasn't any kind of her bad, but it was. She knew that he was married. She had to by now. And if she was staying with him, that meant she didn't care, which meant that I wouldn't care, either.

What I cared about was Lys and how she was going to take it because I would be fucked if I was going to let it continue. I had the driver wait again outside her flower shop and went in, asking Avery behind the counter, "Have you got this?"

"What?" She turned wide green eyes on me.

"I'm going to take Lys home, have you got this?"

"What?" Lys echoed, coming out of the back room.

"Come on, we need to go home." I stood, tapping my foot, impatient and angry, and Lys' expression cooled and turned grim.

She nodded, took a deep breath, let it out slowly and said, "Avery, are you comfortable closing up shop on your own today?"

"Yeah," Avery sounded surprised then got herself together. "Yeah," she said more strongly. "Yeah, no, go on get out of here. Try to enjoy –" she caught my withering look and the words died on her lips. Her expression grew sad, and she nodded and said unequivocally, "I'll be fine."

Lys was studying my face, and dread and dismay crept into her beautiful brown eyes. She went and got her things and followed me out. I held the door to our ride open. She got in without a word.

The six blocks to our apartment were driven in a silence as hard as diamonds. We went upstairs and she rounded on me as soon as I shut our apartment door.

"Tell me," she said, and she was already shaking, expecting the worst, and it killed me that the worst was all I had to fucking give her right now. I pulled out a chair from the dining room table and she sank down into it without being asked. I sat down at the head of the table at a ninety-degree angle and pulled out my phone.

The picture hid the broad's stomach from view behind the big front desk wrap. I turned it toward Lys.

She pulled out her phone and scrolled back and back and back through her photos, to a picture of a man and the same woman at a candlelit table.

"Well, I kind of figured the flowers weren't for me, Golden," she said softly, studying the picture on my phone intently.

I gritted my teeth and was about to set off the bomb when she froze, her gaze becoming intent as she put two fingertips against the screen and opened them up. Her eyes welled and she looked up at me.

I had fucked up. I should have known she was keen, I lived with her, for Christ's sake. She turned the image toward me, and I was looking at the edge of the mistress' computer monitor – and the ultrasound picture taped there.

"She's pregnant?" she asked.

I closed my mouth grimly and licked suddenly-dry lips. I couldn't even bring myself to say it. I simply nodded, cowardly fuck that I am.

She thrust my phone at me abruptly and picked up her own.

"No more flowers for her, he won't be contacting you again," I said and she sniffed and stood up.

"I need a minute," she said and made for her bedroom, her heels making a clipped, sharp sound on the tile. I closed my eyes as she shut her door and I listened to her burst into sobs.

Fuck.

I waited a minute, and got up myself, putting the chairs silently to rights, back in their places, tucked beneath the table, before I went slowly up the hall. I stopped outside her door and called out gently, "Lys?"

"I'm all right," she called back, her voice watered down by her torrent of tears.

I let myself into her room, where she lay sobbing on her side, clutching a pillow to her chest.

"Move over," I ordered, ushering her with my hands. She hesitated, but finally put the pillow back at the top of the bed and eased back to make room for me. I dropped onto the bed on my back and pulled her to me. She rested her head on my shoulder and shuddered, hitching in a fresh set of sobs. I curled my arms around her and buried my hand in the soft fall of her hair, massaging the back of her scalp. I pressed my lips to the top of her head and murmured into her hair, just whatever came to mind.

I let off a string of Spanish, too, telling her how I felt, that she was amazing, that she didn't fuckin' deserve this, no one did, but not once did I tell her to be quiet or not to cry. I didn't know how much she understood of what I was saying. I didn't care, either.

She wet the front of my tee with her tears and I wore it like a badge of honor that I was the one to be here for her. I smoothed my other hand up and down her arm and waited for the tempest to pass. She lay quietly with me for some time, before finally drawing a shuddering breath deep into her lungs. She let it out slowly and pushed up into a sitting position and I let her go.

I looked up at her and asked curiously, "What're you going to do?"

"Call my lawyer," she said and I smiled at the barely-suppressed rage in her voice.

"Atta girl," I said and sat up.

"You don't have to go," she said and reached across me to the bedside table for her phone. She dialed out and put it to her ear and I sat with my forearms braced on my knees as she made her call.

"Deanna Bewley-Davis, please?" she waited a moment. "Yes, this is her client, Alyssa Tanzer." She looked as if she'd tasted something bad when she said her last name and I had a feeling she would be going back to her maiden name when the divorce was final.

"Deanna, hi, yes I know, I'm sorry." She told her lawyer everything and punctuated her story with a demand. "I want everything I can get out of him and double the alimony," she said. Her lawyer sounded optimistic on the other end of the phone, from what I could hear of it.

"Yes, thank you. Um, I haven't formally informed the police of his break –" she stopped when I emphatically nodded. Oh, yes the fuck, she had. "Um, I take that back, apparently I have." She paused. "Yes." Paused again. "Uh-huh, okay." She looked at me, searching my face, her own slightly troubled, but recovering quickly.

"Thank you, Deanna. Yes. Take it to court if you have to, I'll figure it out." She nodded and said, "Uh-huh, thank you again. Bye-bye now." She pulled the phone away from her ear and tapped the screen.

She took another deep, cleansing breath and let it out. I put my hand on her shoulder and rubbed her arm reassuringly, delighted when she didn't jump at my touch, figuring she was just distracted with the disaster at hand.

"You did good, there."

She swallowed hard and said, "Deanna is going to try and argue that I never took any of the orders so I didn't know it was Ray. I think Avery will attest that she didn't know. I mean, I'm not really sure. I guess going through with the deliveries for as long as I have, that it could complicate things."

I shook my head. "None of that matters," I said. "These things are always messy and complicated and never as easy or cut-and-dried as everyone likes to think they are or should be. You've got no guilt, Chica. Not in this."

She swallowed and bowed her head, pressing her fingertips to her forehead between her eyes, pinching the bridge of her nose.

"Headache?" I asked and she nodded. "Yeah, my sister gets 'em too when she cries."

I got up and went into her bathroom, checked her medicine cabinet and plucked down a bottle of Excedrin. I got a glass of water from the tap and went back to her. She took the pills and asked, "So what did you want to ask me? Earlier. You came all the way to the shop to ask me something and then never did."

I smiled kindly and shook my head, "It's not important," I said.

She frowned and looked up at me. "It was important enough for you to walk six blocks just to ask, so yeah, it kind of is." I touched her cheek, flicking my thumb in a light caress along it but she wouldn't be distracted. She kept her eyes locked on mine, searching my face.

"It's not important right now," I told her. "You should take a nap, get settled; I'll get some dinner started."

She swallowed hard and nodded, looking at me like she didn't quite believe me, but I didn't want this hanging over what I had planned in any way, so I would wait and ask her later, when she was well clear of it.

"Thank you," she murmured when I reached her door. I turned

and looked at her and lightly popped the doorframe a couple times with my fist, wishing it was her ex's face and I was punching a lot harder.

"No problem," I said and let her have some alone time. Well, that, and I called some of my buddies down at the station-house to have Ray picked up for violating the protection order – because fuck that guy.

20

Alyssa...

"Dinner?" Kenzie echoed in my ear. I tucked my phone between my neck and shoulder and sighed.

"Not just dinner, Kenzie! Like fancy, like a date."

"How fancy?" she asked suspiciously.

"Like, 'The Grotto' fancy," I said and tried not to wince as I said the restaurant's name. It was someplace I had always wanted to go at least once, but it was oh-my-god expensive. You could easily drop three hundred dollars for a dinner for two, but the place was magic.

"Holy shit, Lys. This guy is taking you to 'The Grotto' on a cop's salary? He's, like, totally sprung on you. What have you been doing? Putting Viagra in his coffee?"

I snorted and shook my head, dropped the phone and bit out a curse. I picked it up off the cement floor and said, "I dropped you," but I don't think Kenzie heard me, she was too busy laughing her ass off on the other end of the phone. I smiled and resisted giving her the satisfaction of joining in. I was trying to be serious here. I was nervous about it.

Kenzie got herself together and said, "When are you supposed to go?"

I clipped the end off of a rose and admitted, "Tonight."

Dead. Silence.

"When did he ask you, again?"

I blushed and said, "Um, the middle of the week, last week."

"You waited a week-and-a-half to tell me about this? Lys, come on!"

"I know, I'm sorry! I guess I was still in shock and couldn't believe that I actually said yes!"

"What are you wearing?" she demanded.

"Can't go wrong with an LBD," I sang out.

"Okay, you have like three little black dresses, which one? You know what, never mind, when are you supposed to go? I'll come over and help you out."

"Tonight, I said that already," I said, exasperated, and Kenzie spluttered.

"Oh, what the fuck, Lys? What time?" she demanded.

I told her and there was more dead silence on the other end of the line, which I rushed to fill.

"I know, I'm sorry! I should have told you about it a lot sooner, and I was thinking the cocktail dress, you know the one –"

"With the slit up to there," we both said in unison. We laughed.

"Yes, that one," I said.

"Good choice! I think you should go, I think you should have a fabulous time, and I think you should let your sexy-as-sin roommate bang your brains out."

"Kenzie!"

"What? There's life after Ray, you know, and you should totally be living it."

I groaned, "Why'd you have to say his name?"

She heaved a heavy sigh on the other end of the line and said, "Lys, I'm worried about you."

"I'm worried about me, too!" I declared.

"Okay, why? Why are you worried?"

I chewed my bottom lip carefully and let out a defeated sigh; I hated talking about me and my feelings. It always felt like I was opening myself up to drama... but this was Kenzie and she hadn't said a thing to make me feel bad about any of this, so I went with it.

"He's my roommate, Kenz. What if I freeze up? What if I'm not ready, and he gets angry or disappointed, and things get awkward? What if I have to find someplace else to live? It feels like an awfully big gamble for a night of fun." Which was what I was really worried about. I didn't do flings. Of course, I was putting the cart before the horse here. Golden hadn't exactly given me any indication that sex was on his brain. It could very well be just dinner.

Oh, come on, Lys! At 'The Grotto' of all places? I derided myself.

"Lys, let me ask you something."

"Yeah?"

"Why'd you say yes?"

Because it was Golden, and I was comfortable around him, and because he'd been so adorably nervous when he'd asked... How could I say no?

"Because my gut said so?" I hazarded.

"Exactly, and if it's one thing I've learned, you should seriously start listening to your gut. I mean, for Christ's sake, Lys!"

She wasn't wrong. I'd had a gut feeling for a long time that things weren't right with me and Ray and I had ignored it. I'd blinded myself to what was, believing that if I just kept focusing on what I wanted it to be, that it would somehow get there. I'd let my hope and my faith blind me. Blind faith wasn't a good thing and if there was anything Golden had been steadily teaching me, it was that if something didn't feel right, then something –wasn't– right.

Except what about when it felt right? I mean, when everything felt absolutely right? What then?

I posed the question to my best friend, and Kenzie sighed, "I think you just answered your own question there, Lys."

"I did, didn't I?" I asked.

"Good things happen too," she reminded me gently and I nodded, checking my watch face on the inside of my wrist.

"Oh, shit, Kenzie, I've got to go if I'm going to have enough time to get ready."

"Right! Shave everything, makeup, hair; the works! Leave him so he doesn't know what hit him. Do me proud!"

"Oh, my god! You sound like one of those creepy southern mothers who just live to make their daughter a debutante and get them married off to give them lots of fat grandbabies!"

"Wow. You have one hell of an imagination, Lys," she said dryly and I laughed. Oh, she totally knew.

"Go!"

"Right! Bye!" I hung up and went for my purse.

~

AN HOUR LATER, I stepped out of my bathroom in my most expensive heels and my fitted cocktail dress. It was sleek and elegant with a slit up one thigh that was just this side of indecent if I moved wrong, giving a glimpse of the garter holding up my stockings. I swallowed nervously and pulled my burned-out velvet black wrap around my shoulders, gripping my classy beaded black clutch in my hands.

Golden appeared at the mouth of the hallway and I froze. He mirrored me, freezing too, and we both just sort of stared at each other for a long time, our gazes roaming over the other. It very much felt like we were sizing the other up, but in that stunned way that said *Oh, my god, this totally wasn't what I expected.*

I knew Golden cleaned up nicely. I'd seen him in uniform probably a hundred times or more, but this was… wow. He wore black slacks and a black shirt. His tie was a shiny indigo satin held by a silver tie bar and the look was slick. He looked like he belonged on the cover of GQ magazine, not standing right in front of me just a few feet away, looking at me looking at him.

I let out a shuddering breath, suddenly nervous as a smile played over his sensual lips. He held out an upturned hand to me and I stepped forward, lightly placing mine atop his, the contact very nearly electric.

"You look beautiful," he breathed and I felt myself blush.

"You don't clean up so bad yourself," I said softly.

"Car's here, come on." He picked up his suit jacket off the back of a dining room chair as we went by and locked up the apartment behind us. I thought it was cute that he took my hand, holding it as we waited for the elevator and even once we were inside.

It didn't stop there, either. He held doors for me and was the perfect gentleman; I hadn't been all that sure he had it in him, to be honest. He was treating me so differently than I had ever seen him treat the other women he'd brought to the apartment, and that gave part of me pause. I didn't want to hope again so soon after…

However, I'd accepted his invitation to dinner, knowing the venue was as fancy as it got with a dress code, and that this was definitely not the type of things that 'just friends' or 'roommates' did with each other.

This was a date. A real date. Even though I was still married, *but separated and who gives a fuck about Ray's feelings!?* Which was true. I didn't, but oh, what was I doing? Was I ready for this? What was this?

I suppose we would talk about whatever it was over dinner, this strange thing between us that had been quietly and steadily growing.

The Grotto was a tall, stone castle façade and little more. Located in the depths of Ridgeview Park, it was only open during the spring through the summer months in good weather and was a singularly unique dining experience. No more than two dozen tables no more than two people per table, and surrounded by natural rock, water fountains, and lush greenery and flowering plants, it was a horticulturist's dream. As a florist, I certainly could appreciate, and it was the main reason I had always wanted to come.

We stepped through the block stone archway to the hostess pedestal, where Golden produced a gold envelope from his inside pocket. He handed it over and the hostess, with a smile, opened it, gave a nod, and said, "Right this way, Mr. Martinez, Ms. Glenn."

I blinked in surprise. I hadn't heard my maiden name in quite some time, and I was actually pleased that he'd thought to use it rather than my married name. The very last thing I wanted on my mind tonight was anything to do with my failed marriage, yet my thoughts lingered far too long on it as we wound down a flagstone garden path, deeper into the beauty of the garden restaurant.

We were seated at a stone table draped in fine linen, candles winking from mason jars hung from the tree above our heads, providing lighting. Lilies bloomed on giant stalks, perfuming the evening with their delicate scent, and nearby, a soothing trickle of water spilled into a stone pool, thick with flowering water plants.

"It's so beautiful," I murmured, and I gazed around myself in wonder.

I expected Golden to be doing the same but his eyes, I was startled to realize, were fixed on me. He licked his lips and said, "I hadn't really noticed, Chica. Can't seem to take my eyes off of you."

I lost my breath as a furious blush overtook my cheeks, across the bridge of my nose. He smiled fondly and I stammered, "I'm not really sure what to say to that," as the waitress, smiling, set two flutes of champagne on the table, each with a ripe strawberry on the rim of the glass. I smiled up at her and murmured a 'Thank you' as she set a silver ice bucket with the bottle on the edge of our table between us. She drifted off up the path and I raised an eyebrow.

"Champagne?"

"Of course, we're celebrating," he said and raised his glass, holding it out. I tapped mine gently against his and the pure note that rang out could only come from crystal. I sipped, and it was probably the best champagne I'd ever tasted. He laughed gently at the surprise on my face, and I found myself blushing again.

"What are we celebrating, then?"

"Your freedom," he answered and I smiled, but it held an edge of sadness.

"I don't really view it that way," I said honestly. "I see it more as a failure."

He shook his head, "It takes two to make a relationship work, Lys. That isn't all on you."

"I know, but..."

"No 'but's' about it. You tried your damnedest. You were the committed one. You didn't run out on him, you didn't abuse him, or try to hurt him for something outside his control. He let his bitterness and anger swallow him whole, you used that bullshit as fertilizer and grew. I admire you for that."

I laughed a little incredulously, "You admire me?"

"Yes." He cocked his head and his look was so very serious, it wiped the smile right off my face. "You've done the impossible, Chica."

"What's that?" I asked softly. The waitress had returned and set the first course, a fennel-and-leek soup, in front of us. The Grotto didn't have a menu. You didn't choose. You ate the marvelous creations the chefs prepared for you and experienced their art the way they meant it to be.

He waited until she drifted away, his dark eyes following her, until he was sure she was out of earshot, his next words meant for me and me alone. He bowed his head, shaking it once and said, "This has a fifty-fifty shot; It's either the best or worst thing I've ever done for a woman." I frowned, and he reached inside his suit jacket and pulled out a single white sheet of trifold paper.

He handed it over. I opened it, and turned it so the light from one of the suspended candles could illuminate it in the failing light of deepening evening. I squinted and read the letterhead *Indigo City General Medicine*. I felt brow furrowing as my eyes drifted down the page.

Test results – Negative for any STI's

I looked up at him, confused.

"Angel's idea, seeing as you probably only see me as a raging manwhore. Which I was, until you made me want to be a better man."

I blinked, open mouthed, and folded the paper, setting it aside.

"Yes, but I didn't think you were a stupid raging manwhore – your words, not mine," I said hastily when he scowled. "I figured you were being safe, I mean," I said gently.

"Yeah?"

"Yeah."

We lapsed into an uncomfortable silence and I thought about it, about everything. I picked up my spoon and filled the silence with soup as I tried to consider the implications.

"This is a really awkward way of telling a woman you would like to sleep with her," I murmured, not sure what else to say.

"Yeah," he agreed, nodding.

More silence elapsed and we ate. Finally he set down his spoon and heaved a sigh, though whether he was impatient with himself, or me, I couldn't tell.

"Lys, the point I'm trying to make with all of this is that you're safe with me."

I flinched and said sharply, "I know that," affronted that I could have given him any other impression.

"So let me treat you right," he said and I stared at him for a long time and tried not to tear up. I wanted what he was offering, but I was scared.

"What are you thinking?" he asked softly, after a time.

"I'm thinking that I really want what you're offering, but I'm scared."

He nodded slowly and looked thoughtful for the moment, "Slow then; I'll go slow. I'm okay with that."

"Really?"

"Really."

I smoothed my lips together and finally nodded carefully and he smiled. I smiled back, bravely and he raised his champagne glass again, holding it out.

"To new beginnings."

I held my glass out.

"To new beginnings," I echoed softly.

The rest of dinner was a waking dream of taste and sound. Music began to play softly as the sun finished its plunge below the horizon. After the main course, but before dessert, Golden got up from the table and came around; he held out his hand to me and I placed mine in his, fighting down a shiver when he caressed his thumb over the backs of my fingers. I stood carefully and he led me onto the path and down the way a little bit, to a courtyard of smooth, polished marble set into the grass.

Two other couples were there and already dancing to the light sounds created by a live string quartet. I had thought the music had been via a hidden speaker system. I went with Golden to the dance floor where he carefully eased himself into my personal space. I let my arms drift around his neck and his hands smoothed gently over my hips and around my waist, settling on my lower back. He took a gentle step to the side and we began to sway.

"Doing okay?" he asked, low and even.

I nodded and stepped slightly closer, resting my head on his shoulder. His hands smoothed up my back and he held me as we gently moved to the light and ethereal notes drifting along the cooling night air. I closed my eyes when he pressed a kiss to my bare shoulder where the wide strap of my dress didn't cover.

The sensation was electric, the chill of the evening quickly forgotten as warmth traveled from the press of his lips out over my skin in a rush of heat that had little to do with any actual temperature change. I let out a shuddering sigh that was half relief that I could. and did. have a reaction to his touch that was so pure, and he held me just a little bit tighter.

The last notes drifted over marble and beautifully-manicured grass and couples broke apart and applauded. Golden and I did, too, although I have to admit we stood closer than most. He put an arm around my waist and we went back to our table along the garden path picked out by twinkling fairy-like lights. The effect was stunning and didn't look like anything modern that I could see, though I was sure it was some form of LED lighting.

He pulled out my chair for me and I sank into it, a bit grateful. My shoes, though stylish, weren't the most comfortable. He retook his seat across from me and dessert was served, our glasses refreshed with the delicious champagne, which I was drinking in moderation. I had no desire to revisit the kind of drunk from my last time behind a bottle. I didn't even want to come close.

By the time we were finished with our cheesecake, night had

completely fallen and the music provided by the string quartet had faded into frog- and cricket-song. We took a walk around the night display of the garden on our way out and by the time we reached the exit, a car was waiting to take us home. Golden had wrapped his suit jacket around my shoulders and I shivered lightly as I got into the back seat of our ride, grateful that it was warmer in the car.

He held my hand lightly between us where it rested on the seat. Warm and alive, he brushed his thumb lightly back and forth over my skin and my heart jumped with every pass. When he let us into our apartment, he gently led me back down the hall toward the bedrooms, and my heart leapt into my throat, my pulse throbbing almost-painfully in the side of my neck. He stopped us outside my bedroom door and lightly touched the side of my neck, his thumb grazing my jaw in a light, sensual touch.

"Here we are, safe and sound at your door," he said gently, and I nodded.

"Thank you," I whispered.

"For?"

"Everything, the whole evening, it was perfect."

He gave me this sexy little smirk and oh god, I wanted him to kiss me. I wanted him to kiss me so badly, because I just wasn't brave enough to do it. Before I knew I was even going to say it the words were out of my mouth.

"Are you going to kiss me? Because I really need you to make the first move if you are. I'm just not brave enough."

He smiled and it was entirely too sexy and made me melt into my heels. He nodded carefully, his other hand rising to capture the other side of my neck, his thumbs beneath my jaw. Tipping my head, just so, he searched my face to make sure that this was really all right while I remained frozen in his grasp. I willed him with my eyes to close the gap, and it felt like he moved towards me agonizingly slowly.

His lips touched mine and I shuddered in his grasp; my own hands went behind his head, gently, his hair softer than it looked. His tongue gently flicked against my lips and I groaned, opening to him, and then we were kissing, my heart racing, my body pulsing with every throb of my heart, blood rushing, breath lost, as the whole world narrowed down to his mouth against mine, his tongue toying with mine, his hands smoothing over my skin and down the silhouette of my body in the little black dress as I crushed my body up against his, desperate for more of this wonderful human contact.

He broke the kiss, his chest heaving, and gasped out, "Your place or mine?"

"Mine," I whispered and he opened my bedroom door and practically carried me through. I laughed against his mouth, committing to his touch as I stumbled back in my heels. I kicked them off and lost several inches as his hands tracked around to my back. His fingertips glided up the seam of the dress's hidden zipper and I shivered with wanting as they traced along my spine through the material, and I worked his tie free of its knot.

He paused and reached up with one hand between us, and popped the first two buttons at his throat, and I could tell he had felt constricted.

"Lys." His voice was a sexy growl, full of need and it stole my breath, not that I needed it anymore. He kissed me again, hauling me tight against his body and I could feel the heat and rigid strength of his erection through his slacks.

The zipper of my dress parted, smooth as water, the slightly cooler air of the room spilling across my skin. One of his fingertips traced a line of heat down my spine as the two cloth halves of the back of the garment separated. I closed my eyes and let myself be enveloped by the sensation of his fingertips gliding over my skin, sending shivers across it. My fingertips struggled with the buttons of his shirt while our mouths tangled, our tongues clashing in a passionate and sensual dance.

His other hand joined the first at my back, and skated up and out, drawing my dress down over my shoulders. I shrugged out of it so that I could get back to pulling his shirt out of his waistband and he gave this little moan against my lips. He broke our kiss and sucked in a shuddering breath as he took a half-step back, his gaze sweeping over me. I felt devoured by those dark eyes of his, but I can't say I didn't return the favor because his arms were something else, each muscle defined in that way that drove any sane woman mad with lust.

I wanted to see more of him. I wanted his black A-shirt off of him, the ribbed material was obstructing my view of his chest and the abs I knew were under it, cutting down to that delicious V that made me want to run my tongue lower and take that bulge in his slacks into my mouth, which was watering just thinking about it.

He drew it over his head, grabbing it from the back between his shoulders and hauling it over his head, and the movement was just so powerful, I pressed my thighs together and sucked in a breath as I felt myself flush, my pussy giving a little throbbing ache of *Want!*. He gave me a reckless sort of grin and reached for me, his arms twining around my waist, bringing me to him his mouth pressing against my chest, just below the hollow of my throat. I wondered if he would go high or low as he walked me the two steps back so the backs of my thighs fetched up against the edge of my bed.

I plunged my hands into his hair and scraped my nails lightly along his scalp and he growled, his lips parting, his teeth scraping lightly along the top of one of my breasts just above the lace of my bra's cup. I moaned in answer, my head falling back, my hair sweeping along my lower back and the top of my ass and I shivered from the unexpected sensuality of the sensation.

Golden was determined to seek out and find every one of my erogenous zones before he went any further in undressing me. I worked at his belt with my hands and shoved them off his hips, his black boxer-briefs a maddening final barrier, hiding him from my sight. I didn't want to rush, but at the same time I was so impatient, so, for now, I settled with smoothing my hands over every exposed, reachable inch of him.

His hands dropped to my lower back, tracing along my skin in a feather-light touch that drove me wild and soothed me at the same time. I sucked in a breath and held it as he plucked at the hooks holding my garter belt. He undid them, the lace giving with a little sigh, and he smiled, going to his knees in front of me, staring up at me like I was some kind of personal goddess for him.

"Sit," he urged, his voice husky, rough with lust and something that sounded like awe. Surely he couldn't really feel that way about me, though? Could he? I sank to the edge of the bed and he peeled the garter belt down as I went, unhooking the back on first one side then the other. He did it by feel, his eyes locked on mine the whole time, the intensity in them unlike anything I had ever seen before. Focused, his energy so calm, so stable, I'd never felt anything quite like it. He was in control and I found it a relief to cede what little I thought I had left, laying it in his hands, which were busy gliding one of my stockings down my thigh.

He leaned in, his eyes still fixed on mine, and pressed a kiss to my knee. His eyes slipped shut and he followed the hosiery's descent, pressing a line of chaste kisses down my shin, along the top of my foot as he pulled it off, half taking the other with it as the garter was still attached. He laughed and I giggled with him and once we were done, he gave the other leg the same treatment.

God, he was such a slow tease. I almost couldn't stand it. He smiled with the devil's own fire in his eyes, knowing the sweet torture he was putting me through and took my toes into his mouth. I gasped, the sensation was so foreign but at the same time, really nice. I swallowed hard and he placed kiss after kiss back up my leg, walking up the bed with his arms on either side of me, overwhelming me so expertly with his sheer presence that I found myself lying back. He kissed along my stomach, up to my chest, pulling down one of the cups on my bra and taking the nipple into his mouth and sucking.

I sighed out, my hands flying from the covers to his head, cradling it gently, pulling him to me, my back arching and thrusting more of my breast into his mouth. My head fell back, my eyes closed, and I captured my bottom lip between my teeth as I let out a passion-filled sigh. I shuddered and whatever tension my body held drained from my muscles, and left me loose and compliant beneath him.

His fingertips traced my collarbones as his mouth migrated to the other breast and gave it the same lavish treatment. His fingers did some walking, sweeping out from my throat, travelling in an upward trajectory to curve around my bra straps, drawing them down off my shoulders. I helped him, bringing my arms out and he continued to feed on my breast, tongue playing along my tight nipple, sending a blush of pleasure through my body and leaving no doubt that I was wet and aching to have him inside me.

He stood and reached down, helping me to sit up, and he made quick work of getting my bra off the rest of the way. I could see him straining at his boxer-briefs and I hooked my fingers in the waistband, pulling them out from his body and sweeping them down his legs boldly. The backs of my knuckles traversed the rough terrain of the scar tissue that created seams in his left thigh, where he'd been shot.

He let me undress him, but bent at the waist and hooked his fingers in the waistband of my panties, preventing me from doing anything beyond that just yet. I lay back and pressed my toes into the floor, arching my hips so he could draw them down my thighs.

He reached down and had me sit back up, but got up onto the bed beside me, walking on his knees so that he knelt behind me before I could do anything. I waited him out patiently as he gathered my hair behind me, up off my neck, and though I couldn't see, I got the distinct impression he brought it to his nose and breathed me in as he let it plunge through his hands. It swept along my back, cascading against my skin in a cool, silky rush that made me shiver, and I couldn't think. His lipswere at my neck, working along the side, pinging that erogenous zone so perfectly, so completely, all thought fled before the onslaught of sensation he wrought.

His hands swept over my body, caressing my stomach, his fingertips delving down my front and I parted my thighs for him. I could feel the hot press of his erection against my lower back, just below my hair, which he gathered with his free hand and swept over my shoulder opposite where his mouth worked the side of my neck.

"Golden!" I gasped as his fingertips found their mark, sliding through my wetness, over my clit. He pressed the pad of his middle finger against it and swirled it in a tantalizing motion and I shuddered against him.

"Lie back," he murmured, and he helped me to lay down in the center of the bed, kneeling between my knees, his mouth back at my chest, kissing down, down, impossibly down, between my breasts, over my stomach, at the top of my mound, just out of reach of where I really wanted him to be. His fingers threaded between mine as he shouldered my legs apart and with those impossibly dark eyes staring at me, he made sure I watched him as he tasted me for the first time.

I made this strangled noise, somewhere between crying out and a gasp, as if the air rushed from me yet my throat forgot to make sound. I fell back, my hands gripping his, holding on to stay grounded, as his tongue worked against the most intimate part of me, lavishing my body with attention long denied it, teasing at my clit and bringing me right up to the edge.

Oh, he was good, keeping me there, right on that edge, but backing off and letting me recover so that he wouldn't send me over, alternating between teasing soft licks of my clit and plunging his tongue just inside my entrance. I shuddered and shook under the onslaught and bit my lip until it very nearly bled.

"Oh, god!" I cried, "Please. Please, please, please!"

"Please, what?" he asked, and his voice was as devilish as his look had been moments before, soft, dark, totally inviting.

"Please, come up here, I want you, I need you inside me."

He chuckled darkly and obliged my begging, but at his pace, on his terms, his cock brushing against the inside of my thigh a couple times on his way up. He grabbed my hips forcefully and bodily brought me up off the bed, sitting on his knees, lining me up with him, checking my expression and my body language to make sure he wasn't doing anything frightening or triggering.

I didn't care, I was too far gone, too drunk on his love-making to be any kind of afraid and it felt so good to let go of all of that and just live totally and completely in this moment with him. He rolled his hips, the head of his cock nudging against my pussy lips and I cried out, stuffing the heel of one of my hands against my mouth to keep quieter, the other hand gripping the blankets at my hips as he found purchase and eased the first inch or so of himself inside me.

"Look at me, Lys," he said and I opened my eyes. He smiled and murmured in Spanish as he eased himself all the way in, so slowly I swore I died a partial, little death, though I hadn't come. Not yet. It was a near thing, though, pressing my walls around him, just there beyond his penis like low-hanging fruit. Just one last final nudge and I would fly apart, I just knew it, and oh, how I wanted it. How I wanted him, and to be like this with him forever.

He stayed inside me, fully-seated, his eyes heavy-lidded with his passion, his breath weighted with his desire as it rushed from his lips and spilled heated over my nude body spread beneath him. I bit my bottom lip and moaned, and he smiled like it was the sound he'd always wanted to hear most. He rolled his hips ever so slightly, moving within me easily, and I gasped, arching.

"Eyes on me, baby," he whispered and I opened them again. He nodded and started, low and slow, rolling his hips carefully, sliding out so carefully before easing back in. He felt so good, so incredibly good, but he was holding me right there on the precipice and wasn't ready to let me over.

I settled into his lovemaking carefully, and he smiled triumphantly, bending over me, fully seated, and laid his lips on mine.

"Good girl," he whispered against my lips and I eased further into the mattress below me. I don't know what I'd done to deserve the small praise, but something about it was so incredibly sexy, I felt myself throb around him. He let out a little gasp and stilled, waiting the fine tremors in my pussy out, and I gasped, which sounded almost petulant. He smiled above me and shook his head slightly.

"Not yet, Lys. I want to make you feel so good, you'll never want another man again."

Despite the possessiveness of the statement, it was so incredibly hot. The tone with which he said it spoke low and soft of other things, of gentleness and safety, of strength and protection.

"Yes," I whispered and he thrust into me a little bit rougher than he had been. I let out a throaty half-moan/half-cry and he looked utterly pleased with himself. I had to admit he'd earned it. Golden was flipping every single one of my switches into the 'On' position and I wasn't quite sure what to make of it.

I didn't get to dwell on it for too long, because he bent over me, and put his mouth on mine and I didn't need to think on anything anymore. It was just pure feeling from there on out. Think or feel, like I could do only do one but not the other, and I was surprisingly relieved to do only the latter.

21

*G*olden...
 I lay my body over the top of hers, kissing her, bracing on one arm to hold the majority of my weight off of her so she wouldn't feel trapped. My other hand drifted over her silky skin, smoothing down her body until I could palm the outside of her knee and raise her leg. I wanted deeper and she groaned against my mouth, complying, wrapping both her legs around my hips, her hands drifting over my back.

She twined around me, my wild blue rose, and pulled me closer, wrapping herself around me, holding me to her petal-soft skin, and I about died and went to heaven. I worked myself in and out of her body with solid, sure, yet slow and measured, strokes, ravaging her completely but as gently as possible. I knew I could be intense, but it wasn't about me tonight. It was about her and making sure she was comfortable, that I made her feel good, safe and loved, appreciated like she hadn't felt in a long time, if ever.

Her passionate breathing, her voice when she moaned or cried out in that cadence and tone that told me I was doing everything right, gave me such a thrill. It was the natural virile high any man should get when he treated his woman right.

I loved how unexpectedly responsive she was, I loved how she kissed me without a second thought, boldly, after I'd gone down on her. She was a princess, a queen, but she also had that down-and-dirty street vibe and I loved that. She cried out and jerked below me, her pussy spasming once around me and I thought *This is it*, that I'd made her come too soon, but she settled and raised her hips to meet my forward thrust and I realized that she was super close, but not there yet.

Good. I wanted to make this last. I wanted to love her until she was languid and loose, and couldn't or wouldn't dream of getting out of this bed for anything for a while. I wanted to make her feel out-of-this-world, because I couldn't be sure she'd ever been fucked so good and –I– wanted to be the one to give her that experience.

She gasped, her eyes closed, her head back, her dark hair fanned across the lavender pillowcase in the amber glow of that pink rock light on her bedside table and it was easily one of the most beautiful things I'd ever laid eyes on. I rolled my hips forward at a slightly different angle and gritted my teeth as she tightened around me. *Close, she's so goddamned close.*

I wanted to see if she was one of the rare ones that could and would come from penetration alone. Most women needed a touch to their clit to go off, but a few didn't. I rode her body into her crisp cotton sheets, thrusting deep, making sure I was fully seated inside her before thrusting just that little bit more. It felt good, the slick slip-and-slide of her silky walls around my shaft, the way her body gripped me, the tease of her hot flesh around the head of my dick. Shit, I wasn't going to last long at this rate and I really needed her to come, I wanted her to come first.

She sucked in a sharp breath on a surprised and startled cry and I worked myself in short hard thrusts against her body. Her pussy grew wetter, tighter, expanding around my head and I felt my lips curve into a triumphant grin as time and space stopped in that perfect moment like the night held its breath completely waiting, *Will she, won't she,* but I had no doubt. I knew I'd unlocked the door and the light she held inside spilled out through it and blew me the fuck away.

She cried out sharply, her arms going around my shoulders as she pulled herself up, stiffening, holding me tightly to her like I was some sort of anchor, keeping her here, keeping her grounded, as her body quivered and shook beneath me. Her body milked me and I groaned, my balls tightening right along with her the higher-strung she got and when she let loose, I detached and flew with her, both of us spiraling out of control, to be held in the velvet palm of night's gentle grasp.

I saw stars, I came so hard, and when the white flashes and starbursts of light cleared from my vision, it was to Lys' smiling face, her bottom lip captured seductively between her teeth, her brown eyes sparkling with an unbridled joy I'd never seen on any woman's face before. I stared at her in wonder, smoothing some of her wild mane back from her cheek and I think I fell in love right then and there.

I mean, I couldn't exactly be sure on that because I wasn't one-hundred on what love was supposed to be, but I almost had to believe that's what it was because I had certainly never felt anything like it before.

"You okay?" she asked softly, her expression tempered with concern.

"I'm perfect," I said, my voice husky with untamed growth of whatever this emotion was.

To prove it, I lowered my mouth to hers, kissing her, my blood hot and racing through my veins, my heart throbbing so hard in my chest I could feel it in my back. No sooner had my cock started to go soft inside her than it was already growing hard again, and I took advantage of it, slowly rolling my hips. Her breath picked up almost as soon as she'd caught it again, her moan of surprise quickly turning to one of decadent ardor.

I knew the feeling. Recognized it myself. I couldn't, and I don't think I would, ever be able to get enough of Alyssa Glenn.

22

*A*lyssa...

We loved each other into a state of perfect exhaustion, until all that was left was laying sated in my bed, my head on his chest, the warm subtle glow of my salt lamp matching the ambience of the outside to what I was feeling on the inside. I didn't think that things could get any more perfect or serene.

He held me, his arm around my back, his free hand tracing up and down my arm in a soothing, light, vaguely-ticklish touch. I lay in an exhausted state of happiness and let my fingers wander over his body, tracing the ridges and planes of his musculature, as if memorizing him as completely as I could by feel as well as sight... because who knew if this would ever happen again? Golden struck me as a conqueror and I very well could be just the latest in the long line of conquests. I didn't know, and I was too afraid to ask. I just wanted to bask in the afterglow, enjoy the moment and rest, safe in his arms, before facing any more ugly realities.

Those realities would be there come the morning, but this? I didn't know where we were supposed to go from here. That made me sad, in a way, but I didn't let my distress show. Still, he somehow picked up on it because he asked me suddenly, "Whatcha thinkin', Chica?"

"Mm, I don't know if I should say," I told him, honestly.

"Why not?" He stiffened slightly beneath me, his body tensing as he went on high alert and I sighed, a little exasperated, because knowing Golden, he wouldn't let it go until he knew, until I talked.

"I was wondering what happens now?"

He chuckled and the rigidity of his posture eased again. His fingertips, which had stopped at my words, resumed their lazy travels over my skin.

"Now, we lay here and enjoy this, we sleep, maybe go at it again in the morning."

"I meant after that," I said softly, and his hand drifted up from my back to bury itself in my hair as he held me tenderly.

"Whatever you want to have happen, I'm game, baby."

I pushed up and looked at him, to see if I heard him right. His expression was stone cold serious, and I frowned slightly.

"I don't know what I want," I said softly. He reached up and grazed my cheek with his thumb lightly. My eyes slipped shut as I concentrated on the feel of it, such a tender gesture, full of promise, full of meaning, full of potential, but I just didn't know... which wasn't fair to him. It wasn't fair at all.

"Talk to me," he whispered.

"I don't know what I want, Golden. Everything feels so far up in the air, right now." I swallowed hard and opened my eyes. He was looking at me, a soft, charmed smile playing along his lips.

"You don't have to worry about hurting my feelings, babe. We do this at your pace."

"Yeah, but I don't even know what 'this' is," I said, and unhappy frustration crept into my voice.

"Shhh," he soothed. "You don't have to define it. It doesn't need a name or a label. You want your space, you tell me to get the fuck out and go to my room."

I choked on a shocked little laugh.

"I'm not grounding you," I said.

He chuckled, "Didn't work anyway, even when I was a kid, but I mean it. You want time to yourself or some space, just tell me you need your space. Otherwise, I figure I can stay with you at night, we can fool around if you want. If you don't, we don't."

"That sounds an awful lot like a relationship," I said suspiciously.

"It does, doesn't it?"

"You don't do relationships," I said dryly.

"Correction, I didn't want to do relationships."

"And now all of a sudden you do?" I asked, stunned, wondering how on earth plain old me could suddenly change his mind.

"I wouldn't mind giving it a go, if it's what you want."

"You would change for me, just like that?"

"Not for you," he said softly. "I only change for me. You just came along and made it seem like it might be a good idea."

I stared at him, mystified as to how that could possibly even be a thing. He reached up and pulled me down gently so that he could kiss me. I closed my eyes again and sank into it, bathing in the sensation, in his warmth, and clean, masculine scent. I lay back down, my ear over his heart and listened to the steady thrum of it. Strong, sure, and even, the way he'd been for me since I'd come clean about what'd happened to me before we'd met.

"I don't understand that at all," I said softly.

"I don't always get it myself, but what's honestly not to like about you, babe? You're beautiful, you're smart, you don't take any shit, you keep the place clean, you're a half-decent cook when it's your nights to cook, and my family likes you."

I scoffed. "Pretty sure Maria hates me."

He laughed. "Maria is bound to hate everyone I choose but she hasn't screamed at you or tried to knock your block off; that pretty much means she likes you. Plus, I was more going off what Manolo thinks of you, and my twin. If Angel didn't like you, that'd pretty much be it. Dude's like a dog that way. He likes you, you're good people; he doesn't, and, well, sorry, you gotta go."

I giggled and stuffed a hand against my mouth to keep from

outright laughing. Golden's chest shuddered beneath me with a laugh of his own.

"What's so funny?"

"I'm sorry, it's just… with as much as you sleep around, you compare your twin to being a dog?"

He laughed outright then and said, "Okay, okay, I'll give you that one." I swallowed hard and he tipped my chin so I would look up at him. His eyes were very serious when he asked, "What was that for?"

"You promise I'm not boring in that department?"

He smiled and it was genuine. "Baby, you're my new favorite thing to do."

I felt my face crack into an unexpected smile and he sat up, turning me onto my back, kissing and nuzzling the side of my neck until my breath caught, and fell ragged from my lips.

"Let me show you again," he whispered in my ear and drove every bit of self-consciousness out of my head with his lips, hands, and well-placed gentle nips of his teeth. One thing I had to give him was that he was definitely good at sex.

∽

THE NEXT MORNING I woke to Golden settling himself on the edge of my bed, a cup of coffee in his hands.

"Hi," I murmured sleepily. "What time is it?"

"Hey, and it's nine-thirty."

"Mm, guess I'm not going in today," I murmured.

He chuckled, "Good thing you told Avery it was a possibility?"

I swore and groped for my phone while he waited patiently for me to call in. I talked to Avery briefly; she laughingly brushed me off, saying I was the boss and I really didn't have to be there every Saturday. I laughed and admitted that was true. She had Sunday and Monday off, Jeremy was only Monday through Friday. I really only needed to be there on Monday and four other days of the week. Things had eased up enough that I really could contemplate making my sixth working day of the week an administrative day from home, crunching numbers, paying suppliers, dealing with all the things that didn't require my presence at the shop to do.

I hung up and set my phone aside and took the proffered coffee from my lover's hands. I smiled around the rim of the mug as I took that first, blissful, caffeinated sip. His hand, once free, naturally gravitated to the outside of my thigh, kneading through the blankets from my hip to just above my knee and back again. I sighed in contentment, and after enjoying it a minute, carefully shoved myself up into a sitting position so I could enjoy my coffee more and look him in the eye.

He raised an eyebrow and I smiled impishly once more from around the rim of my coffee mug when the sheet slipped and I didn't bother with trying to cover up. I mean, why? He'd seen it all only hours ago and hadn't given me a bit of cause to regret it. *At least not yet.* I shoved the pessimistic thought aside and simply tried to enjoy it.

"Any thoughts on what you would like to do today?" he asked smoothly.

"None, actually. I have a really bad habit lately of not making plans or thinking beyond the next few minutes."

He gave me an amused look, "Nothing wrong with that."

"I guess not," I said, but I still didn't know how things were going to work from now on, with us living together and these latest developments, I mean, *Yikes*.

"How long have you even been up?" I asked, changing the subject.

"An hour or so. Figured we could get a shower, maybe go grab something to eat. What do you say?"

"I say that sounds fantastic. I'm starving."

"You care for some company in the shower, or..?" he trailed off, raising an eyebrow and I realized he was seriously not taking anything for granted, that he really intended to ask or give me some sort of notice for anything intimate. I appreciated that more than words could say, so I didn't say anything. I leaned forward and put my lips to his and hoped he couldn't taste the slightly bitter edge of sadness to it.

It hurt my heart that he felt he had to go to such lengths, and it hurt my heart even more that he honestly wasn't wrong to feel that way. The sadness was chased back by a pang of anger at Ray for breaking me down so far and locking me into a prison of fear and mistrust. I vowed that I wouldn't stay. I could escape those confines, couldn't I?

"Hey, what's going on in there?" Golden asked softly, his fingertips caressing over my unkempt hair, his thumb sliding gently along my temple.

I closed my eyes and decided that the first order of business for this particular prison break was trust. I told him what I'd been thinking, and he smiled slightly and nodded.

"You're an incredible woman, you know that?" he asked.

"No."

"Well, you are. Incredibly self-aware, and that takes a hell of a lot of bravery."

I swallowed hard and again tried to change the subject by saying, "I think I would very much like that shower together," and his smile grew.

"Your place or mine?" he asked.

I smiled and said, "Mine."

"Okay, go get it started and I'll meet you in there."

I smiled back, "Sounds good."

I finished my coffee in three big gulps as he stood and went across the hall into his room wearing nothing but his boxer-briefs from the night before. I slid out of my bed and took the time to make it really quickly before grabbing down two of my towels from my closet and going into my bathroom. I started the water running and he slipped into the bathroom behind me with towels of his own, making an appreciative noise as I bent over to pull up on the little knob on top of the faucet to start the shower.

I laughed and straightened, whisking the curtain closed against the spray. His hands fell on my shoulders and he stepped up warm against me, placing a chaste kiss against one.

"You're a beautiful woman, Lys."

"Thank you," I said softly. "You're a devilishly handsome man."

"Devilishly, huh?" he asked, amusement in his voice.

"Mm-hm."

"That's cool, I'll take it."

He held back the curtain so that I could get in then joined me, pulling it shut. His hands went to my waist and he stepped into my space and I welcomed him with open arms. We kissed as the shower spray wet my hair, slicking it back from my face and plastering the strands to my back.

We didn't go much beyond kissing or heavy petting because I was sort of tender and sore from the night before, and he was totally cool with that, which was nice. When we finished up and went to get out, he handed me my towels first.

"Dress for the ride and not for the slide, Chica," he said with a wink, opening the bathroom door. I smiled and laughed a little as I finished running my brush through my wet hair.

"A ride sounds lovely," I called after him, despite how I ached where my legs met my body.

I took the time to put my hair into a French braid before going to my room. I dressed in jeans and a nice blouse, swishing hangers along the rod until I came to my leather coat. I shrugged into it and slung my purse across my chest just as he knocked on my doorframe.

"Ready to go?"

"Yeah," I agreed and he held out his hand. I took it and stepped across the carpet in the same pair of boots he'd selected for me the last time he'd taken me out on the bike.

We walked at a leisurely pace to the garage and chatted comfortably about how to spend the rest of the day, both agreeing that a lazy Sunday was in order. Even though it was Saturday by the calendar, it was Sunday for us. Although, I was sorely tempted to make mine a three-day-weekend. Even though he had work tomorrow night, I felt like I could use some time to decompress.

That wasn't to say I wasn't loving every minute of the time I got to spend with Golden, because I was; I just had some introverted tendencies. Likely, it was the byproduct of spending so much of my time alone in the last couple of years during my marriage to Ray. Maybe, I'd always been this way. I don't know, I couldn't ever remember a time where I didn't take time to get lost in a book or a show by myself, after spending time with other people. It was like I needed it to recharge. Likewise, if I spent too much time alone or on my own, I started to crave human contact and cuddles. I didn't know what it meant, I just knew it was how I was and that sometimes it was hard for me, because I always seemed to be lacking in either one or the other with little balance.

"You're thinking awfully hard over there," Golden remarked as we prepared to get on his motorcycle in the garage.

"It's like I can't stop worrying about everything, I don't know what my problem is," I told him truthfully.

"Sounds like anxiety, and I get it, believe me, I do. You've been catching a lot of curve balls out of life in a pretty short amount of time." He picked up my hand from where it was loose at my side and raised it to his lips, lightly kissing the pad of each fingertip while never taking those dark, obsidian eyes off of mine.

I felt my pussy clench and the vague soreness that accompanied it reminded me I needed a time out for a while. I wasn't used to so much sex after not having any for so long. I blushed furiously and he winked.

"Bet you'll feel more yourself after some food; it's been a while since dinner last night."

"You're probably right," I said. "Where are we going?"

"Saturday brunch at the 10-13. Reflash puts on one hell of a spread, anything your heart could desire." He got on his bike and patted the seat behind him as he started it up. I got on and held on and he patted my hands where they rested on his stomach, and took us up and out of the garage.

The ride to the 10-13 was far too short and I realized I really, really, loved riding with him. It was something I hoped we would be able to do more of and I was startled to realize I wanted that. I wanted to be able to make plans beyond the next few hours or days. I was just scared to. I'd done it once and it'd ended so badly…

"Woah-ho! Twice, bringing the same beautiful lady through our door. That's gotta be some kind of a record, son."

"Yeah, shut it, old man,"

I smiled at the older Hispanic man who was behind the bar, dropping a steel bin of pancakes into a frame over some sterno.

He dropped a stainless-steel domed lid on it and grinning said, "Get yourself some plates and get it while it's hot. Go on up into the banquet room, we're a full house this morning."

"You got it, VP."

"Come see you in a minute," he called back, going into the kitchen. I looked around and he was right. It was pretty full in here, the bar set up like a buffet. Golden fell into line and handed me a plate and silverware.

I smiled at him and nodded and helped myself to pancakes, breakfast sausage, and fresh fruit. Golden fixed himself a plate of eggs, sausage, and bacon with a couple of English muffins and jam. He waited for me while I got a little stainless-steel mini-pitcher of maple syrup and then wound his way through the people waiting to get their food towards the fishbowl they'd had their meeting in. He held the door for me and I slipped through and when it shut behind us, it was blessedly quieter.

"Have a seat anywhere, Chica."

I slid into one of the many vacant seats along the smooth, glossy table and he joined me, taking a seat beside mine. The food was really good, the companionship quiet and comfortable. I sighed in contented satisfaction and Golden looked at me, a happy expression of chill contentment mirrored in his eyes. We broke into a fit of nonsensical giggles.

"Food good?" he asked just as the door scraped open. We both looked up and the cook came through, smiling.

"I heard that, and I'd really like to know, little lady."

"Oh, it's fantastic," I said, finishing a bite of pancake.

"All right! That's what I like to hear!" He pulled out a chair at the end of the table and sat down with a gusty sigh.

"Long morning?" I asked, smiling, trying to be polite.

"Yeah, always is around here. Name's Reflash." He held out a hand and I smiled and took it, shaking warmly.

"Alyssa, but everyone calls me Lys."

"Nice to meet you, Lys. You know you got the lot of us curious."

"I do?"

Golden interjected, "Come on, man, give her a break," he said, rolling his eyes. He turned to me and said, "Reflash is the Indigo Knights' vice president. He owns half this place with our president, Skids."

"Oh, that must be nice," I said, and cringed inwardly at how lame it must have sounded.

"Yeah, we've been best friends for thirty years or more."

"Oh, wow."

"They might as well be married to each other," Golden cracked.

"Well, if we are, it's one of them poly situations, because both of us is married to this place, first."

I laughed. "Sort of the nature of owning your own business," I agreed.

"You got your own?" he asked.

I nodded, "I own a florist shop. A little place, only me and two employees."

"Oh, yeah? Where at?"

"Around six blocks from our place," Golden said and I was surprised. He'd said 'our' place, not 'his' place, and the phrasing suffused me with warmth at the same time my nerves fizzed to life.

Was it too soon? Should I even be going there? I mean, maybe he didn't mean it that way. Technically I live there, so it is 'ours' in that I pay rent, too. Yeah, that's all he meant. You're reading far too much into this, girl. Slow down.

Slow down.

Easier said than done.

23

*G*olden...
 She'd suddenly become quieter, more subdued after the short chat with Reflash and I could almost see the wheels turning in her head. Not only that, I was pretty sure I detected some smoke. I knew she had to be going through a lot inside. The girl was pro at second- and third-guessing herself, and after what her douchebag ex pulled, I didn't think she would ever trust anyone completely again. I had to be patient, but patience wasn't my strong suit. That was my twin's department.

 I didn't say anything. Not at the restaurant, not on the ride home, not on the walk from the garage to the apartment, and not even when we closed the door on the outside world again. I simply stood in my living room with Lys's hand in mine and searched her face, waiting her out. She didn't look like she knew what to do with herself, and honestly, that made two of us. She looked tired and I suggested, "You should go put something comfortable on, maybe take a nap."

 She nodded and said, "I feel tired, not bad, just tired, and pajamas sound fabulous. I feel like I ate way too much."

 I laughed a little and said, "Easy to do, when it comes to food prepared by Reflash's kitchen. What do you say? Your place or mine?"

"How about ours?" she suggested softly.

Ah. I think I figured out what was bothering her. I touched the side of her face gently and smiled. "As in, maybe cuddle on the couch, and find something on TV?"

She smiled broadly. "You're a mind reader."

"Shh, don't tell anyone." I winked and she laughed and it was a good sound.

"Go on, go get changed. I will, too."

"Okay," she said softly, almost shyly and she moved for her room. I figured it was going to be this way. Three steps forward, two steps back. Still, even knowing, it wasn't any less frustrating. I didn't know how to broach the topic, so for now, I let it lie, but questioned myself over whether it was the right thing to do. I mean, not communicating about these things could lead to some serious problems, but we were having such a nice weekend together, I didn't want to bring anything up that could or would fuck it up.

It was a tough call, either way was going to lead to some form of discomfort. I just wanted to pick the way that put the burden more on me and less on her. She'd carried enough already. I texted Angel the problem and set my phone on my dresser so I could change. It buzzed as I pulled a worn, comfortable tee over my head.

Angel: Tough call bro. Leave it for now and enjoy the rest of the weekend but def talk to her about it soon. She's probably just working her issues with her ex. Probably doesn't have anything to do with you specifically. Just take it slow.

I rolled my eyes. I mean, *did he even know me?*

Me: Thx bro.

Angel: NP – good luck.

I set my phone back on the dresser and went out into the living room. Lys was already curled up on the couch in one of the man-shirts she liked to wear to bed. God, that shit was sexy as fuck, but it would only be sexier if it were my fucking shirt. *One of my uniform shirts. Yeah.*

"Hey," she said softly.

"Hey." I dropped onto one end of the couch and turned, sliding down so my head rested on the overstuffed leather arm. I reached out to her, and open and closed my hands in the classic sign for 'Gimme', and she giggled and came over. I settled one leg along the back of the couch as she turned on her side and carefully wedged herself between my legs. I appreciated the care with which she took not to crush the family jewels as she settled against my chest, her ear over my heart.

I pulled the plaid throw down off the back of the couch and put it over her, and picked up the remote from the coffee table. Her eyes were already closed and a soft smile played on her sexy lips as she listened to the cadence of my heart. I swear, she probably heard it cease as I raised my chin and looked over at the TV, but if she did, she didn't say anything. Still, the image of her laying on me like that was so sweet and so beautiful to me, it caused me this flash of real, visceral, physical pain right in the center of my chest. It was something the likes I had never experienced before.

I put my arms around her, holding her loosely, and I don't think she lasted three minutes and she was out. I smiled to myself, closed my eyes, and rather than actually try to find something to put on the TV, I just let whatever it was that was on, go. I didn't care anyway. I was more focused on this, on how I wanted this to be a regular thing, a lazy Sunday spent cuddled with Lys, napping on the couch.

∞

I WAS WOKEN up sharply by pounding on the front door. Lys sat bolt upright and I pushed up into a sitting position. She and I exchanged a look and I didn't like how she'd gone pale on me. Then again, I was thinking the same thing. The only people who knocked like that were angry exes or the cops.

I got up and went to the door, checking through the peephole and sure enough, there was a uniformed patrolman on my doorstep. I frowned and waved Lys down who stood by the couch, clutching the throw in her hands fearfully. She visibly relaxed and I opened the door.

"What's up, man?" I asked the uni on the other side.

"Looking for Rodrigo Martinez?"

"Yeah, that's me."

"Sorry to bother you, Officer Martinez." He stepped aside and Manolo beamed up at me from behind him.

"See, I told you my uncle was a cop."

I scowled and demanded, "What's he done?"

"Nothing, the boy was with his father, who we just picked up on an outstanding warrant."

"Oh, yeah? Didn't know he was out of jail."

"Yeah, well, he's back in now. We tried to reach the boy's mother but she didn't answer her phone, so as a professional courtesy, we decided to give you a go before phoning it in to social services."

"I told you," Manolo said, rolling his eyes, "Mom's at work and they don't let her have her phone."

I reached out and took Manolo by the shoulder, and said, "Get in here, learn some respect for the badge, little man." I shook my head and sighed. "He's right though, you tried calling me?"

"Yeah, you didn't pick up, either."

"Yeah, sorry about that, I was napping on the couch, phone's in the bedroom. What was the warrant for?" I asked.

"Burglary."

I shook my head. "Right, got it. Thanks for going the extra mile, man." I stuck out my hand. He shook it.

"Well, when your name came up we had to try. You're a legend over at the – "

I held up my hand and stopped him, "I just did what any other cop in my situation would have done, bro. Nothing more, nothing less, that doesn't make me any kind of special."

"We'll have to agree to disagree there, sir."

"Hey, I'm a beat cop, just like you. It's Rod, or Martinez, not 'sir', okay?"

"Okay, sure," he said, surprised, his eyebrows going up under his patrol cap.

"What's your name? I didn't catch it," I said gently.

"Roark," he answered.

I nodded. "Thank you for bringing my nephew over, Roark. I sure do appreciate it."

"Anytime, man. Anytime."

I nodded and shook his hand again; he looked past me to Lys and gave a nod. "Ma'am."

She smiled and said, "Thank you, Officer."

Manolo was nowhere to be seen so I had to guess he was in my room. I closed the door and sighed, dropping my head. Lys looked sympathetic and I gave a helpless little shrug. Her smile and the understanding that radiated from her face made me want to march over to her and kiss her, but I had to go be an adult and get the full meal deal out of Manolo.

Dammit.

"If you need anything, I'll be in my room," she said gently and laying the throw over the arm of the couch, she drifted down the hall and disappeared into her doorway. I looked at the time and realized we'd gotten a solid two-and-a-half-hour nap in. I shrugged off the last of my tiredness and went to deal with my nephew and his latest family drama.

I found him sitting cross-legged on my bed, a comic book open on his lap. Where the hell he'd got that from, I had no idea.

"Hey, Hombrecito, what happened, eh?" I asked.

"I'm not little," he complained, and rolled his eyes.

"I'm not your enemy, little homie, so you get that disrespect right outta your mouth when it comes to me. Now, what the hell's going on?"

"Papá got arrested. They said he stole some stuff. One minute we were going down to the bodega for an ice cream and then there were cops like everywhere, man. They slammed him against a car and everybody was screaming and yelling. It was stupid."

"Hombrecito..." I let out a frustrated noise and hung my head. I didn't know how to do this, tell a kid his dad was a piece of shit. Ultimately, I decided it wasn't my place. That yeah, his dad was a deadbeat douchebag, but he was still Manolo's father and nothing was going to change that. I just wished Maria would wise up and stop trying to save the dude and would just focus on saving herself and her son instead, because this shit was killing Manolo.

"I told you, I'm not little," he said and sniffed, barely holding back tears. I pulled him into a hug and held him tight.

"Scared you, huh?" I asked.

"Yeah," he said, his voice warbling and warped with his crying.

"It's okay, man. It's okay," I lied, because none of it was really okay. I mean, he was eight, getting jerked this way and that, dad in and out of jail, mom working all the time… it wasn't good for him. Kids needed structure and stability. Not to watch their pops get put in cuffs and hauled to jail, Mom not reachable by phone, getting dropped off by uni's at random on my doorstep.

Like I'm a stellar parental figure…

I caught a glimpse of movement out of the corner of my eye as Lys leaned a shoulder against the doorframe leading into my room. She'd put on jeans under her blue nightshirt and the effect was pretty hot, with her brown hair falling in waves around her face. She looked both empathetic and concerned as I comforted my nephew, and I jerked a chin over my head. She nodded and followed my silent direction, disappearing from the doorway and drifting silently on bare feet up the hall toward the living room.

Manolo calmed down after a minute and I asked him, "You good, Hombrecito?"

"Yeah," he said sullenly, with a hiccup.

We had a long talk, he and I, about a lot of things. About respecting authority, for one. About working hard and earning an honest living. About selfishness versus being a good man and the difference between being a good man and a hero. The talk wound its way around curves and bends, and was good, like a long solo ride on old roads lined with nothing but green.

"Feel better?"

"Yeah," he said with a nod.

"Come on, let's feed you."

"'Kay."

We got up and went out the bedroom door. Lys stood by the dining room table; she looked at us imperiously and said, "Gentlemen, choose your weapons." She did this Vanna White handwave over the table. There was something under a dishcloth and an assortment of spoons laying on it. I raised an eyebrow and looked at Manolo, who looked back up at me and shrugged.

"A pain like this deserves the straight-from-the-carton treatment." She said it to Manolo, but she was looking straight at me as she whisked aside the dishcloth. I had been covering three pints of ice cream. I tried like a son of a bitch not to laugh, and failed miserably as she winked at Manolo.

"Ice cream, for dinner?"

"After the day you've had, Hombrecito, why the f– not?" I stopped myself from cussing by the skin of my teeth, at Lys' warning look.

"Awesome!" he cried and chose his weapon. I went for a big spoon and let him have his pick from the different flavors on the table. I let Lys choose next, and was perfectly happy with the butter pecan left behind. I mouthed 'Thank you' at her over Manolo's head, and when she was sure he wasn't looking, she pursed her lips in a silent long-distance kiss.

"Movie?" she asked out loud.

"*Desperado*?" Manolo asked hopefully.

"What about *Once Upon A Time in Mexico*?" she asked.

"What's that?" he demanded.

"Oh, my god. Did your uncle never show you the sequel to *Desperado*?"

"There's no sequel!" Manolo scoffed and I laughed, shoving a spoonful of ice cream into my face.

"Actually, bud, there is. I just didn't like it."

"Wow. All that talk of respect and you been holding out on me?" My sister's kid let out a gusty sigh and finished with, "Man."

Lys lost it, and I shook my head. Yeah, he was feeling better. Right back to being his plucky self.

"all right, all right, we'll watch it, and you can see how awful it is for yourself."

We were halfway through our ice cream when the pounding started on my front door. I rolled my eyes and tossed my spoon in my carton, setting it aside on my coffee table. Before I could even get to the front door, my sister had keyed open the lock and was shouting at me.

"Where is he, please tell me he's with you!"

"Calm down, he's right here," I growled at her.

"You think this is my fault?" she asked, her back going straight, and I felt one of her epic tirades coming on. She started railing at me in Spanish while Manolo and Lys looked on, wide-eyed, from the couch.

"Manolo!" my sister snarled, and then in Spanish told him roughly to get his shit and they were leaving. My nephew snapped to it, and I could see the heartbreak on Lys's face.

She spoke up calmly, but saying anything at all with an angry Latina in the room only drew her fire.

"Maria, no one thinks any of this is your fault –" Lys tried to say but my sister rounded on her, and what she said set me off.

"Shut up, puta!"

"Hey!" I bellowed, and Lys flinched and shrank back. I cursed my knee-jerk reaction, but she had to know she wasn't the one I was pissed at. I was staring my sister down and keeping a lid on it, barely.

"You're in my house, Maria, and when you're in my house you'll treat the people in it with respect. I just got done having this conversation with Manolo and don't think I won't school you the same, little sister. So, do you want to try again?" I demanded. She stood there staring at me wide-eyed, her chest heaving, and Manolo slunk out from behind me and the direction of the hall, dragging his feet and shrugging into his coat.

Maria grabbed his arm and towed him toward the front door. Manolo cried out and I barked, "Maria!" She slowed and I told her, "You can be pissed at me, you can be pissed at yourself, but by god – you will not take it out on that boy."

"Or what?" she demanded. "I am his mother!"

"Then act like it!" I snapped.

She scoffed at me, towed her son out the door and slammed it behind her. I went for my phone while Lys just stood there, her hands pressed to her chest over her likely-thudding heart, her eyes wide and brimming with tears.

"You okay?" I asked, and she nodded mutely, a bit too rapidly.

"I'm sorry you had to see that," I said, raising my phone to my ear.

"Who are you calling?" she asked. But it took her a couple of tries to get the words out.

"My brother," I answered. "He's the peacemaker."

She nodded and mechanically started cleaning up.

"Leave it," I said. "It's okay."

She shook her head, but I was distracted by Angel picking up on the other end of the line.

"Golden, what's up?"

I sighed and filled him in.

24

*A*lyssa...

Golden had had to leave quickly, but before he went he'd told me, "Leave your bedroom door open if you want me to join you; if you need your space, close it. I'll understand either way, Chica." I'd nodded and even though I was still rattled from the screaming and yelling, I'd asked him before he could walk out the door, "Aren't you going to kiss me?"

The gentle side of his soul had come out and he'd smiled at me so sweetly. His hands had been gentle where they'd smoothed along my ribs in a light caress through my nightshirt and his lips on mine had been warm and soft in the barest of kisses. I'd gone from overwhelmed to safe within a matter of seconds, and it had been such a relief.

Still, as soon as he was gone, the dread and anxiety had crept back in even though I knew with my heart, and the front of my head, that I had nothing at all to fear or worry about when it came to Golden. I knew it, but I couldn't seem to shut my lizard brain off, I couldn't seem to get the fear to stop. I felt like I was caught in a hamster wheel, running, running, running, and like I'd stumbled or fallen, and was sucked into the vortex of that spinning wheel, helpless, going over, and over, and over again.

It was an ugly feeling, and I needed to work through it, to process it, and so I cleaned up our ice cream mess, putting the pints back in the freezer, and the spoons in the dishwasher, and I shut off the lights in the living room. I left the bedside lamp in Golden's room on for him, and a note for him on his pillow, begging him not to take it personally, but I needed to sleep by myself tonight.

I then went to bed, and I tossed and turned for what felt like forever, until I finally managed to fall into an uneasy sleep.

I didn't stay asleep. I dreamt, and I don't know what it was, but it was bad, because I woke, screaming, Golden kneeling by my bedside and holding my arms firmly, but as gently as he could. I stopped, my face slick with hot tears and stared at him, wide-eyed and frightened, unsure what had happened.

His voice was low and intense, yet softly sweet and soothing to the ear.

"Hey, hey, hey; it's okay, Lys. It's all right. Breathe, baby. Just breathe."

I was taking in great and gasping breaths and still didn't feel as if I was getting any air into my lungs. He caught my eyes with his and took exaggerated breaths, in slowly, out slowly, bidding me to mimic him. I did, and things slowed and calmed and pretty soon, I was back in control.

"I'm sorry," I stammered, and he shook his head. "No, really I am, I don't know what's wrong with me, that's never happened before, I'm so sorry, I –"

"Lys, shh; stop, just stop. Its fine, you're fine, just breathe for me, and try to relax."

I swallowed hard and felt my eyes well, his image blurring for a moment, before more hot moisture slipped down my cheeks in scalding lines. He brushed a thumb uselessly through the tears on my face and wiped it on his jeans. He looked around and grabbed some Kleenex from the box on the bedside table and pressed them into my shaking hands.

"I'm sorry," I repeated. "I feel crazy, I don't know what's wrong with me."

"You're having a panic attack, but it's going to be okay, I promise. I've seen this before, ain't my first rodeo," he said, laughing a little bit. I smiled through the pain and he nodded.

"That's my girl, come on. Over, move over," he stood and made a shooing motion and I scooted over in the bed. He didn't bother taking off his pants, or his socks, but he didn't have a shirt on at least, as he slipped between the covers and cuddled me into his side.

I laid my head on his shoulder and sniffed, taking some final swipes at my eyes and face with the soggy Kleenexes.

"Think you might have some post-traumatic stress disorder going on, babe," he said after a few quiet moments, when my heart had returned to a thrum somewhat resembling normal.

"How do I fix it?" I asked quietly.

"Time, meds, knowing your triggers and avoiding them, but there's no real fixing it, Chica. It's a part of you, now." He punctuated that last by pressing a kiss against my forehead and I didn't know what it was about it, but it was the most comforting thing, and I just melted from it.

He held me tight and showered me with chaste little kisses until I squirmed and giggled, and once he had me laughing, he kissed me for real and the laughter turned to moaning and the moaning to heavy breathing, but it never went further than that. He stopped us, despite how hot and hard he pressed against the front of his jeans, and he murmured next to my ear, "Try to sleep, Babe. I'm not going anywhere."

I nodded, and closed my eyes, thinking sleep would be an impossible thing, but Golden's presence fought my demons and I fell asleep once more and there was nothing fitful about it this time, but only by virtue of my exhaustion.

∽

I slogged through work the next day. When I'd woken up that morning to my alarm, it'd been to an empty bed. I'd been disappointed, but that disappointment quickly evaporated when I found the note on my bedside table.

Respecting your space, like you asked. I get it. I'm right across the hall. Kiss me before you go.

-G.

I'd gotten ready for work, showered and dressed, but lost my nerve when it came to actually waking him up to kiss him good-bye. It seemed silly waking him up, disturbing him, just for that. I'd dropped my hand from where it had been poised to knock on his door, but I only made it as far as the leading edge of the dining table when his door opened.

I turned around and looked over my shoulder. He leaned against the doorjamb, hair tousled, in just his boxer-briefs, looking warm and inviting. He smiled, a sexy little smirk, and asked me the same thing I'd asked him the night before: "Aren't you going to kiss me good-bye?"

I'd practically run to him and had kissed him with everything I'd had in me. His arms had gone around my body and hauled it up against his much stronger, much firmer one, and I'd melted all over again. When he'd let me go, I'd been dizzy, almost drunk, on his kiss, but he'd wisely sent me on my way, but not without a light smack on my ass.

That kiss and the gentle, patient, strength he'd shown me the night before, when I'd been nearly at my absolute worst, carried me through the day. At every turn when I'd looked at the clock and realized it'd only been moments since I'd looked the last time, I'd draw from the pleasant memories of the weekend and let it carry me through.

I was on my own in the shop today, and it was slow, so I'd worked on fresh arrangements for the wedding coming that Tuesday, wondering to myself *Who got married on a Tuesday?*

At long last, it was quitting time, and all I wanted to do was go home and go to bed. I was starving, and I probably should eat something, but I was also too damn tired to care. I locked up the shop and, my hands buried deep in my jacket pockets against the cooler evening air, set off towards home. I made the turn at the proper corner, and blue and red lights lit up behind me and a siren chirped. I jumped and damn near came out of my skin at the unexpected noise and sound, to masculine laughter.

"You all right?" a familiar voice called. I turned and looked.

"You scared me half to death!"

Golden, who was in the passenger seat and leaning out the window said, "We paced you from the shop, Chica. Didn't know how else to get your attention. I called your name a few times."

I scrubbed my face with my hands and groaned, "Oh, God! I'm sorry. I'm just so tired."

"Come on." He jumped out of the car and opened the back door, waving me in. "We'll give you a lift home."

"You can do that?" I asked, frowning.

"Call it in, Pruitt," Golden said, and his partner, Pruitt, picked up the radio and said something about a meal break into it.

"Now, come on, we have a half an hour and need to eat, too." He waved the door back and forth on its hinges and I slid into the back seat of the patrol car, snorting a giggle when he put his hand on the top of my head to guide me in.

"Shit, sorry," he muttered and my smile grew.

"Habits are habits," I said, and he flashed me a smile before shutting the door. I was honestly just grateful not to have to walk the last four blocks.

The seat was hard and plastic, warm from the engine somehow, and I was surprised to find there were strange slots in the back that made getting comfortable leaning back impossible. I blinked stupidly when it dawned on me that the grooves in the back of the hard seat were meant to accommodate someone with their arms cuffed behind their back.

Pruitt pulled up smoothly against the curb in front of our apartment building in the loading zone and put it into 'Park.'

I realized there weren't any handles to open the car door back here, *Because, of course, there aren't*, but Golden didn't waste any time jumping out of the car and opening the door for me.

"Thanks," I murmured and he smiled at me.

"No problem, Chica."

"Hey, grab the food," Pruitt called, and Golden gave a little start.

"Oh, right." He ducked back in the passenger-side door and came up with a plastic grocery bag tied at the top, holding three Styrofoam clamshells. I smiled and he winked at me. I led the way into our building, the guys following me. I stopped and got the mail and we went upstairs. As soon as we were in the apartment, Pruitt went to the fridge and pulled out three sodas.

Golden silently pulled out a chair for me at the dining table and I sank into it grateful for food I didn't have to cook myself, and that I wouldn't be crashing hungry. He set one of the clamshells in front of me and I opened it to a heavenly French dip sandwich, a side of au jus in a Styrofoam bowl with a plastic lid on it.

"You guys really know how to treat a lady," I said dryly and Pruitt smiled, dropping into a seat of his own across from me. Golden took a seat at the head of the table between us and I smiled as I took a bite. He opened up the can of Coke in front of me for me and I smiled a little more.

I had once complained how I was always afraid of breaking a nail when I opened a can of soda and he'd been doing it for me ever since. Now any time I went for a can of anything anymore, if he were home, I would just take it to him and he would open it and hand it back. I tried to remember when we'd started doing that, but I couldn't. It just felt like something that always was.

We ate in comfortable silence, and I appreciated the fact that Golden and his partner didn't feel the need to drag me into a conversation to fill it, that they just let me be and didn't make me try to think, because I was seriously all out of brain left to brain with. Thinking, beyond dragging myself out of my clothes and into bed, just wasn't going to happen.

"Mm, we gotta get back on the clock," Pruitt muttered and Golden sighed, sitting back from his demolished sandwich and fries.

"Go, go, go," I said, waving them off. "I'll clean this up. It's the least I can do after the rescue you provided me. I'm dead on my feet."

"Thanks," Pruitt said. "I'm gonna use the can and we can get out of here."

"First door on the right," Golden told him. He ducked into my bathroom, turned on the light, and shut the door. I turned back to Golden, who was looking me over, a soft look in his eyes, genuine affection radiating from them.

"Do me a favor, if you're up to it?" he asked quietly, so as not to be overheard by his partner.

"Sure," I murmured.

"Go find one of my shirts, and let me find you in my bed when I get home, one of these nights."

I smiled gently and nodded. "I think I can do that," I whispered.

He smiled and leaned in, pressing his lips to mine gently in a gentle kiss. He whispered against them, "Bonus points if it's one of my uniform shirts."

I laughed and he leaned back with a smug look on his face as Pruitt came out of the bathroom.

"What's so funny?" Pruitt demanded.

"Inside joke," Golden said immediately and winked at me. I rose and quickly began to clear the table, so I could keep my back to Pruitt to hide my blush.

"Right," Pruitt said like he didn't believe him. I bit my bottom lip and threw the Styrofoam in the trash before putting my leftovers in the fridge.

"See you when I get home, Chica."

"Nice to see you again, Lys."

"Be careful out there, boys," I said, and smiled at them both affectionately.

"Always," Pruitt said, tipping his patrol cap at me. As soon as Pruitt turned his back, Golden pursed his lips in a kiss and winked at me. I bit my lips together, the feel of his last real kiss still lingering on my lips.

As soon as the door shut behind them, I felt my shoulders sag and the last of my mustered energy fled. I leaned heavily against the nearest countertop and heaved a tired sigh, trying to rally just enough to finish the meager cleanup left before I could drag myself off to bed.

As I drifted down the hallway just a few moments later, I paused outside our bedroom doors. I took a deep breath, and twisted the doorknob to Golden's room and let myself in.

I felt strange standing in his space. I'd never come in here before, both as a sign of respect for his boundaries, and because I didn't feel as if I belonged here at all, especially with the parade of women that had been through.

I swallowed hard, knowing there was something different when it came to me, that he had broken almost all of his rules when it came to us and that he was serious about me where he hadn't been serious about any of the other women he'd brought here but still… I may have managed to let myself into his closet, I may have found one of his uniform shirts, but I didn't think I was ready to spend any more time than that in here. Not yet. I fled to my room, shutting his bedroom door tightly behind me.

Standing just inside the threshold to my own space, I felt like a coward. I felt marginally better when I raised the shirt in my hands to my nose and breathed deeply. It smelled like him, subtly of clean laundry and his cologne, the scents I had found so comforting the night before, after my bad dream, which I couldn't for the life of me remember. Just that there had been yelling and arguing and pain.

I stripped swiftly and slipped into the long-sleeved uniform shirt. I rolled the sleeves to my elbows and buttoned it from about the third button all the way to the bottom. It didn't fit like one of my nightshirts. It was loose on me, but wasn't nearly long enough. I felt naked and vulnerable from the waist down, so I went to my panty drawer and selected a pair of simple black cotton bikini-cut briefs and slipped them on.

I lit my salt lamp by the bed by thumbing the little dial on the cord's switch and turned out the overhead light. The light from the little lamp was soothing, and not bright enough to keep me awake, but bright enough to see by. I left my bedroom door wide in invitation like we had discussed and climbed into bed and I swear I was asleep before my head hit the pillow.

25

olden...

I leaned against her open doorway, still in my uniform, and watched her sleep. She was out, but so beautiful, so serene, and she was wearing my shirt. She wasn't in my bed, but the invitation was clear. I couldn't drag my eyes off of her to get a shower and a change of clothes for myself. She was just too much and I couldn't stop staring.

Fuck me.

I had it bad for her and the sharp, sweet ache in the center of my chest as my heart swelled looking at her was echoed by the deep throbbing of my cock in my pants. My eyes swept over her sleeping face, her long dark hair fanned out over the pillow behind her, following the curve of the one lock of it where it lay against the collar of my shirt, down to where the neckline plunged, giving a tantalizing glimpse of her cleavage.

I don't know how I managed, but I finally pulled myself away. I went across the hall and got myself into a hot shower where I gripped my dick in one hand and stroked it, the vision of her lying there, waiting for me in my shirt, halfway to what I asked, burned into my brain. I grunted, biting my bottom lip and bowing my head as my cock surged, spurting my load, hot and sticky, over my fingers.

Somehow, I didn't think jerking off was going to be enough tonight. I wanted her, needed her like I'd never needed anyone before. I closed my eyes and let the shower water beat on my head, but there was no getting Lys out of it. I didn't want to wake her, but I didn't know if I would be able to sleep next to her looking like that and not take her. I'd give anything to see her stretched out beneath me again, or better yet, above me.

I let out a breath and finished washing up, making sure to shave off the rough five-o'-clock shadow that'd come in on me. I wiped off my face and checked for missed spots in the mirror and, satisfied, dried off completely. I whipped a quick comb through my hair and went out to my bedroom, looking through my open doorway, leaning back to look through hers. Just a short, less than three-foot width of hall between my door and hers, yet it might as well be worlds apart. Patience wasn't my strongest suit, but I managed to hold onto it where she was concerned.

I pulled on a pair of boxer-briefs and padded barefoot across the floor and into her room. I closed the door gently, silently as I could, and turned to drink in her beauty from the soft amber glow of her pink rock light. She hadn't moved an inch. She was sleeping so peacefully, like an angel, and it took me three tries to get my feet to work, to move me around the foot of the bed and up the other side, between it and the dresser.

I watched her back rise and fall as she lay curled on her side, closing my eyes and listening to her soft breathing, like music from another room, gentle and indistinct, but still beautiful in its faint cadence. I lifted the blankets and got between her crisp, lavender sheets, carefully scooting across the bed closer to her, settling behind her, a big spoon to her little. When I draped an arm over her, she sucked in a breath, her voice tremulous as she asked, "Golden?"

"Yeah, it's me, Chica."

"What time is it?"

"A little after twelve-thirty."

"Mm. I missed you." She cuddled back into me and I held her close, sticking my nose into her hair behind her ear and breathing her in. She hummed in pleasure and I placed a light kiss there.

"I missed you, too," I confessed.

She let out a little crooning hum of satisfaction and I smiled, kissing the side of her neck. She cringed slightly and giggled softly, and to take the tickle out of my kiss, I nipped her lightly. Her giggle turned into a sultry gasp of pleasure and if I hadn't been hard already, it would have brought me around instantly.

"God, you're so fucking beautiful," I growled. "So sexy and tempting."

She gave another sultry little laugh and asked me, "You know the best way to get rid of temptation, don't you?"

"Hmm." I ran my nose along the side of her neck and kissed the pulse in the side of her neck, gathering her hair lightly with my fingers and sweeping it away from her skin, taking the fragrant silky final barrier from between my lips and her skin. She held her breath and I flicked out my tongue, tasting her pulse. She gasped and it turned to a throaty little moan.

"What's the best way to get rid of it, Chica?"

"What?" she asked, her voice far away.

"Temptation, what's the best way to get rid of it?"

Her arm came up, her hand cradling the back of my head as she twisted and arched her back provocatively.

She met my eyes over her shoulder and whispered: "Give in to it."

Fuck. It was all the permission I needed. I covered her mouth with mine and damn near devoured her.

I slipped a hand into the open neckline of my shirt and captured her breast, kneading it as she rocked her hips, grinding her gorgeous ass against my cock unconsciously, even as her hand pressed to the back of my head, holding my mouth to hers. Her body was taut, tighter than a bowstring, quivering, eager, and I wanted her so bad.

She tore her mouth from mine and begged in a raspy voice, rough with need and soft with desire, "Make love to me."

I slid the arm pinned between me and the mattress under her

neck, capturing her across her chest above her breasts and pulling her back, tight against my chest. She reached back and shoved down at the waistband of my underwear and I let her free my cock while I reached down the front of her panties and slid a finger between her legs.

Aw, fuck, she was wet. Wet and hot and slick, just waiting for me to be inside her. I swallowed my unbridled passion and forced myself to slow down and not get carried away, not too far, not too fast. Not yet. I didn't want to scare her. I never wanted the prospect of more tomorrows to end. I never wanted to hurt her or make her cry. I never wanted any look, but the one of desire and euphoria she wore now, cast in my direction during an intimate moment like this.

I shoved her panties down out of the way in front and had to bring my hand around back and pull them down so I could gain access. They didn't need to go far. This was perfect. She was perfect, and the anticipation of pressing myself at her opening, that first moment of penetration had me damn near panting like a dog.

She whimpered and writhed so beautifully, like a vine twining along me, using me as a trellis. I reached between us and forced my cock down, she pressed back against me and I slipped into her hot waiting pussy like it was meant to be, despite the unconventional angle, and it felt like coming home more than I'd ever felt walking through my apartment door.

Her mouth dropped open and she made this sound, like her breath had been stolen, yet she couldn't help but cry out. A light, gasping little cry that I found beyond sexy as I pumped in and out of her body, the heat between us and my pulse rising in unison. I drove into her balls-deep and she rode me, her pelvis shifting back and forth in a wanton, writhing dance that drove me absolutely wild.

Everything about Lys was organic. The way she moved, the way she breathed, the sounds she made, everything. It was beautiful to behold and something I think my soul craved. Her natural beauty in everything she did, everything she said, how she treated the people around her... I was drawn to it, watered by it, nourished. She was life and light, food for my soul and I hadn't realized how starved I was for something like that until I'd opened myself up to her. Best decision I'd ever made.

"Golden!" She cried my name like it was some sort of prayer and I closed my eyes, concentrating on the feel of her in my arms, around my cock, against my lips. I breathed her in as my balls tightened and I was on the brink, as close as she was, hanging on by a tenuous thread.

Everything felt so good, so amazing, but as awesome as it was, it was like we were both caught on the brink and just suspended there. Neither one of us reaching climax, the satisfaction it would bring, maddeningly just out of reach. While I was content to just live there, Lys was going wild, until she finally couldn't stand it anymore. She dragged herself away from me, my cock slipping out of her and she stood by the bed, ditching her panties altogether.

She got back onto the bed, walking on her knees across the mattress, her hands on my chest, pressing me back, as if the one thing I had managed to obliterate, along with the last vestiges of her sanity, was any inhibitions she might have held. She threw a leg over me, settling her pussy over the top of my cock where it lay against my stomach. She ground against me, teasing, my hands going to her hips, working her back and forth, up and down, delicious friction between her slick folds and my hard shaft, kicking the passion between us into high gear.

She was beautiful, wicked, a siren, with the way her breath and voice fell from her lips in the seductive song of sex. All natural beauty, her face free of makeup, her hair tumbling around her shoulders as she threw her head back her eyes closed, feeling as much as listening, she drove me to the brink all over again and I wasn't even inside her, this time.

"God, baby. You drive me fucking crazy," I growled and she bit her bottom lip, dropping her chin, staring at me with mischief in her eyes, and I loved that she would let go like this with me. She reached between us, raising my cock off my stomach and slipping down over it, sheathing it tight and perfect in her wet little cunt, and I swear to fucking god it was like she was made for me.

My hands flew to the buttons on my shirt, working them free as she rolled her hips, rising and falling over the top of me gently, as I opened up my ICPD uniform shirt, a tantalizing swathe of her light skin revealed with every button I let loose. She had closed her eyes again, her head tilted with passion, her high perfect breasts still covered by the deep indigo fabric of my shirt, my eyes drawn by the pale glimpse of skin cast golden by the light of her rock lamp, from her beautiful face, down her body, to where both of ours met.

She was like a dream made real, her voice like an angel's, heavy with passion as she moaned every time my cock did its job and hit the right spot inside her. She ground on top of me, taking her own pleasure until I thought my mind would explode from the torture of just not getting anywhere myself, but then she would rise and fall, working me just right, and all I could do was fall back into the pillows and let her have her way with me.

She was by no means an expert at sex, but she was completely and totally a natural at it, which made her something like a thousand times sexier in my book. She just had an otherworldly harmonious way about her, utilizing instinct rather than skill, and it was absolutely out of this world.

I wasn't going to be able to hold off much longer, not that a guy was ever really good at that in the first place. Your body wanted to come, it was going to come; there wasn't a whole lot we really got to say about it. I smoothed my hands over her hips beneath my shirt and let my thumb drift to the cleft at the top of her sex. She was so hot, so slick and ready, the both of us were a damn mess, but that's what made it fun.

I teased her there, thumb against her clit and she threw her head back with a sweet cry. She stilled a moment, pussy gripping around my shaft and I thrust up into her, my hips jerking involuntarily as I tried to hold back but couldn't. I jerked under her, driving into her with short little strokes as I pumped my load deep up in her pussy and with a cry that was honey to my ears, her body spasmed and contracted around me and she came apart beautifully.

Jesus Christ. I was done. Alyssa had me smitten. She wasn't only beautiful, she was soft and perfect, and legitimately the best, most intoxicating sex I had had in a long while – if ever.

She bowed over the top of me, and I took her into my arms, holding her hair back from her face. I kissed her, and hoped like hell that she would have me, and let herself be the last woman that I would ever kiss, because I didn't think I would ever find anyone that could compare.

26

*A*lyssa...

    I laid my head beside his, too languid, too loose, to even want to move yet and enjoying the feel of him still inside me. I smiled and kissed the side of his neck, as he chuckled lightly and cuddled me close, his big arms around me, holding me close. Our chests matched up just right, and I could feel the pounding swell of his heart reaching up to meet mine, which surged down to meet his.

I closed my eyes and let my lips play along the side of his neck as I concentrated on the beating of our hearts as they slowed and returned to normal. It felt as though even they were reluctant to leave one another, and it was the kind of intimate I couldn't even begin to describe.

I sucked in a sharp breath when his warm hands delved under his shirt to meet my body skin-on-skin. He stroked them over my flesh, feeling over every inch of me in firm but light caresses, not meant to tickle, but meant to titillate, and they did the job admirably. I raised my head and found his mouth with mine, our kisses growing in intensity as the fires of our passion reignited, stoked into a cheery blaze.

"Want to try a different position?" he said roughly, and I nodded.

"Which one?" I asked softly, my hips already beginning to rise and fall over his fresh erection.

"You good with from behind?" he asked.

I nodded, "Yeah."

"'Kay, on your knees, baby."

I reluctantly let him up, swinging a leg over him and shivering as he slipped out of me. I felt the loss of him keenly and took the position he asked for quickly so that I could have him again. While he got onto his knees, I shrugged out of his shirt and laid it forlorn, off to the side on the edge of the bed.

He put his hands on my hips, smoothing his hands over my skin, caressing my ass, admiring my body thoroughly, and damn if it didn't feel good. I felt beautiful, appreciated, as if the skin I was in were being looked upon as if it were a classic work of art. It elevated me, made me feel genuinely gorgeous, and I hadn't felt anything but – less– in so long that it nearly brought tears to my eyes.

He caressed my pussy with his fingers and I arched low to the bed like a cat, moaning, pressing my body into his hand, begging silently for his cock. I wanted him inside me again. I wanted to feel him, like velvet-covered steel, stroking against my walls, stoking the fires of my passions. I wanted to rise high into the night and crash back to earth, into his arms, and I wanted to live there, where everything was good and safe, and I felt like nothing could or would hurt me again.

Golden groaned in appreciation, as if looking at me caused him an exquisite pain. I bit my bottom lip to keep from moaning, just at the sound. When he first nudged my outer pussy lips with the swollen head of his cock, I gasped and my hips jerked back to meet him and he uttered into the intimate, close dark, "Oh, God, Lys…"

He pressed into me and I cried out, writhing subtly, trying to contain my movements for fear of him slipping out. I wanted him so badly, I needed him to stroke deep, I wanted to feel him completely, immerse myself in him, leave the world behind and bathe in our mutual existence as we simply lived for one another and attained that next level of pleasure in each other's arms.

"Golden, please," I begged and he grunted, rolling his hips, surging forward, but controlling his pace so as not to bottom out against my cervix, not yet, like he knew we had to work up to that.

"Mm, more, please, more," I begged and I gripped the bottom sheet in my fists, resting on my forearms, arching my back low, opening myself to him. He grasped my hips and, panting with the sight of it, lost himself in me, surging forward powerfully. I cried out, it felt so good. I thrust my hips back to meet him, wanting, needing more. I wanted him to take me. I wanted him to possess me, own me, as crazy as it sounded. I wanted to, just for a little while, give it all up to him and cede my hard-won control and just let him take care of me.

He didn't disappoint. He rocked into me, found the cadence that made me insane with love and lust, brought my body to a whole new height. He held me, caressed me, made love to me so completely, I didn't know up from down, my inside from my outside, and I simply didn't care. His strong arms reached under me and brought me up on my knees, I leaned back against his chest, his cock seated deep inside me, captured so completely, as one of his big hands palmed my breasts and the fingertips on the other delved between my folds at the top of my sex and mercilessly teased the orgasm out of me.

I died in his arms and he brought me back to life with his kiss. My arms twined back around his neck, my fingers played in the short soft strands of his hair at the back of his head, I held his mouth to mine as our passions cooled incrementally with every little aftershock of my pussy twitching around his cock, getting further and further from one to the next to the last.

"You're so incredible," he whispered in my ear and I laughed, a throaty, sultry sound I barely believed I could make.

"I'm pretty sure that was all you," I murmured.

"No, Chica. That was –us–."

His words stole my breath and he kissed the top of my shoulder, once, twice, each subsequent kiss creeping across my skin towards that erogenous zone on my neck. I beat him to it, turning my lips in the way, and we kissed, the fires stoked all over again.

Walking to work in the morning would definitely be interesting. Maybe I would just take a car.

~

A FEW WEEKS LATER, Kenzie stared at me, open-mouthed from the other end of her couch and held out her wine glass. I laughed and clicked mine against hers, and she tried to find her big-girl words and use them. Her jaw worked up and down, yet no sound came out, her wide eyes making her appear like a landed fish.

"I don't know whether to be proud of you, or super jealous!" she finally cried.

"Mm," I swallowed a sip of the crisp, sweet, white wine in my glass and said, "Oh my god, both, please. It's been forever since I feel like I've been the one to talk about with good news."

"Wow. A real, honest-to-god Latin lover. I am jealous."

I laughed and settled back on her couch, in the corner that the arm of it made with the back.

"It's really nice," I confessed.

"I'm just so glad to see you happy again," she said.

I nodded carefully and said, "I am. I really am. I mean, I don't know what the future holds at all, but I'm okay with that, for now."

"Well, a toast to your future, girl, because from what I can tell it holds a lot of some really hot sex with a guy who, by all accounts, is over the moon for you!"

I cringed a bit, face screwed up into a look of skepticism and asked, "You really think so?"

She heaved a heavy sigh as if heartbroken for me and set aside her glass, "Lys," she said folding her hands in her lap, "I don't think so, I know so. While giving you his STD test results over dinner was kind of fail, I can concede his point. With everything you've been through, you don't have any reason to trust anyone ever again. The fact he was even willing to go that extra mile is extremely telling, don't you think?"

I did. I mean, really I did, but... "I guess it's just so monumentally hard to believe that anyone would do all of what he has for me," I murmured and she let out a rush of breath that spoke of frustration and anger, but I could see it on her face what was about to come out of her mouth and I let her have it, because I knew it wasn't wrong.

"Your measuring stick for this type of thing is so broken," she said, scowling. I hadn't quite expected that, so I blinked at her, stunned with surprise.

"I hadn't really thought about it..."

"Well, you should, and while I know we agreed not to invoke his name, it's Ray's fault, it really is, but it's also yours, for letting him get away with warping your world view as much as you have."

I pressed my lips together, biting down on them to keep from saying anything, before I really thought through all of what she was saying. I swallowed hard and nodded. She wasn't exactly wrong, but I mean, it was kind of hard for me to see things from an outside perspective, you know? I told her as much.

She rolled her eyes at me, exasperated and said, "Sweetie, baby, honey, my best friend, light of my life – I'm not knocking you at all, I'm knocking him, but I am telling you that this is a thing you need to work on. You deserve to be happy. This guy is making you happy, take it, hold onto it, and don't let what Ray did to you dictate too much about how you feel about it. That is what I am trying to get at here."

I teared up, feeling so grateful and so loved by her it wasn't even funny.

"I'm so lucky to have you to talk sense into me," I said, sniffing.

"Oh!" she said, startled, and laughed. She held out her arms and I set my glass aside and went to her, hugging her tight.

"He seems like a real catch, which is surprising as hell, given everything he did in the beginning."

"I know, right?" I asked.

She laughed and sat back and said, "Hang onto this. See where it goes, but don't rush. There's no need and it sounds like Golden isn't in any hurry. Just go with the flow like you've been doing, and enjoy things."

"Thank you," I said, wiping under my eyes.

She picked up her wine and I followed suit.

"Seriously, to new beginnings," she raised her glass.

"To new beginnings," I agreed and we clicked glasses again.

We talked late into the night and I felt more relaxed, more connected than I had in ages. We had intended to watch a romantic comedy at her place, but we'd gotten our wine and had started talking, and pretty soon we had switched off the TV and had just caught up.

All too soon, the first bottle of wine was empty, takeout had been ordered, and now we were finished eating and halfway through the second bottle. I sighed, happy and sated and more than a little tipsy.

"Thinking about getting out of here?" she asked.

"Mm, it is pretty late."

"What's lover-boy up to tonight?" she asked, and I rolled my eyes.

"Why do I feel like we're better entertainment than one of your smutty romance novels?" I asked.

"Because you totally are. Don't start holding out on me now." She nudged my knee with her stocking-covered toes and I laughed.

"He's with his twin on his twin's boat or something," I said.

"Wait, he has a twin? Oh my god! You are holding out on me!" I waved her down.

"Yes, he has an identical twin brother, Angel, who works as an EMT with the ICFD."

"Wait, hot fireman and a hot cop?"

I rolled my eyes.

"Hot paramedic," I corrected.

She sighed and said dryly, "Well, that's fantasy fuel for days."

I finished off my wine and nearly choked on it, from trying not to laugh.

"Okay, now that's a little weird," I told her.

"What?"

"They're twins; brothers, you don't think a threesome with them would be, I don't know, a little incestuous?"

I raised my eyebrows.

She cringed, making a grossed-out face, "Ew, well, when you put it that way."

"Uh-huh!" I said and nodded.

She gave an exaggerated, exasperated sigh. "Fine! Crush my feeble fantasies."

"Mm, if ever there was one that needed to be crushed..." I shuddered.

Her mouth dropped open and she smiled super big. "You're jealous I would fantasize over your man, aren't you?" she asked excitedly.

"What? No!" I reached for the bottle of wine, rattled. I poured myself a little more. This bore a little more exploration. I mean, was I?

"You totally are," she said judiciously, and I hadn't realized I'd said anything out loud. She sniffed and waved me off, saying, "You didn't say it out loud, but your face says it all. You totally are, and I am happy for you," she said.

"You are?" I asked confused.

"Yes! You really feel for this guy, Lys. If you didn't, then you wouldn't be jealous. The fact that you are tells me this is serious."

I downed the wine in my glass in one big swallow and she pulled her head back raising an eyebrow.

"I'm not even divorced yet. Should I be getting so serious so soon?"

She gave me a flat look like *Seriously?*

I frowned.

"What?"

"Honey, he-who-shall-not-be-named was serious about another woman enough to knock her ass up before you guys even declared you were getting a divorce. You're just fine."

I winced, "Thanks for the perspective."

She raised her glass, gave me a smile, and downed the rest of her wine, holding out her glass as she swallowed and waggling it back and forth. I poured the last of the bottle for her and she nodded.

"Thank you."

"You're welcome," I said absently, my mind turning over the probability that my feelings for Golden went deeper than even I realized. I was surprised more over the fact that I wasn't surprised to find she was right.

"Go home, Lys. Get laid, fall asleep in your lover's arms, and tell me you aren't as sprung over him as he obviously is over you."

I pulled out my phone and opened the ride-share app, requesting a ride.

"You're crazy," I told her and she smiled sweetly at me.

"Oh, I know, but what does that make you, sweetie? After all, you know, and you're my best friend."

"Touché," I told her and she put up her arms and gave a little seated wiggle in a victory dance.

I laughed and got my purse and coat on after I put on my shoes. I took a bow and said, "Thank you for a lovely evening."

"Any time, girlfriend. We need to do this more often."

"Agreed," I said with a gusty sigh.

"Your place next time," she said with an impish grin and I laughed. My phone buzzed in my hand.

"Well, that was fast," I muttered. "My ride is already here."

"Go!" she cried, making a shooing motion with one hand. "Call me tomorrow and tell me all about it!"

"Right, will do!" I let myself out and made my way quickly downstairs and got into the back of the waiting Prius.

I texted Golden that I was on my way home like he'd asked, and let him know I was fairly buzzed from the wine and to hide the whiskey. He LOL'ed back at me and said he'd see me when I got there and no joke, he was waiting at the curb when the car pulled up.

He opened my door for me and before he shut it behind me, he'd bent and kissed me, murmuring against my lips, "I missed you."

"I missed you, too," I said softly, and I had no trouble admitting to myself that it was true.

"Come on," he said, and, tucking my hand into the crook of his arm, led me to the lobby door. He escorted us to our apartment and as he opened the front door, asked me, "Your place or mine?"

I smiled softly that he still gave me the choice, even this many weeks later and decided that he had more than earned my trust. I think I still surprised him, though, when I said, "Yours."

He stopped in his living room, right before the hallway and turned to me, searching my face. His hand drifted up and caressed my cheek and I smiled at him, wondering what was wrong. He said to me, his voice rough with emotion, "No offense, Chica, but when I take you to my bed, I'd like for the both of us to be stone-cold-sober."

I felt my eyes widen in surprise and thought about it for only a half-a-second. I nodded and reached out, putting my arms around his neck and pulling myself to him. I kissed him fiercely and tried to put just how much his proclamation meant to me into it. He kissed me back, hands smoothing over my body through the fabric of my clothing and I shuddered, really wanting it to be skin-on-skin.

"My place works just fine," I said breathlessly and he picked me up. I gave a little leap, twining my legs around his waist, and let him carry me to my bedroom.

27

Golden...

I was balls-deep in Lys, one arm hooked behind one of her legs so I could get that much deeper, when the pounding started out on our front door.

"Shit!" I put some serious feeling behind the word and looked down into her surprised face. She looked up at me, blinking owlishly, still a little bit tipsy, and a little fear slid behind her eyes.

"Who is that?" she asked and I shook my head and pulled out of her, standing. I pulled the sheet over her and was looking for my pants. We both froze again as the front door opened.

"Golden!" I felt my shoulders drop.

"Jesus Christ, it's Angel," I muttered.

"Um, might want to stop him from getting back here before he sees me naked," she said, stifling a giggle. I jumped into the first leg of my jeans, hopping up and down on one foot as I tried to get the other leg on.

"Yeah, Angel! Hold up. Don't come back here!"

I heard him bite out a curse, low and in Spanish.

"Get dressed, baby." I leaned over her and kissed her quick before I went out.

"Where's the fucking fire at?" I demanded.

Angel sighed. "Our sister just got arrested in a drug sweep in the warehouse district."

"What?" I demanded, dropping heavily onto the arm of my couch.

"Yeah. Manolo's with social services. They need one of us to take custody."

"Shit," I muttered, and Lys stepped out from the hallway.

She took one look at me and demanded crisply, "What's wrong?"

I didn't answer; I was still trying to wrap my head around this shit.

I looked at Angel and said what was on my mind, "Man, you can't take him. You live on a boat."

"You know I will," he said defensively, and I shook my head.

"Guys, what's wrong?" Lys demanded. I turned to her.

"Maria just went up on drug charges, big ones. Trafficking." I felt sick to my stomach.

"Oh, my god." Lys' face sobered instantly. She padded barefoot across the faux wood floor tiles and wrapped her arms around me, pressing my head to her chest as if to protect me. She kissed the top of my head and I hoped and prayed, for the first time in a long time, that she would stay with me, that she might help me, because Maria was looking at hard time and there was no fucking way that Angel and I could put up bail in a case like this. This was probably fucking RICO , a set of United States federal laws that provide for extended criminal penalties for people involved in organized crime. If she was caught packaging drugs, then this was most definitely RICO, and meant bail would be astronomical.

Shit, lawyer fees, alone, were going to wipe us the fuck out. I had some substantial savings, but they were supposed to be for in the event I had a family. You know? I'd always called it a 'rainy day' fund and I guess when it rained it poured.

Fuck me.

I let Lys hold me and took strength from it.That was rich. Me, taking strength from her. I pursed my lips and derided myself for even thinking for a minute that she couldn't be the strong one. Shit. She sure as fuck had gone through more than I had lately.

I took a deep breath and let it out slow, and she stepped back from me, giving me a slight nod. I turned to Angel who had a weird little smile on his face.

"I'll take him. Where is he?"

"I don't know, I just know Social Services has him by now. Maria used her one phone call to call me and let me know what's up. I guess her cleaning job has been a scam for, like, the last eight months. She got fired for some bullshit reason, and rather than ask us for help, she went to work for the Mariana Reyes cartel."

"Motherfucker," I swore. "The Ice Queen, herself?"

"Yeah."

"Will she turn?" I asked.

"Man, you know she does that, she dies."

"I know she doesn't, she goes to prison for the rest of her goddamn life."

"Either way, Manolo grows up without a mother," Lys said, the sorrow in her voice apparent.

"Right, first things first. Find Manolo and get him out of there. Then I'll talk to Maria."

"I'll get dressed," Lys said.

"Chica, you don't have to do this…" I started, but trailed off at her baleful look.

"Yes," she said intrepidly. "I do."

"Thanks," Angel said, cutting off my coming argument with a pointed look.

She kissed my forehead and went back down the hall toward her room. Meanwhile, I had an entire silent conversation with my twin.

I shot him a look, *Really?*

He rolled his eyes in exasperation and shot me one back that clearly said, *Not now.*

I scowled. *Then when?*

He scowled back. *When the immediate threat is over.*

I rolled my eyes. *Fine.*

He scowled deeper. *Damn right, it's fine.* He jerked his chin at the hallway. *Now get your ass dressed.*

I chuckled, my shoulders bouncing with silent laughter. *Sí, Madre.*

He flipped me off; no interpretation was needed there. I hauled my ass to my feet and went down to my room to find some real clothes.

I found Lys dressed and ready to go, quietly talking with Angel in the living room when I got out.

"I was just saying we should take a car," she said, but the light blush across her cheeks said she had been saying anything but. The look Angel was shooting me from behind her back was telling me, *Bro, she's a keeper.*

I smiled, *I know,* at him and nodded. "Looks like I'm gonna have to get a car when all this shit is said and done." I heaved a heavy sigh, not exactly sure I was ready to become a parent overnight, but one-hundred-percent committed to the fact that I was about to become a full time parent. Over. Night.

Maria, what the fuck were you thinking? I silently asked.

"Come on, let's go find Manolo. I'm sure he's terrified," Lys said and that galvanized both me and Angel into action.

"Come on, I doubt he's even been processed into the system, yet."

At least I knew where to go.

I looked up the address to the building I wanted and pulled up the rideshare app on my phone, punching it in as we went down to the street. We only had to stand around a few minutes before our driver showed up.

The ride went by in a grim silence, made better when Lys threaded her fingers through the spaces between mine. We got out at the department for Manolo's neighborhood and I ran in to talk to the desk sergeant.

"Do I look like the Department of Health and Welfare?" he demanded.

I scowled at him, and pulled my badge out of my back pocket.

"Do I look like your typical street thug, now?" I demanded.

He got real fuckin' helpful after that. I didn't get any nicer. He called around and said after a minute, "Social Services ain't got him yet. They were on their way here to meet with an officer for an escort to the projects your nephew lives in. According to his ma, he's staying with a neighbor, his grandma."

I nodded and said, "Yeah, his dad's mom."

"You wanna wait here, the social worker should be comin' any minute."

"That'd be great, thanks."

I went back out front to the street and filled Angel and Lys in on what was what. They followed me back into the lobby. We waited probably half-an-hour more until an official-looking woman in a neat pantsuit walked in, and by the look of her, she screamed Children's Services.

"You Child Services?" the desk sergeant asked.

"Yes, I'm Donna Williams. Do you have that escort ready?"

"Do you one better," I said. "You got family and a police escort rolled into one." I held out my credentials to her and she looked them over.

"You're the minor child's..?"

"Uncle. This is my twin brother, Ramiro, and this is my live-in girlfriend, Alyssa Glenn."

"Hi," Lys said quietly while Angel just gave a respectful nod.

"I see. This is highly unusual," she said. "I've never had family meet me at the police station before, and I've been doing this for eighteen years."

She raised her chin, blue eyes flashing from behind her glasses, and I knew an old battle-axe when I saw one. I could appreciate that, too. It meant she would be looking out for Manolo. Now it was just up to us to convince her that she didn't have to worry about us, that we were right there with her.

"Who was planning on taking custody of the minor child?" she demanded.

"That would be me," I said without hesitation.

"I live on a boat," Angel said with a shrug. "I'm good for a night or two, but stability-wise, Rodrigo and Lys are better set up and equipped."

"I see..."

Didn't sound like she did. Let the games begin, first person through the red tape was the winner. Thing was, I saw this for what it was: a marathon, not a sprint.

That woman put all of us through our paces. She expected us to have answers to everything, and any time I even came close to failing to have one of those answers, Lys was right there, like she was some kind of seasoned pro at motherhood, even though she'd never had one of her own. It was like she'd dreamt of it often enough and long enough, she knew how everything was supposed to go. I can't tell you how much that shit broke me, but at the same time, I also can't tell you how grateful I was she was here.

Finally, we were allowed to go along with the social worker to get my nephew. Angel had a key to Maria's place. We all did; I'd just forgotten mine at home. We all stood grim outside his abuela's door and waited for it to open. When it did, Manolo looked up at all of us and his easy smile fell off his face.

Shit.

The kid knew. He was too smart not to know what was up. The disappointment on his face fuckin' crushed me, but Lys, once again, saved the day. She knelt down and with a smile said, "Hey, you need to do us a favor and tell your grandma we're here to get you and that you're going to be staying with me and your uncle Rodrigo tonight. Okay, bud?"

"Where's my mom?" he asked, his voice quavering and eyes filling.

"Oh, hey, no, don't cry, honey, she's okay. Your mom's fine. You're just going to come stay with your uncle Rodrigo and me for a while, that's all."

"Where is she?" he demanded.

The social worker heaved a tired sigh and said, "She's in jail,

Manolo. I'm Miss Williams from the Indigo City Department of Family Services. Do you know what that means?"

"You're gonna put me in foster care?" he demanded.

She shook her head.

"No, we don't do that when you have family."

"I'd never let that happen to you, buddy. Never in a million years."

"Hello, who are you? Oh!" Rita, Manolo's abuela, his dad's mother, walked up to the door. Finding four people on her doorstep rather than just the social worker startled her a little.

"Hey, Rita," Angel said, and she looked taken aback as the wheels and gears turned as to what our presence meant.

"Maria?" she asked, surprised, knowing her son was still locked up.

Everything went off in a flurry of Spanish as we explained what had happened. Rita waved Lys inside with Manolo, but barred the social worker's way with the flat of her held-up hand. This was the 'hood. You didn't let anyone official past your door, if you could help it. Lys wasn't official, so she got the okay.

She returned with Manolo, his backpack, and his coat. Rita, in tears, hugged her grandson and begged us to bring him to see her every once in a while. I told her I didn't hold anything against her, and absolutely, that we were family, and family didn't cut each other out or turn our backs, no matter what was up.

The social worker took notes, and even though she was a güera, I guessed that made her all right. She was one of the good ones, as far as I could tell, one of the ones who, despite their insane workload, still cared. There weren't a lot like her left. I could respect that, even though this time around we were on opposite sides of the tape.

Shit, maybe I was hanging around Chrissy and Yale too much. I was starting to get their lawyer thing.

We left Rita's and went down two floors to Maria's apartment to pack up a bunch of Manolo's things. Angel called one of the guys with a car, to get us and the shit moved to my place, and I did some serious thinking. My place wasn't suited for this long-term, but for now, we could make it work. I shoved that to the back of my mind and tried real hard not to think about it too much.

We got home, we got Manolo to bed, as it was fucking late as hell and the kid had school in the morning, and then I dropped in a heap onto my couch and put my face into my hands and took a minute to feel overwhelmed and to work through that shit. Lys sat down gently on the arm of the couch and rubbed my back through my tee shirt comfortingly.

"You didn't sign up for this, Chica. I wouldn't blame you if you bailed." She smiled but it held hurt which she tried like hell to hide.

"You didn't sign up to take my problems on, either," she reminded me, gently.

"Yeah, well, not the same thing."

"I disagree," she said. "It's exactly the same thing."

I pulled her down into my lap and she wrapped her arms around my neck. Her face was soft and lovely as she let her gaze roam over mine, and I closed my eyes and rested my forehead against hers.

"I don't know how to do this," I confessed, and I heard her smile.

"Being an adult is easy when it's just you; when you bring other people into it, it becomes infinitely harder. Yet for all of the millions and billions of people who have gone before… still, no one has written an instruction manual on how not to be a shitty parent."

I laughed softly and she kissed me. I kissed her back and took solace in her gentle touches.

"One day at a time, I guess."

"Starting with tomorrow," she agreed.

"What would you do?" I asked.

"Well, I'll help get him up and get him to school. I can also go get him from school and watch him until you get home from work. I'll just rearrange my schedule some."

"You don't have to do that," I said.

"You're right, I don't, but I want to."

"I don't really know what I would do without you right now."

"That goes both ways," she said and she kissed me again.

We curled on the couch together and talked until so late it was early. She had time for a little under three hours of sleep before she had to be awake to take Manolo to school and get to work. I tucked her in, and felt nothing but regret that I couldn't crawl in there with her. Instead, I took my ass back out to the couch.

I'd made the decision to not rush Manolo into our lives as a couple. He was used to us having our own rooms and I didn't want to put too much by the way of change onto his small shoulders at once.

I woke up to Lys getting him up for school.

She had him sit at the dining room table and I lay, pretending to be asleep and listened.

"So," she asked him, "does your mom fix you breakfast in the morning?"

"Sometimes, not all the time."

"Oh yeah, when she fixes it, what does she make?"

"Pancakes, or French toast."

"Is that during the week, or only on the weekends?"

"On the weekends."

"What about during the week?"

"Sometimes she makes me toast and orange juice, most of the time, I just have a bowl of cereal."

Lys asked all these questions and was an expert at getting the full meal deal out of my kid nephew. She fixed them both oatmeal while she talked and made herself coffee. Manolo was subdued, and pretty cranky over the fact she was making him go to school, but she fielded that one like a pro, too.

After he'd eaten, he walked away from the table, dragging his feet to go in and get dressed mumbling in Spanish. I caught him calling her a bitch and I pursed my lips, giving him a half-second to think he'd gotten away with it, before calling out in Spanish, "Manolo, get that disrespect out of your mouth, little man!"

"Sorry, Tío Rodrigo!"

"Get out here when you get dressed."

You better believe I dressed him down over it. By the time I was done, he tearfully apologized to Lys, who hugged him and told him it was okay, that she understood and she wasn't mad. That then led into a discussion about better ways to deal with anger and frustration. I hadn't even thought about that last part. Not only did she school Manolo, she schooled me without even knowing it.

I needed to marry her, like yesterday.

Slow down there, turbo. She ain't even divorced yet.

Shit.

I'd fucking forgotten all about it. Her divorce hearing was next week and here I was taking up all of her time with my family's drama. I wiped a hand over my face and looked over to where Manolo was shouldering his backpack.

"C'mere, Hombrecito."

He came over, as mopey and as sullen as an eight year old can get, and it didn't matter that he was a kid who was way older than his years – he was still a kid. I hugged him tight and told him, "I love you, kid."

"I love you, too."

"We'll get this thing with your mom figured out as best we can."

"Promise?"

If I'd learned one thing as a beat cop, it was 'Don't make promises you can't keep'. I gave his shoulder a squeeze and told him the truth. "I can't promise everything will be okay, bud. That's not how things like this work. I can promise not to lie to you about it, and I can promise we'll all do everything we can, but your mom, she made a big mistake this time."

"Bigger than my dad does?"

I nodded. "Way bigger."

He nodded and let out a huge sigh weighted with way more disappointment an eight-year-old should ever have to carry. He nodded and I let his shoulder go.

"You know which school?" I asked to be sure, and Lys smiled serenely and said, "I've got it."

"Okay, text me," I said.

"Get some sleep," she ordered gently.

Manolo rolled his eyes. "Come on, I'm gonna be late."

"You didn't even want to go a minute ago," I said, accusingly.

"Yeah, now I can't wait to get out of here, and away from you two!"

I put my face in my hands while Lys shut the door on her laughter.

That kid was going to kill me, once he really ramped up and got used to being here.

28

*A*lyssa...

"All rise; the court of the Honorable Judge Daniel Arken is adjourned."

We all stood and the judge left the courtroom. I turned to Deanna, my lawyer and she smiled at me broadly. I hugged her. I know it wasn't professional, but she deserved it. She had argued my case better than perfectly and had convinced one of the hardest judges there was so well that he'd given us everything we'd asked for and more.

"Thank you," I murmured and she gave my shoulders a squeeze and beamed at me from arm's length.

"You did remarkably well," she said, then asked, "Are you okay?"

"I am, thank you," I said with a laugh, and turned towards the gallery. Golden smiled from one of the back rows. Ray glared at me and followed my gaze, turning nearly incandescent when he saw who I was looking at.

I thought to myself, quite out of character, *And here you were thinking —you— were the one to trade up. It's spelled K-A-R-M-A and its pronounced 'Ha ha, fuck you, Ray.'*

I waited for him to leave the courtroom, exchanged a few more words with my lawyer, and went to meet Golden where he waited for me at the end of the aisle between the galleries' seats. He took my hand when I reached him and tucked it into the crook of his arm. It was so old-fashioned, so gentlemanly, and I loved that about him.

He'd told me that his father used to do it for his mother all of the time when he was growing up, before his father had died, and that the gesture had stuck with him. It had been a tough week or so with Manolo in the apartment, somewhat testing boundaries and acting-out. The situation with his mother didn't look good and Golden had committed for the long haul when it came to his nephew.

"Well, that went better than expected," he said, with a dark chuckle that bordered on vindictive.

I smiled and nodded slowly.

"Yes it did."

"So, you're a free agent, now."

I laughed and shook my head slightly as he opened the courtroom door for me. I let my bottom lip go from between my teeth and said, "No. No, I am not. At least as far as any other man is concerned." He paused and gave an impressed look like, *All right!*

I laughed and he put his hand on the small of my back. We stepped through, out into the courthouse hallway. Ray looked in our direction and looked positively murderous. My heart leapt in my chest and stuck in my throat until Golden took my hand and tucked it firmly into the crook of his arm again, laying his opposite hand over the top of it. Ray straightened and looked down his nose at us and we walked away.

"I don't expect he'll do half of what he's supposed to," I murmured.

"Like keep you on his health insurance?"

"Or pay his alimony on time, if at all."

"It'll come back to bite him," he said.

"That's his problem. He's definitely not my problem anymore, I'll be fine."

Golden laughed softly and smiled proudly at me. "Now, that, is my girl."

I smiled broadly myself, and we took the elevator down to the first floor. As we stepped off, we ran into someone we knew.

"Yale," Golden greeted.

"Hey, what are you two doing here?"

"Final divorce hearing," I answered.

"Oh, I'm sorry to hear that. How did it go?"

"Oh, don't be! I'm not," I said, laughing. "I got everything I asked for, and then some."

"Really? Well, congratulations. Must have had Judge Kellerman."

"Arken, actually."

Yale gave a low whistle and said, "Your husband fucked up, then."

"Spectacularly," I agreed.

"So, what are you guys off to do now?" he asked.

"Well, my nephew is with my brother," Golden said, and in a lowered voice, his gaze darting around to make sure he wasn't overheard, he added, "So I figured I'd get it while the gettin' is good; take her home and fuck her brains out."

I blinked surprised and Yale burst out laughing. I was surprisingly on board with this plan.

We took a cab home, and our mouths were like magnets, locked together as soon as the elevator doors closed. We rushed down the hall to our door and he fumbled with keys. As soon as the door was shut behind us, the clothes started coming off.

The last time we'd had sex, we'd been interrupted; then we'd had to put everything in the deep freeze. Over a week's worth of pent-up desire and frustration rushed to the surface and we were both ready to explode. Angel had Manolo for now, so we were definitely taking advantage of the situation.

"Your place or mine?" he asked harshly, breathless with need.

I stopped cold. I couldn't help it. Maybe it was my new-found freedom, the fact that I really felt free. Maybe it was the fact that so much had been turned upside-down and inside-out over such a short amount of time, but I stopped and looked up at Golden with a stunned realization.

"No more 'your place', no more 'my place'... What about 'our place'? Like, for real?"

He stopped and cocked his head, looking at me. Really looking at me.

"Like, move?"

"We can't pretend forever, Golden. He's going to figure it out, if he hasn't already, and we can't keep paying for ride services to take him to school every morning and home every afternoon forever. It adds up, it's too much."

"What are you suggesting?" he asked, his expression carefully neutral.

"I'm saying we're going to have to move... Manolo needs his own space; we need ours."

"Ours?"

"Yes, ours."

"So, like a two-bedroom with Manolo in his room..."

I laughed and finished, "And us in ours. Yes. That is what I'm talking about."

"You're sure?"

"I'm sure."

"God, you're amazing!"

I laughed and he renewed attacking the side of my neck with vigor, licking and sucking all of the right places, until I was putty in his hands.

29

*G*olden...

"Thanks, man." I took the beer Skids handed me over the bar and he nodded. I swiveled on my barstool, taking a drink, and faced my twin, who raised his eyebrows expectantly.

"So what's up?" he asked.

"I think I'm ready, dude."

"Ready for what?" he asked, scowling slightly.

"Ready to buy a place."

"Wait, what? No shit?"

"Yeah, man. No time like the present. I got Manolo full-time and I don't think shit's gonna end well for Maria. Minimum, I think she's looking at ten years, dude. She ain't got nothing to fight with, either, so this is going to be short and brutal."

"Shit." I saw the heartbreak I felt mirrored on my twin's face, only unlike Angel, I didn't tear up. I was the harder of the two us, but I wouldn't wish that hardness on my brother. He was cool, just the way he was.

"Mom's gotta be rolling in her grave right about now," he said.

"Abuela and Papa, too," I agreed. We both drank.

"Manolo could be graduated from high school before she's out."

"I know that, bro, believe me."

"That was cartel shit, too, wasn't it?" he asked. I nodded. "Shit," he said, low and with feeling. I nodded again.

"She going away under RICO?" he asked.

I shook my head. "That's about the only thing she's actually got going for her," I told him. "In the grand scheme of things, she's just a peon, so no RICO for her. Still, they got her dead to rights for trafficking, not a simple possession with the intent to distribute, and the bust they snatched her up at? That was a damn near forty-kilo bust. She's fucked. Even as a first offense, no judge in their right mind is gonna give her anything less than ten."

Angel sat back and I let the harsh reality of what our sister had done to herself and her family sink in. We drank and sat in silence for a while, marinating in it. Maria had fucked herself sideways, and there wasn't a fuckin' thing either of us could do about it without ruining ourselves, too.

"So, what, you want to buy a house?" he asked finally, changing the subject.

"Ah, I got my eye on a couple of places, actually."

"Yeah? Where at?"

"Well, there's a house out near Youngblood's place up for sale, but I don't want to move that far out of the city, for either my or Lys' jobs."

"So, where else you look?"

"I was actually looking at one of the brownstones on Backdraft's street."

"Can you afford one?"

"I have quite a bit put away for a rainy day, man. Enough I think I could pull it off. Still, if I went for it, I'm going to need help from you and the rest of the guys on renovations and shit. I don't have Lil's deep pockets to contract it out."

Angel smiled and shook his head. "None of us have Lil's kind of money."

"Anyway, I'm just looking right now. Whatever I get, I want a yard, or a garden. That's why I was thinking the brownstone. They have back yards. Not super-big, but enough for some flowerbeds and shit."

"Lys?" he asked.

"Yeah, she likes to grow things, but hasn't been able to in years."

"You going to marry this woman?" he asked, raising his eyebrows again.

"Not anytime soon, we're cool with sweating her ex for alimony for a few years first."

"Holy shit. You've talked about that shit. You're really serious about her, aren't you?"

"Well, yeah, man."

Angel sat back on his stool and said, "Color me jealous, bro."

"What?"

"Not going to lie, I always thought I'd find it before you."

"What?" I demanded, scowling.

"Love, you jackass!"

I jerked back like he'd said something shitty about our mother and thought about it. I mean, I don't think I'd ever been in love with a chick before and then it hit me, Lys wasn't a chick. She was a woman. She was the woman you wanted to marry, the one you wanted to raise your children; she was so much more than a random hookup or a chick for now.

I nodded slowly and said, "Well, if love is wanting to move her into your house, wake up with her in your bed every morning, and have her be the only woman you fuck for the rest of your life, then yeah, I guess that's where it's at," I said. Angel's shoulders were shaking with silent laughter that he just couldn't keep quiet anymore. He laughed until he had to wipe tears out of the corners of his eyes.

"You're a fucking barbarian," he said finally, catching his breath.

"Never really put much thought into the hearts-and-flowers portion of the program. That's what I got you for."

He shook his head and said, "Yeah, and I can tell you're gonna need me, man. Holy shit."

"Fuck off," I muttered, and finished off my beer.

"I'm with Angel, brother. A poet you are not. Don't quit your day job, now," Skids called, from not too far down the bar. I rolled my eyes at him.

"Seriously," I said. "The brownstone, what do you think?"

"I think, yeah, if you can afford it, go for it. You know we'll back you up."

I nodded and said, "I'll look into it more in-depth tomorrow."

"I wouldn't buy without taking her with you, if you're serious about it," Skids called out.

I nodded and said, "Thanks guys."

"For what?" Angel asked.

"Not giving me too hard of a time and not shooting me down is a good start."

"I'm a medic, it's my job to patch your ass back together after you get shot down."

"True that," I said, and Skids set down a fresh beer in front of me just in time for me to drink to it.

"So, what are your plans the rest of the night?" Angel asked.

"Going to finish having a beer with my brother, and go home to my unexpected family."

"Now that is worth drinking to," he said, and we drank again.

30

Alyssa...

"Where's Manolo?" he asked, leaning against the counter, just in time for a mighty splash and the sound of his nephew playing to come from behind the closed door of my bathroom. He grinned at me and came around into the kitchen to put his hands to my hips and draw me in close.

"Have a good visit with your brother?" I asked.

"Yeah, you were right, I needed a bit of a break."

I smiled and his lips descended onto mine. I kissed him quietly and ached a little inside. I missed having him hold me at night and I wished there was some way around the awkward conversation with Manolo about it.

He sighed and held me close and we stole what moment we could before Manolo shouted out, "Hey, Lys?"

"Yeah, Hombrecito, what is it?" Golden called out.

"Can I get out now?"

With a soft sigh Golden reluctantly let me go and stepped back, I checked my watch rolled my eyes and nodded.

"Yeah, Bud! You can get out now."

"Boys," I muttered and Golden laughed slightly. The struggle was real, keeping Manolo in a bath for longer than five minutes. It was a phase, but one I couldn't wait for him to outgrow. He opened up the bathroom door a minute later in his pajama pants and strolled right across to Golden's room. We fought not to laugh.

"That's your cue," I murmured.

"Pretty soon he's going to be too old to want his uncle to tuck him in and tell him stories."

"Mm," I nodded in agreement. I went into my bathroom to clean up. There almost always seemed to be more water on the floor and the edges of the tub than there was draining out of the bottom of it. I picked up Manolo's discarded towel and mopped things up, turning on the overhead fan to make sure the moisture was well ventilated. I dreaded coming up with a mold or mildew problem in here.

As I went to step across the hall to the laundry closet and deposit Manolo's towel in the wash, I heard him talking to his uncle, my name giving me pause.

"...do you like Lys?"

There was silence for a moment, then Golden laughed a little, "Of course I do, Hombrecito."

"No, I mean, do you like-her, like her?"

"Bud, what are you asking me?"

"I guess I'm asking, do you love her?"

A quiet pause then, "Yeah, Manolo. Yeah, I do."

A little overwhelming, but not too bad. I bit my lips together, but my smile wouldn't be contained. I jumped when Manolo shouted, "Hey, Lys!"

I went to the doorway to Golden's room and leaned against the doorjamb. "Yes?"

"You like my uncle?"

I laughed a little and said, "Of course I do, why?"

"You love him?"

I blushed and nodded.

"Yeah," I said quietly. "Yes, I do."

The little guy perked up like it was the best news he heard all night and said, "Great! You can sleep in Lys' room and I can have the bed all to myself!"

I turned around and walked away before I could laugh, but Golden lost it, and I couldn't help it, I followed suit. *Out of the mouths of children.* I couldn't say I faulted his eight-year-old logic completely, but at the same time, I don't think he quite grasped that wasn't technically how things worked.

What are you talking about? He's not off the mark at all, and you know it.

I deposited his towel in the washing machine and closed the sliding doors, shaking my head. Golden came out of his room a moment later, closing the door behind him. We took one look at each other and both of us tried valiantly to squelch our giggles as we moved carefully away from the door and into the living room.

"Wow," I said, my voice low and careful.

Golden snorted a laugh and nodded. "'Wow' is right."

"How'd you handle it?" I asked.

"I kind of didn't, I just told him good night, tucked him in, and came out here."

I stifled a giggle behind my hand and he pulled me into his arms, another stolen moment which was all we limited ourselves to lately... But maybe we didn't have to, anymore.

"I guess the cat is out of the bag," I whispered.

"Mm." Golden's eyes roamed my face.

I cocked my head to the side and asked, "What is it?"

"Did you mean it?" he asked softly.

"Did you?"

"Not fair, I asked first."

I smiled and nodded. "I meant it," I whispered, carefully looking anywhere but his face. Not wanting to see it when he said something like how he was just telling Manolo what he wanted to hear... *what you wanted to hear,* my mind corrected me.

He tipped my chin with gentle fingers and brought me back around to look him in the eyes. I bit my lips together and tried not to cringe, but he smiled and said, "I meant it. I love you, Lys. It may not be the family you dreamed of, baby, but it's here, if you want it."

"Are you asking me to marry you?" I asked, a frisson of fear travelling down my spine. It would be way too soon for that. I mean, I only just finalized my divorce!

"No, when I get around to asking you that, there'll be a ring involved. We had this talk. We're not done with your ex, yet."

I smiled in spite of myself and said, "Things sometimes have a strange way of working out, don't they?"

He smiled at me and lowered his lips to mine and it was the best kiss. So gentle, so perfect, so loaded with promise that I could actually believe in. I put my arms around him and molded myself to the front of his body; his hands smoothing over my body through my clothes were enough to drive me crazy.

"You better learn to be quiet," he said roughly against my lips. "Because as soon as he's out, I'm making love to you."

The words stole my breath, but I couldn't say I was opposed to the notion. I nodded carefully and he smiled, stepping back and letting me go. I moved to the kitchen to finish cleaning up from dinner and Golden swatted me playfully on the ass, following me in to help.

"So, I talked to my brother," he said.

"And?"

He sighed heavily and said, "I'm a realist. Maria is going to do some time. Some serious time. The official minimum sentence for her is five years without the possibility of parole, but I don't see that happening. With the way they're getting tough on drugs around here, I see her doing ten years minimum, easy."

"Oh, my god... even though it's her first offense?"

I nodded, "Babe, these are trafficking charges. This is going to be short and brutal. Even if we could find her a decent lawyer, the financial load alone would wipe both me and Angel out so bad... I have a choice here. I can either take what I have stashed for a rainy day, and put a hefty down-payment on a place to provide for Manolo, or I can try and get Maria off with a good lawyer and still go into debt up to my ass after burning through what I've got saved."

"I hate the thought of leaving her to her fate with a public defender," I murmured.

"I do too, but Maria made her bed with this one. I hate to sound harsh, but she's gotta lie in it. Kids come first, always, and I'm not about to screw Manolo over any more than his dad and my sister have. It's just not fair."

I nodded and could see the lines of tiredness and distress etched around his mouth and eyes. I leaned back against the cabinets and heaved a heavy, emotional sigh.

"I don't envy you your position at all," I said.

"It's a damn mess, that's for sure."

"It sounds as though you've made your decision, though."

"No telling if it's the right one," he said softly, "but it's no contest. Manolo comes first, and I don't think Maria would disagree with that assessment."

"Still haven't gone to see her?" I asked. I knew he hadn't but still, it needed to be talked about. He shook his head and stayed silent on the matter. "Why not?" I asked, gently prying.

"I'm so fucking pissed at her," he confessed and hung his head, dragging on the back of his head with one hand to ease the tension in his neck. I put a gentle hand to his back and propelled him to the living room. He went with me, and I sat on the couch and waved him to the floor in front of me. He sat and sighed out, and I began to work at his knotted shoulders and neck.

"I understand that you're angry, but don't you think this is a discussion that needs to be had with her?"

He was silent for a minute and said, "Yeah, but I know how it's going to go down and I'm not looking forward to it. She's going to be pissed the fuck off and feel like I've thrown her to the goddamn wolves."

"I know this sounds awful," I said. "But she's going to have plenty of time to think about it; she'll come around eventually."

The dark chuckle he let out, followed by a groan as I found the spot of tension in his muscles giving him the most trouble, vibrated through my quickly-tiring fingers and I smiled. I worked on massaging him until my own hands hurt and when I couldn't do anymore, I simply draped myself over his broad shoulders and hugged him back into me. He sighed and brought his arms up, holding mine to his chest. We sat like that for a long time.

He bowed his head and kissed my arms, and I smiled and asked, "Are you ready for bed?"

"Mm, never been more ready in my life, Chica."

I sat up, relinquishing my hold on him. He got up and held a hand down to me, and I let him pull me up off the couch.

He followed me to my bedroom, his hands on my hips, gently guiding me up the hall and through my door. The anticipation building, the wanting, the need, overrode my better judgment to not have sex when Manolo was here and could potentially wake up and catch us in the act.

Golden shut the bedroom door and flipped the lock, and I felt a little silly for forgetting that the doorknob even had a lock on it, even if it was one of the cheap and cheesy ones easily bypassed with a paperclip from the outside.

He came back to me and cupped my face with his hands, kissing me long and slow as I gathered the hem of his tee in my hands. He raised his arms for me and let me pull it from his body, his fingers immediately going to the front of my women's blue oxford shirt and working the buttons out of their holes.

I sighed contentedly as he worked to undress me, letting my hands wander over his warm skin, exploring him with light and gentle touching while he worked the last button free. He pushed the shirt back off of my shoulders and down my arms, effectively cutting my explorations of his hard body short. Once free of the button-down, I grasped the hem of the white cotton camisole I wore underneath and drew it up over my head.

Our mouths naturally gravitated to one another and we kissed, pressing skin-on-skin, our upper bodies needing the intimate contact even as he unhooked my bra at the back and pulled it out from between us. My hands went for his belt as he guided his fingers down to the waistband of my dark grey yoga leggings, catching my panties under them and sweeping them down my legs. Smooth as butter, when I stepped out of each leg, he managed to get my socks, too. I stood nude before him, he on his knees looking up at me.

It was a strange feeling.

He was always the one that seemed so powerful and in-control out of the two of us. He was always the one with the plan and the know-how, yet here he was, kneeling at my feet, fingertips ghosting up the backs of my legs, nudging them apart just a little bit more, his somber dark gaze looking up at me in worship as he leaned in and dipped his tongue at the apex of my thighs.

My head fell back, a deep gasp of surprised pleasure falling from between my lips as his hands found the globes of my ass and pressed me closer to his probing tongue. My hands fell to his hair, fingers burying themselves into it as I trembled at the delicious sensations his mouth wrought on my most intimate parts.

"I don't think I can stand much longer," I confessed, my knees feeling weak. He stood swiftly, his own knees letting out twin painful-sounding cracks into the confines of the room, though he didn't seem to pay them any mind. He picked me up and carefully tossed me onto the bed where I bounced, laughing quietly, as he stripped his belt from the loops on his jeans.

"One of these times, if you're okay with it, I want to tie you to the bed."

I raised an eyebrow and said, "Kinky."

"Sometimes," he agreed.

I smiled, and put my hands together and held out my wrists, trusting him. He grinned and looped the belt around them, pulling it tight. He gave the long end of the braided leather a loop around the center, tightening the belt around my wrists, and threaded it through, locking them into place.

"Lie back," he whispered and I did, and he raised my arms above my head and tied the long tail of the belt left remaining around one of the bars of the old-fashioned, wrought iron headboard.

I tugged on my hands and found them held fast as he climbed up onto the bed between my legs and nudged them apart with his shoulders.

"I'm going to eat you out, make you come at least twice, then I'm going to give you the ride of your life," he promised.

I watched with fascinated heat while he slowly stripped out of the denim of his jeans, peeling them down his muscular thighs, my gaze lingering for just a moment on the indented silvery spider work of the old scar from where he'd been shot, long before we'd ever met. He knelt on the bed, his cock bobbing and swaying, fully engorged, as he settled on his stomach between my legs, taking it from my sight, his dark eyes filling my field of vision as he licked a deliberate, slow, wet line from my opening to my clit.

I gasped, jerking against my bonds and the fact that I was trapped and at his mercy sent such a thrill through me. I knew I was safe, because I knew I was loved, and because I knew that if I asked, he would let me go. I wouldn't ask, though. I wanted this. I wanted to feel him inside me, I wanted him to do his worst, which in this scenario, translated to his very, very best.

"Oh, god," I said, and he chuckled darkly against my body, making me gasp.

"Quiet, Chica," he murmured against my pussy, reminding me, and I bit my lips together to stifle the next moan he ripped from me. I closed my eyes and let my head fall back and concentrated very hard on simply breathing and not letting my voice come into play as he made it extremely hard to remember and incredibly easy to forget all things.

He slid a finger inside of me and teased that spot inside while working my clit with his mouth from the outside and fireworks went off behind my closed eyelids. I shuddered and gasped, panted and attempted to writhe, but his arm across my hips put a quick stop to that last. I swallowed hard, gritted my teeth against making any sounds and gave myself over to just feeling, and it was a cascading rush of pleasure that left me exquisitely shattered in its wake.

I lay panting, beautifully devastated in the wake of it, as Golden climbed my body with light touches and kisses,planting seeds of desire with every scant press of his lips against my overheated, oversensitive skin. I gasped, sucking in and holding sharp little breaths every time he made contact with me. His smile grew with every kiss until he knelt above me, hovering over me and smoothing my hair back from my face.

"How do you feel?" he whispered, checking in on me.

"Amazing," I whispered back and he kissed my lips. I closed my eyes and drowned myself in the warm euphoria he brought over me.

"Ready for round two?" he asked softly.

"No," I said, but I think he could taste the lie when I smiled. I mean, I felt good, why go further?

"Hm," he chuckled darkly. "Be right back, baby."

He settled down between my quivering legs and lapped at my pussy. I gasped, a whimper escaping my mouth before I could stop it. I'd barely come back from the last earth-shattering orgasm and he was already sending me back into space. The pleasure mounted, the full feeling returned to my pelvic region as he sucked at my clitoris, teasing it with his tongue, his fingers pumping in and out of my wetness as I strained at my bonds, the feeling of being at his mercy incredibly sexy and surprisingly freeing.

I just couldn't get enough.

31

*G*olden...

Her second orgasm was choice. It was like she crashed hard into a quivering wreck in the middle of the bed and when I pulled my fingers out of her, licking them clean, she looked up at me with lust-filled brown eyes that told me that she was having a blast. I pulled her legs apart and walked up the bed on my knees, collapsing over her, holding myself up on one arm over her shoulder. I gazed into her eyes from inches away and she panted, struggling at her bonds a little. I could tell she wanted to touch me, but not yet. I wasn't done playing with her.

"I believe I promised you one hell of a ride, Chica."

She raised an eyebrow in challenge. "So what are you waiting for?"

I grabbed her around the thighs and pulled her towards me; her arms snapped taut above her head and she let out a surprised yip, but her smile and her laugh followed it and I knew she was in a good place. Hopefully, I was about to make it better.

I shoved into her hot, wet cunt in one deft stroke and she was ready for me. She bit her bottom lip and let out a harsh breath with just the edge of a decadent murmured sound. I pulled her onto my cock to meet the surge of my hips and it was rough and brutal and I fucking loved it.

We'd talked about her ex, what he'd done, in detail, so I had figured this was worth a try, seeing as it was the opposite to how she'd been assaulted. I was glad I'd given it a go because the unbridled joy on her face was worth everything.

"Harder," she murmured and I obliged. I wasn't going to last long, not like this, this was something too hot for me to hold off. I gritted my teeth and felt a surge of triumph when she came around my dick. The squeeze of her soft body around my shaft sent me right over the edge.

We both gasped for breath, her arms twisting against her bonds as she begged me breathlessly, "Let me go."

I knelt up and undid her bonds, working the leather off from around her wrists, massaging them and her hands until she shook them out of my grasp and captured my face between them, dragging my face to hers. I fell over the top of her, cradling her under the protection of my body as she clung to me and kissed me breathless all over again.

"Stay with me," she murmured and I nodded carefully. Manolo seemed like he didn't have a problem with it, and I could use a decent night's sleep that didn't involve the kid kicking me in the middle of the night, or waking up with a plastic dinosaur digging into my ribs from between the couch cushions.

She kissed me again, slower, more luxurious than before, full of weight and meaning, before whispering, "I love you."

My heart swelled so damn big in my chest it damn near hurt and I put my forehead against hers and whispered back, "I love you, too, Lys. I love you, too."

∼

She lay on my chest in the close dark, her fingertips playing along my skin, her skin hidden beneath one of those damn nightshirts of hers, but it wouldn't do for Manolo to walk in on us in nothing but the sheets. We'd already tempted fate once that night. She sighed out and it was the most satisfied sound I'd ever made a woman make. I smiled and kissed her head and she cuddled closer.

"Life has a funny way of working out, doesn't it?" I asked.

She practically purred when she snickered.

"Mm, it does," she agreed.

"I've been thinking about some things," I murmured.

"Like?" she asked.

"A beat cop's salary is okay for one guy, but when it comes to raising a family? A mortgage? Not so much."

"You know I'll help," she said, her tone slightly injured.

"I know, baby, I know... it's just the department has been after me since I joined up to take another position, and now I'm seriously thinking about it."

"What position would that be?" she asked and I could tell it piqued her interest.

"Well, when I was overseas, I was trained to do things like bust down doors and extract the bad guys. All the things the ICPD look for in a SWAT member. They were trying to court me onto the SWAT team when shit went sideways serving that warrant and I got shot."

I laughed a little and she raised her head, smiling a little wanting in on the joke asking, "What's so funny?"

"All the tours of duty I pulled over there, I didn't once even come close to getting tagged by a bullet. Come home, and I get shot in the leg inside my first eight months on the job."

She swallowed hard and I could see the wheels in her pretty head turning. It was my turn to ask her, "What?"

"Tactical situations are dangerous..."

I could hear the 'but' coming so I said, "...But?"

"So is being a cop on the street, especially nowadays, right?"

"Actually, statistically, crime is lower than it's ever been," I told her. She looked at me like I was crazy. I laughed, "No, really, it is! It's just that everybody has a damn camera in their hand now, so things that wouldn't normally make the news, they get put up on social media and then go viral and everybody hears about more and sees more than they used to. At least, that's my explanation for it, anyway." I gave a light shrug.

"Are you asking me for permission?" she asked, after mulling it over for a while.

"Well, yeah, kind of, I guess. I don't want to just go off and make a decision that might affect you or Manolo negatively."

"I suppose it's really a matter of pay, isn't it?" she asked.

"How do you mean?"

"I mean, is the pay they're offering worth the extra risk you would be taking?"

"Yeah, but that's not necessarily why I am considering taking the job," I told her.

"Why did you resist it before?" she asked.

It was a fair question, so I answered, "Because it's a lot of training, a lot of sitting around and waiting and then short bursts of activity. The street, while pretty boring, I'm at least doing something all the time."

"Are you saying that SWAT is too low-key for you?" she asked, amused.

"Eh, kind of. I mean, it's a lot more dangerous, but those spates of danger are few and far between, comparatively, and I would still be on patrol, I would just be more on certain taskforces, which is sort of how I ended up shot the first time."

"Look," she said dryly, "let's not phrase it that way, shall we? It's just how you got shot – there is no the first time. Getting shot needs to be a one-time deal, if at all possible. I'm not sure my heart would take it if you managed to get shot again. Not on my watch, handsome."

I smiled and she pushed up enough to kiss me. We made out for a little bit and I said, "So I'm not hearing that you're opposed to me making a move up the food and income chain."

"Hmm, would it mean more money? Yes. The thing I worry about is, would it mean less time?"

"Less time?"

"With me and with Manolo," she murmured. I smoothed my lips together and nodded slowly.

"It could," I said.

She shook her head, "Then, no. Money doesn't buy happiness, and if we can make it for a while with the help of the alimony, fine, but we need to strike a balance. Do some financial planning so we don't become dependent on it, but there has to be another way. You know? One where you're happier with what you earn, but not having to sacrifice your time off or the happiness of your family. Does that make sense?"

"Yeah, it does, Chica. Which is why I asked. It was just an idea I was kicking around but if it doesn't make you happy, fuckin' forget it."

"You're sure?" she asked, and her tone was so careful, so controlled I rolled my eyes.

"Out with it. What're you afraid of?"

She smiled and laughed slightly, but whether because she was amused I had her pegged, or whether to buy herself a little time, I didn't know.

Her face sobered and she said, "You're sure you won't resent me for telling you you should say 'No?'"

I caressed her cheek and said, "No, babe. Your reasons are valid. Your concerns, while not ones I immediately thought of, are pretty solid. I was on the fence before I even brought it up, which is why I brought it up. You helped me make my decision. 'No' to moving up for the money, but I'm still going to try and score a day-shift without losing my shift differential."

She wrinkled her nose slightly. "What's a shift differential?" she asked.

"Never heard of one?"

"Husband was white collar our entire marriage, I sort of am, owning my own business, plus, florist shop," she reminded me.

"Maybe it's a blue-collar working-stiff thing, and yeah, I could see how it wouldn't apply. Anyway, I earn a little bit more per hour working swing than the day guys do, and graveyard earns the most. It's incentive to take on a less popular shift."

"How much would the drop in pay be for dropping down to day

shift? That's basically what you're saying, right? That you would have to take a pay cut?"

"Yeah, well, I mean –" I told her and she nodded carefully, and I could tell she was struggling to do the math in her head.

"Well, it would mean we would have to somehow pay less for housing than we do in rent now to make up for it somehow. I don't know that I see that happening."

I nodded. "Never know, depends on how much of a deposit you make and interest and all that happy horse shit."

She giggled softly and said, "True, that's true."

"I guess the first stop would be talking to a real estate guy. I don't know, I've never bought a house."

"Yes, you would need to find an agent," she agreed.

"Okay," I said gently.

"Where would you want to live?" she asked.

"What do you mean?"

"Well, inside the city, outside? Condo or house? Townhouse?"

"You know, what about you?" I asked.

"What about me?" she asked, surprised.

"What was the one thing you always wanted in a place but never got?"

She sighed out and said, "Truthfully? A yard. Didn't even have to be a big one. Or barring a yard, what about just a couple of planter boxes on a balcony or along the window ledge?"

I chuckled, the brownstone looking better and better, if a little big for just the three of us.

"I want to take you and Manolo to go look at a place," I said.

"Oh, yeah?"

"Yeah."

"Okay, when?"

"Soon as I can arrange it."

"Okay," she said evenly and carefully.

I laughed slightly and said, "I think you'll like it, Chica. It's got the best of all our worlds. I just need to check out a few more things."

"Where is it?" she asked.

"A neighborhood over from Old Bayside," I said.

She gave a low whistle. "Sounds expensive."

I shook my head, "Needs too much work; the neighborhood fell hard, and it's just now crawling its way out by way of gentrification." Indigo City's latest rounds of growing pains was seeing low-income folks being pushed further out to the fringes. I hated being part of that problem but I had to look out for my family first and above all else.

"It's getting there, but if we get in now it's doable."

"Then I guess, if you have your heart set on it, we should go look soon."

"Yeah, I do, kind of," I said.

"Why?"

"Can't give it all away at once,"

She smiled, "I suppose that's fair enough." she kissed me softly and we held each other, drifting off to sleep and effectively ending the conversation. I was hoping that we got to go see the place I was talking about soon, because every time I talked about it her eyes lit up with excitement. I noticed there wasn't much that did that for her, so when it did happen, it ignited my joy just a little bit.

I loved this apartment, and being here with her. I couldn't deny that I was going to miss it and it was doable, staying here with Manolo, with a bit of rearranging but... she avoided my room, my bed, for a reason. I'd noticed. I figured it didn't feel like the place for her, with how many other girls had been through it, and maybe it was petty, maybe it was selfish of me to be a little upset about that, but it was how she felt and I could respect that.

In a new place, it wouldn't be like that. I mean, I know it would be the same bed but it wouldn't be the same space. Instead of 'your place' or 'my place' it would be the definition of 'our place' and I was surprised to realize just how much I wanted that, how much I ached to be a part of something bigger than myself, a family, even though it wasn't *my* family. It was my sister's and Manolo would always be Maria's son. Lys wouldn't replace that. She couldn't.

Still, the last few weeks of her helping and being part of mine and

Hombrecito's life had been the most contentment I had ever felt. It felt right, and yet, still a modicum of guilt came with it. I felt so terrible that Maria was missing out on her son's life and would be for years to come, by the sounds of it. For one mistake that she *knew* not to make! As pissed as I was about that, I couldn't deny that it was a mistake she likely felt trapped into committing for several socio-economic reasons, reasons that, though I had been blessed and privileged my entire adult life not to have experienced any of them myself, I could understand from the point of view of we grew up on the same damn streets in the same damn projects.

I think Angel could too, except he was quicker to forgiveness than me. Angel was the one to see her and report to me, and though I didn't feel that was necessarily right, I knew it was for the best. Lys gently urged me to make the trip to the jail, but I wasn't ready and I knew if I went, my temper would get the best of me and make things far harder and worse than they needed to be.

I slid into sleep hoping that all would eventually work out for the best, like so much seemed to have worked out for me since Lys had come into my life.

32

Golden...

"Angel!" I called out and my twin ducked his head out from below-deck on his live-aboard boat.

"What's up, man?" he started to say, then looked over at me, and with a much-sobered look said, "Oh."

"Got any beer?" I asked.

"Yup, come on board."

I stepped up onto the edge of his boat, careful in the dress shoes I was in, and dropped down onto the work-in-progress that was his deck.

"Looks like you almost got her finished," I said.

"Yup, phase one is almost complete." He ducked back down below and came up with two bottles as I pulled my indigo blue satin tie loose from around my neck and popped the top two buttons on my collar.

"Take it you went to see Maria?"

"Yup."

"Also take it that it didn't go to well?" He twisted off the top of the first beer and handed it over.

"Nope."

"Lys?" he asked softly. I gave him a scowl and he nodded.

"I get it," I said. "I totally do. If he were my son I wouldn't want another man raising him. It'd burn me up just thinking about it, but what pissed me off wasn't the fact she was pissed about another woman being around her son –"

"It's the fact that Lys isn't Latina," he finished for me and twisted the cap off his own beer. "I saw that coming."

"Shit, man. Maria was raised same as you and me. Where does she get this shit from?" I demanded.

"No fucking idea, man. Mamma and Abuela both would be fit to be tied if they were still alive."

I huffed a bit of a laugh and said, "I know she never met him, but fuck, she's just like Papa."

"I was just about to say that," he said and held out his beer. We clicked bottles.

"I'm supposed to take Lys and Manolo to check out one of the brownstones in a few hours," I told him.

"Busy Saturday," he remarked.

"Yeah, I just needed a minute to cool off before I went back home. Lys is like a bloodhound when something ain't sittin' right with me, and she won't let it go until I talk to her."

"Sounds like a good woman," Angel said, and took a drink.

"Yeah, but I'm afraid this one would hurt her and I really don't want to ruin the day."

"So here you are, drinking a beer at nine-thirty in the morning with me, makes sense."

"Some things you just get, bro."

"Some things will always just be you and me," he said and smiled. I nodded. He was right. It was nothing against anyone else, it just was a twin thing.

"Yeah, I'd straight like to keep it that way, too," I muttered and we clicked bottles again.

"So, how are things with instant family, just add hot roommate and erstwhile nephew?"

"Butt-hurt you couldn't take him?" I asked.

"Man, if it were next year, I could have and you know I would have, but I get it. You're way better equipped to deal than me. A drafty boat in the winter ain't no place for a kid."

"You can take him off our hands any time you want, bro. I could use the time with Lys, you know. Plus, I can't be his only male role model. That's a disaster waiting to happen."

Angel laughed and said, "You're not as bad at it as you'd like to think. That, and I think everything happens for a reason. Like I said, this time next year, this baby would be sold and I'd be on one of those."

He tipped the neck of his bottle and I followed where he pointed, to one of the nicer houseboats moored up the way.

I shook my head, "No, thank you. I couldn't deal with one of the storms we get out here and the anxiety of *What if my house sinks.* You're legit crazy and I don't know where the fuck you got this crack-ass affinity for being on the water."

Angel shrugged and mumbled, "I dunno, maybe a past life or some shit."

I laughed and shook my head, "I don't believe in that mystical mumbo-jumbo, plus you're Catholic, you shouldn't either, technically. We die, we go one of three places, Heaven, Hell, or Purgatory, and according to how we were raised? Shit, we either go to Hell or Purgatory." While Hell sucked balls and Purgatory was just to get your shit straight, Purgatory didn't exactly sound like a gas. And Heaven? Shit, the way we had it set up, it was a bitch and a half to get into, so you might as well forget it and just pack your bags for an extended stay in Purgatory if you were lucky. Which is pretty much why I said fuck all of it and just didn't want to believe any of it. Angel, though? He'd somehow stuck to it. I still wasn't sure why.

Angel looked at me surprised and crossed himself. "It's a miracle! You actually did pay attention!"

"Shut up," I grumbled. "I was actually thinking, though. Might not be a bad idea you took Hombrecito to church with you on Sundays."

"Wait, what?"

"Religion may be a bunch of bullshit in my book, but it did at least instill some sort of set of values in me."

"I think Ma and Abuela had more to do with that," he said honestly. I scowled at him and he put up his hands. "Yeah, no, I have no problem taking Manolo to church with me on Sundays. Sundays can be our thing."

"Cool."

"Anything else you wanna get off your chest?" he asked after some silence.

I sighed. "I don't know what to do about Manolo visiting his mom while she's in that place, dude. I don't think it's a good idea."

Angel huffed out a big breath and said, "It's another hard choice, man. You keep him away Maria could spiral; you let him see her, it could cause him issues, but then again, maybe not, you know?"

I nodded, "I'm pissed at her, but the last thing I wanna do is deprive her of seeing her kid. Jesus Christ, she's made such a fucking mess of things."

Angel nodded slowly and said, "I think we both sit him down and talk to him, and find out what he wants."

I nodded and said, "He's way too old for his age, ain't he?"

"Yeah, but so were we. Maria was the baby and maybe you, me, Mama, and Abuela sheltered her just too damn much. She was spoiled, didn't figure she could do any wrong, and when she did we were always there to get her out of it."

"Can't do shit this time," I muttered and I felt some guilt over that.

Angel snorted. "You're doing more than enough right now, my man."

"Yeah, well, I wish I could do more."

"Look," he sighed harshly, "divide and conquer, bro. Like we've always done. You worry about Manolo and Lys. I've got Maria. You can't and shouldn't try to do it all. You've got more than enough on your plate and I feel really fucking bad that. Once again, it's your life being upended the hardest."

"Don't," I said. "Don't you dare feel bad about it, seriously. Despite the total shit-show that is Maria and her baby-daddy, Lys and Manolo are some of the best shit to ever happen to me. He's resilient. He's doing fabulous, even with all this going on. It's like all that kid needed was a set of rules and some fucking structure to thrive."

"That's usually the case, man."

"Yeah, well, I didn't know anything about it. I never figured I'd be like the uncle to do this if the shit ever went down. I always figured it'd be you."

My brother laughed and nodded saying, "Me, too, but you're surprisingly ahead of the curve on all of it."

I shook my head. "If it weren't for Lys, this would be a total disaster, bro."

"You always did have the devil's own luck," he said, with a hint of jealousy.

"Motherfucker, I'm the one that got shot," I reminded him. "What kind of luck is that?"

"Motherfucker, you're the one who lived," he shot back, and I couldn't really argue with him there.

We finished off our beers in grim silence, and I could tell he was thinking about the dudes that couldn't be saved that night as much as I was. I shook my head and filled him in on mine and Lys' conversation about potentially joining up with SWAT. He sat back on his seat and shook his head.

"I really like her, bro. She's a keeper."

I nodded and said, "I'm pretty fuckin' impressed, myself."

"Speaking of – ain't you gotta be somewhere?" I checked my watch, handed him my empty bottle and nodded.

"Good talk," I said, and he smiled at me.

"Any time, bro. Can't wait to see the new place and get started."

I laughed, "Putting the cart before the horse there aren't you?"

"I got a good feeling about it!" he called after me, but I was already striding up his dock. I waved a hand over my shoulder and kept moving. I'd stayed a little too long and was cutting it awful close. I called Lys and gave her the address, told her to bring Manolo and take a car, I'd meet her there.

She'd asked what was wrong and I smiled, "Just spent too long talking to Angel. Needed to decompress some before coming home."

"Okay," she drawled. "Is everything all right? With Maria?"

"Everything's good, babe. I promise."

"Okay," she murmured, but it didn't sound like she believed me.

"Just meet me there, okay?"

"Okay, I love you."

"Love you, too."

"Bye."

"See you soon."

I fired up the bike and rode over to Backdraft's neighborhood. He and Lil were waiting for me at the curb, and looked surprised when I pulled up solo.

I parked the bike and shut it off and said by way of greeting, "Lys and Hombrecito are on their way. I had them take a car to meet me. I was running late."

"Oh, that explains it," Lil said, all relieved smiles.

Backdraft and I embraced first then I hugged Lil. I let out a gusty sigh, feeling surprisingly nervous.

"Well, which one is the one they're gonna have us look at?" I asked.

"Two doors down from us, that way," Backdraft pointed.

I nodded and asked, "How many are left?"

"One. Two doors down from us, that way," he said.

I swallowed hard.

"Shit, they went fast."

"They did," Lil agreed, and her smile was a little too big. I felt the first stirrings of suspicion.

"Here they are," she said, and inclined her head to a Prius pulling up to the curb in front of the brownstone they'd indicated. Manolo hopped out of the back and Lys got out right behind him.

"Uncle Rodrigo! This place is cool-looking!" he cried and came running over to me.

The Prius pulled away, leaving Lys standing alone at the curb looking up at the building's old, but beautiful, façade.

Her face held a combination of surprise and wonder, both of which I hoped turned to smiles and joy once she saw the entire place.

"All we're missing is the agent," Lil said excitedly.

"Yep," I said and we all trooped up the street to where Lys was standing, a harried-looking woman with a briefcase striding down the sidewalk from the opposite direction.

"Hello! I'm sorry I'm a little bit late, it's been a bit of a crazy morning. I'm Laura." She stuck out her hand and Lys took it.

"Its fine, we only just got here ourselves," Lys said pleasantly.

"Hi. Rodrigo Martinez," I introduced myself.

"I'm Manolo Gutiérrez!" Manolo piped up and shook her hand.

She laughed and said,

"It's very nice to meet you all." I took note that she didn't ask Lys' name, and she made a weird face at Manolo's last name not matching mine. I was a little worried that Manolo and I might not necessarily be white enough for her, but I held my tongue. I didn't want to jump to conclusions, but it was hella easy to lately.

"Well, come on in," Laura said warmly, after Lil and Backdraft introduced themselves as our friends and hopeful new neighbors. Laura seemed a little more relaxed after that and I felt disappointed. It looked like my initial conclusion wasn't terribly far off the mark.

I worried, but I kept it to myself. There was no guarantee Lys would even like the place. She might think it was too big, and I wouldn't blame her. I was a little worried about that myself. We would just have to see.

We went in the front door and I blinked, surprised at how far along the construction work had gone. The walls were all up and painted white and the space seemed huge. We went through the basement, which was fairly close to finished into a laundry room and had a wall knocked out to make the garage bigger. I liked that. I could work on the bike and we would have a place to not only park it, but for a car for Lys, too; we would need to get one. It was a fair distance from the flower shop for her.

The kitchen was still draped in thin plastic over the countertops, no light fixtures were up, and I grew nervous. This was –way– more finished than I expected it to be, which meant that it probably had a price tag to go with it.

Laura opened the French doors off the open space next to the kitchen, meant for a smaller dining room table, and Lys gasped, stepping out onto the stone deck with its wide, low steps leading down into the garden.

Lys looked like Alice stepping into Wonderland and I could see *Sold!* in her eyes. It made me a strange mix of joyful and doubled-down on the nerves. She looked up and around, and took one look at me, and burst into a chatter of plans and plant types, talking about climbing vines and trellises. She was almost talking too fast for me to track in her excitement. Lil and Backdraft exchanged a secret look and Manolo's mouth even dropped open.

"Uncle, I've never heard Lys talk so much or so fast," he said and the adults laughed. Lys shut her mouth and blushed furiously, stepping down into the narrow, but long, fenced yard.

"There's so much I could do here," she said in wonder and I made a mental note to have a quiet talk with Manolo about making people self-conscious and thinking before he spoke.

Still, there was no erasing the flush of excitement across Lys' nose and cheeks and I decided right then and there, come Hell, I would figure out a way to make this place ours.

She deserved to live someplace that make her feel safe and happy. She deserved to live someplace as beautiful as she was.

"Let's show you the upstairs, shall we?" Laura asked, beaming. She knew a sale when she saw one, and she knew she had us on the hook. I nodded and we went up to the next floor, which had two bedrooms and an office or library-looking room that could be a second living room or TV room if we wanted, or maybe an office for Lys to do her bookkeeping and shit from home.

Manolo picked out his room right away and asked, "Can we paint it?"

"I don't see why not, if we buy it," I told him. "Slow your roll just a little bit, Hombrecito. This is the first place we've looked at."

"Your uncle is right," Lys said quietly, much more reserved in her excitement from the kitchen and garden. "I still have to research the schools around here for you."

Manolo looked taken aback. "I have to switch schools? But – all my friends!"

"Exactly," I said, trying to head off a potential meltdown. "Let's just see the rest of the place, and we'll talk about it tonight, over dinner," I said.

He harrumphed and looked a lot less enthusiastic, but he went through the rest of the place with us. As I expected, Lys fell in love with the little balcony on this floor, overlooking the garden, and the little alcove that was perfect for a kitchenette to make coffee or tea just off to the one side of it. The master suite up top really did her in with the bank of windows and all of the light they let in, the high ceilings, and the private bath for the two of us, with not just a shower but a bathtub as well.

We exchanged a look and I knew she was sold on the first try. I turned to Laura and asked, "Do you have any information on the schools and surrounding neighborhood?" The agent smiled and handed over a packet of information she had at the ready. I looked it over and handed it to Lys who immediately began to devour the pages with her eyes, her brow wrinkled with her critical-thinking face.

"Do you love it?" Lil asked, and looked way too excited.

I nodded carefully, and she and Backdraft exchanged grins that put the hair up on the back of my neck, tripping my cop-sense hard, that something was up. I just didn't know what, yet.

"Thank you, Laura," Lys said, catching my eye. "I think we'll be in touch."

"These brownstones have been a hot commodity, so you'd better make it soon…" she went into hard-sell mode and we nodded along, and followed her out. We parted ways at the sidewalk, and Backdraft and Lil urged us in the direction of their brownstone.

"I really don't think I'm going to be able to afford it," I said sadly. "There's way more work that's been done to it than I expected. That just adds to the price tag."

"Well, what are they asking for it?" Lys asked. I flipped pages on the informational packet the agent handed us, and frowned.

"This can't be right. The owner still wants the same asking price as what it was before."

Lil grinned. "Okay, I can't stand it anymore. That's because I own it. I bought them all, and we really want you to have it. With the way the others sold, I won't be taking a loss. We really want you guys to be our neighbors, so please say yes!"

"Babe!" Backdraft chided, laughing, and I stared at her.

"You're serious."

"As a heart attack, bro. When you said you needed to start looking, and I suggested it, Lil had the workers come in to make it livable for you right away."

Lys and I exchanged a look.

"And you seriously only want this much for it?"

"Seriously."

"I don't know… it might look weird to the department, like I'm taking a bribe or some shit."

"We thought of that," Backdraft said. "Department knows. Way ahead of you, bro."

"They do?"

"They do."

Fuck. "I don't know what to say…"

"Say yes!" Lil cried, and she looked like she was about to burst from excitement.

"Uh, Lys?" I looked to my woman for a little guidance, here.

"What about my school?" Manolo asked.

I went down on one knee and said, "Bud, we can't keep you in your school and live here, and I know you're going to miss your friends, but you'll still see them when you go stay with your abuela, and a new school means new friends, right?"

He crumbled and looked like he was about to cry, but looked back at the brownstone and along its face.

"I get to paint my room however I want, right?"

"I can agree with that, Hombrecito."

"And my friends can come over, on like my birthday and stuff, right?"

"Absolutely," Lys agreed, gently.

He wiped his nose on his sleeve and sucked it up. Brave kid.

"Okay," he agreed, and stuck out his hand.

"Okay," I said and shook it.

"Yay!" Lil cried and Backdraft grinned down at us.

"Welcome home, brother."

I looked up at the building and then at Lys.

"What do you think of our place, Chica?"

"I think I'm going to love it as much as I love you," she declared and just like that, my nerves were put to rest over it.

I could do this. We could do this... and so we did.

33

Alyssa...

Moving day had been the day before and Golden and I had collapsed into bed too exhausted to so much as kiss. I was extremely grateful to the rest of his club; the Indigo Knights had shown up, a tour de force, and had us moved so fast I hadn't realized what had hit me. They'd simply put me in a car, said 'See you on the other side', and shipped me over to the brownstone.

I'd stepped out of the car in front of our new place to find most of the club's girlfriends waiting and ready to help me put things away once they arrived. Manolo had been with his father's mother, hanging out with his friends and just generally being a kid while we accomplished everything, and though I loved the kid, I was grateful to be able to get things accomplished without him underfoot.

It took the guys a while to get to us, mostly because they had to detour to Maria's and clean out her apartment in addition to ours. The bulk of it went into storage, but Manolo's things were on their way here, too.

Chrissy, Aly, Lil, and Aly's friend Dawnie helped me put the kitchen to rights first while the rest of the furniture and big things were brought in. Pasquale mostly made sure the boys were refreshed and made sexually-suggestive comments that had us all laughing until we cried when the boys couldn't hear him.

Today had mostly been me and Manolo, unpacking his room and the living room downstairs. Golden had helped as much as he could, but sadly, he couldn't get any time off tonight and had to go into work, leaving around one, to make his shift at two.

After dinner, I'd helped Manolo with his homework at the dining room table, which was now the informal kitchen table, before it was time for his bath and bed. He'd gone to sleep relatively easily tonight, for which I was grateful. I was tired.

I was on the back stone deck, lounging on a folding lounge chair someone had found somewhere, drinking a glass of wine, and just waiting for Golden to come home. It was nice out, school was nearly over, and so with the warm evening, I'd thrown the doors to the kitchen wide, the lights from behind me illuminating the tangle of yard that I couldn't wait to get sorted.

I heard him before I saw him, the heavy tread and scrape of his boot as he stepped out of the brownstone and onto the deck.

"Lys?" he called softly, and I realized he couldn't see me, slouched as I was. I raised a hand and waved, and he came around to stand beside me, his gun still in its bag slung across his chest. I took a sip of wine and smiled up at him and he grinned down at me.

"Look at you, right at home," he said.

"Mm, I really think you should put up your gun, change clothes, and come join me," I said.

"Oh, yeah?"

"Mm-hm. You want a drink?"

"Dunno, what're you drinking?"

"Moscato."

He made a bit of a face, and said, "Sure. I'll have what you're having, why not?"

I smiled and got up, kissing him hello. He held me to him and we lost ourselves in it for a little while. He licked his lips, tasting the inside of his mouth and nodded.

"Yeah, I'll have what you're having," he said and I laughed.

"Go slip into something more comfortable," I murmured, and I know it came out seductive.

He looked me up and down and grunted like he wanted some of me as soon as he got back. I wasn't opposed, though I thought he was being funny. I had on a pair of cut-off shorts and a thin V-neck tee with no bra. I was home, Manolo was asleep, and I wanted to be comfortable.

"Manolo go down without a fuss?" he asked, turning back from the doorway.

"You know, the usual. He wanted to stay up until you got home, but he didn't fight with me over it too hard. I think he was tired."

"Good deal, and probably. It's been a busy couple of days. Be right back."

"Going to look in on him?"

"You know it," he called over his shoulder softly and I smiled.

I'd wait a bit to pour more wine for me and a glass for him. I finished my glass in the meantime and sighed contentedly, debating on a second. I got up to get his glass just as he rounded the bottom of the stairs. I smiled at him; he was dressed as simply as I was, in an old ICPD white tee and matching cut-off ICPD indigo sweatpants. They'd been shorn off at the knee and yet still managed to look stylish. If I had to bet, I would bet Oz had a hand in that. Even helping us move he was very put together and fashionable.

"I'm not sure I want another full glass," I said and he said, "Just pour the one, we can share."

I refilled my glass and handed it to him. He took a mouthful, rolling it around and swallowing, the entire time making eye contact with me, turning the simple act of drinking some wine extraordinarily sexually suggestive in a way that sent my pussy throbbing with wanting.

"Not as sweet," he said darkly and I think I lost my breath.

Holy hotness. "I missed you," I whispered.

"Not as much as I missed you, Chica. Come on." He held out his hand and I took it while he led us back out onto the back deck, into the night.

He settled onto the lawn chair first and pulled me down so I sat between his knees and lounged back against his chest. He handed me the wine and I took a sip, before handing him back the glass.

He heaved a huge, cleansing breath, and I swear I could almost feel him leaving work off, letting it fall from his shoulders as if he was shrugging off a great weight, and just like that, he was here with me and there was nothing and no one else.

"Welcome home," I murmured, lacing my fingers through his, leaning back against his chest. He took a drink of the sweet wine from our glass and held me tight, swallowing then kissing the top of my head.

"There's no place I'd rather be than here with you, baby. There's no place I'd rather be."

I chuckled and leaned way back, offering my mouth to his. He kissed me without complaint and we lay under the stars, bathed in the warm glow of our home behind us, the smell of green and growing things around us, the light, lazy chirp of cricket and frog song surrounding us.

That made two of us, because there was no place I would rather be either.

THE END

ALSO BY A.J. DOWNEY

The Sacred Hearts MC

1. Shattered & Scarred

2. Broken & Burned

3. Cracked & Crushed

3.5 Masked & Miserable (a novella)

4. Tattered & Torn

5. Fractured & Formidable

6. Damaged & Dangerous

The Virtues

1. Cutter's Hope

2. Marlin's Faith

3. Charity for Nothing

The Sacred Brotherhood

1. Brother to Brother

2. Her Brother's Keeper

3. Brother In Arms

4. Between Brothers

5. A Brother's Secret

6. A Brother At My Back

Indigo Knights

1. Her Thin Blue Lifeline

2. His Cold Blue Command

3. A Low Blue Flame

Paranormal Romance (with Ryan Kells)

1. I Am The Alpha

2. Omega's Run

3. Hunter's End

ABOUT THE AUTHOR

A.J. Downey is the internationally bestselling author of The Sacred Hearts Motorcycle Club romance series. She is a born and raised Seattle, WA Native. She finds inspiration from her surroundings, through the people she meets, and likely as a byproduct of way too much caffeine.

She has lived many places and done many things, though mostly through her own imagination…An avid reader all of her life, it's now her turn to try and give back a little, entertaining as she has been entertained.

Stalker Information:
www.ajdowney.com

Made in the USA
Columbia, SC
01 December 2023